Jessica Gadziala

Cover Image Credit=
shuttershock.com/Viorel Sima

CASH

•

Dedication:

To my GoodReads ladies who kept (and keep!) me motivated:

Dusti, Tanya, Olga, Whit,
Michelle, Sivy, Lelyana, Tink, Nadre, MJ, Lilly,
Dianne, Sabrina (x3, the three of you)

CASH

PROLOGUE

Summer

Reign had church at the compound like he did every Friday. He had left ten minutes before, dropping a nine millimeter on the kitchen counter beside me and kissing down the side of my neck.

"Give me an hour then you get your ass in the truck and drive to the compound," he said, squeezing my ass before he moved away.

I listened to his bike rumble off as I looked down at the gun. Reign wasn't exactly a romantic and I never expected that to change. But he showed me he loved me in his own ways - like when he left me alone but always made sure he left me with a gun. It was his version of flowers and candy. Protection. Safety. They were some of the things I came to appreciate most about being with him. I may not be some withering flower, but it always gave me the warm and tinglies to know that he prized me enough to want to make sure I was always safe.

The abrupt tap tap tap on the sliding glass door in the dining room had my heart flying into my throat and my hand automatically grabbing for the gun, pulling off the safety, and aiming it into the darkness.

I moved slowly out of the kitchen, reaching my free hand into my back pocket for my phone and hitting Reign's number.

Whoever was at the door was in all black, making them all but invisible in the darkness. But then a white hand slid out of the sleeve and reached upward, pulling the hood off their head.

Janie. From Hailstorm, the survivalist camp on the hill. I had met her a little over a year before when she and her leader, Lo, helped Reign, Cash, and Wolf save me from the skin trading psycho called "V" who had kidnapped and tortured me for months to try to get my father to agree to some kind of deal involving using my father's shipping containers. V had been under my father the cocaine kingpin's care (read: imprisonment) since then. My dad and I had managed to make amends despite him lying to me my whole life about being a normal, upstanding businessman. Hell, who was I to judge? I fell in love with a gun running biker who had proved quite adept at taking lives.

But ever since that night, I had never even caught sight of anyone from Hailstorm. Not even Lo. From what I could tell, Reign and the others hadn't heard from them either.

Janie being at the backdoor... I had no idea if that was good or bad.

"Babe... the fuck could you need to talk to me about already? I just left..." Reign's voice found my ear.

Janie's eyes found mine and she said something while watching me, most of which I couldn't make out. But I caught one word. Help.

Then she pointed to the phone by my ear then brought her finger to her lips in a shushing motion.

Shit.

I didn't do that. I didn't keep things from Reign. That wasn't how our relationship worked. But there was a woman who once helped save me at my back door asking for help and asking me to keep it quiet.

"Summer," Reign's voice cut in, sounding concerned.

"Oh, oops," I said into the phone, trying to sound flustered. "Sorry. I didn't mean to call you."

There was a short pause. "You sure? Everything alright?"

"Yep fine. Just trying to crack the code to the safe and find the fun guns," I said, teasing him.

"Summer I swear to fucking Christ if you touch one of the..."

"I'm joking," I laughed, rolling my eyes as Janie watched me, head tilted to the side. I still had the gun aimed at her. Maybe she saved me once, but I learned my lesson in blindly trusting people.

"Wouldn't put it past you," Reign grumbled, likely remembering the time he let me use a fully automatic AK for the first time. I hadn't realized how much of a kick it would have and ended up stumbling and accidentally shooting the side of the compound. No one got hurt or anything, but he never let me live that down.

"Go to church," I said, shaking my head. "I'll talk to you later."

"Promise me there won't be any new holes in my house when I get there."

"No promises, but it's unlikely."

Reign sighed and I could just picture him raking a hand down his face. "Alright. I gotta go."

"Love you," I said, the words still heavy with meaning. It wasn't the flippant love ya' people fed each other to end a phone call. I meant it. I felt it down to my bones. And my words echoed that.

"Love you too," he said in a matching tone before he hung up.

I took a deep breath, tucking the phone back into my pocket and walking toward the back door. I flicked on the porch light and reached for the lock. As she reached for the handle, I backed away, gun still raised. I was good with a gun, so was Janie, but she had me beat on any other kind of fight. I wasn't letting her get near me until I knew what was going on.

"What are you doing here?" I asked as she walked in, closed the door, and sat down at our dining room table like she had done it a hundred times before.

"I'm... in a situation and I need your help."

"I'll call Reign back..." I started, reaching for my phone.

"No," she said, almost a little hysterically. It was such an unexpected, out of character tone for her that I froze.

"What's going on Janie?"

"I can't tell you that without getting you involved. But I need you to do something without telling anyone that I have asked you to do it."

"You want me to lie to Reign?" Again.

"Yes. But it will keep him safe. And Cash, Wolf, the rest of The Henchmen, and your dad."

My dad? And all of The Henchmen. Christ. What the hell did she get herself into?

"Does Lo know about this?"

"No," she said, her blue eyes boring into mine as she ran a hand through her long dark hair. "And she can't know."

"Janie..." I tried to reason, noticing a slight tremble in her words. If she was doing something on her own, without Lo and the rest of Hailstorm behind her...

"I just need you to invite your dad, Cash, Wolf, and Lo here one night, Summer. That's all I need from you. Just throw a fit until they all agree and get them here. That's it."

"Janie if you need help..."

"This is as much for you and your people as it is for me, Summer. Just say yes. All you have to do is invite them here and keep them here for a couple hours."

"Are you going to be safe?" I asked, lowering the gun finally but keeping it in my hand.

Janie took a slow breath, one of her small shoulders rising and falling in a casual shrug. "Probably. Hopefully. I don't know. But that's not your problem," she said, standing, and slipping her hood back up. "Here," she said, slipping a piece of paper out of her pocket and placing it on the dining room table.

"Janie. Seriously... if you are in over your head..."

"Don't worry about me. I'll get by. I always do," she said, pulling the door open and disappearing into the night.

I walked over to the dining table, grabbed the piece of paper which gave me a date and time, and locked the back door.

It looked like I had a dinner party to plan.

And an epic fit to throw if I was going to get anyone to agree to come...

ONE

Cash

Reign's driveway had never held so many cars before. Up until a year ago, no one even knew where his place was except me. I pulled my bike up to the side of Wolf's mammoth truck and climbed off. I pounded my fist into the side of a black rape van as I passed, making Janie jump and turn toward me, gun raised. It was a dick move, but she was fun to rile up. I mean, who didn't enjoy poking a sleeping bear once in a while? And Janie, the twenty-something, tatted, dark-haired, blue-eyed slip of a girl who was actually one of the best tactical minds inside the survivalist camp known as Hailstorm, yeah, she was a sleeping fucking bear.

"Jesus Christ, Cash," she sighed, shaking her head. "I could have shot you in the head. I mean... not that I think the brain damage would be noticed or anything but..."

"You coming in?" I asked, nodding toward Reign's house.

"No. I was just dropping Lo off."

CASH

Lo was her boss, as in Lo was the woman behind Hailstorm which, along with being a weird survivalist camp, also did work catching skippers, did private security, and carried out contract killing.

"Lo is here?" I asked, feeling my smile fall slightly.

I liked me a whole smorgasbord of pussy. Tall, short, thick, thin, blonde, brunette, purple-haired. Twenty. Forty. I didn't give a fuck. I loved them all.

All except fucking Lo, man.

While I might have admired the way that woman held a gun and spoke her mind, I couldn't get behind the fact that she and her people engaged in hits on any civilian for money. I was okay with killing: for family, for friends, for brotherhood, for business, hell, even for your country. But killing just for the fuck of it, because the paycheck was high enough? Hell fucking no.

Granted, I had friends that did that shit. I had friends who broke kneecaps or worse. I had a friend who was the best goddamn sniper in the country and used those skills. And I could go out with them, I could pound drinks, I could place bets on which one of us would land the hottest chick, but I didn't get involved with that shit.

And fucking a woman, even just for a night, meant you were involved.

"You know," Janie said, cutting into my thoughts. "I watched you shoot a man right between the eyes. You didn't even flinch."

I reached into the open window and chucked her chin. "It's different, kid. You and I both know that. Lo doesn't."

I turned to keep walking but heard Janie say quietly, as if to herself, "Maybe I don't either."

I shrugged it off as I made my way to the door, pulling it open and walking in.

"I'm just going to go ahead and say what everyone else here is thinking," I said as I looked around. "This has got to be the weirdest fucking dinner party that has ever happened."

And it had to be.

We were in the home of a my brother, gun running biker leader with his wife who had an almost alarming love of said guns. Her father, a notorious cocaine crime lord was standing in a corner in a three-thousand dollar suit looking wholly uncomfortable. Wolf, Reign and my oldest friend, was leaning against the kitchen counter, arms crossed, looking scary as fuck with his long dark beard and haunting eyes. It didn't help that the fucker never said more than a handful of words at a time. I turned my head slightly to find Lo watching me.

Seeing her was like a kick to the gut. First, because she was gorgeous- tall, long blonde hair, a face full of sharp edges and keen brown eyes. She had long legs, great hips, and a fucking phenomenal rack. She was a couple years older than me and she was probably the sexiest woman I'd ever seen. She was just not the kind of person I wanted to have anything to do with. Unfortunately, my cock did not get the message about that second thing. I was half hard just looking at her in her tight light wash jeans and white tee with a gun strapped around her thigh.

Holy fucking shit she was hot.

A slow, knowing smile spread across her features as she watched me looking her over. "Tuck your tongue back in your mouth, Cash," she said, tipping her beer up at me before taking a swig.

"Oh, sweetheart," I said, smirking. "If you had any idea what I could do with my tongue, there's no way you'd be telling me to tuck it back into my mouth."

I was rewarded by her choking hard, beer spurting out of her mouth as she coughed.

"If you could try to refrain from killing my guests," Summer said, handing a paper towel to Lo, "I would really appreciate it."

"Hey there, gorgeous," I said, smiling at her before swinging her off her feet and swirling her in a circle.

I had a soft spot for Summer. Maybe it was because she was the first woman in a long time that I had never had any sexual interest in. It wasn't that she wasn't gorgeous with her long red hair and her delicate face, but it had been clear from day one that she belonged to my brother. Lord knew the man needed some softness in his life and that was exactly what Summer gave him. She helped smooth his rough edges. She also kept him on his toes. There wasn't a day that went by that they weren't arguing and making up, when they weren't challenging and comforting one another.

She gave my brother someone to come home to, someone to remind him to shrug the weight of leadership every now and then. For that, I would always feel like I owed her. Which was why I was at her asinine dinner party in the first place.

It didn't hurt that she threw an absolute shit-fit when any of us had tried to come up with excuses to not show up.

"Hands off my woman," Reign said, walking up as I put his woman down, wrapping an arm around her waist, half gluing her body to his. "You gonna behave?" he asked me, giving an almost imperceptible chin-jerk toward Lo who was squatted down, wiping her spilled beer off the floor.

I gave him a smirk. "Oh, you know me. Fucking angel, man," I said, clapping him on the shoulder and moving over toward Wolf.

"'Sup Wolf?" I asked, reaching behind him for a beer.

"Weird fuckin' party," he said, using as few words as possible, as was his nature.

Wolf was a lot of things, not one of them being talkative.

"Yeah. If Repo and about three dozen armed psychopaths were here, it'd be like a fucking reunion."

"I get us," Wolf started, waving a hand toward himself, me, and Reign. "Don't get them," he said, gesturing toward Lo and Richard Lyon, Summer's cocaine kingpin father.

"Well, he is her dad," I shrugged.

"And Lo?"

That was a good point. "Maybe Summer feels like she owes her? Lo was really the only reason we could go in there and get her out."

Lord knew we, The Henchmen, owed Lo and Hailstorm a big, bloody fucking favor in the future, a fact that had been weighing more heavy on me than Reign for some reason. I guess he figured that whatever it was, would be worth having the woman he loved back.

"All together?" Wolf asked, turning his light, fathomless eyes at me.

That was another good point. Sure, it made sense for Summer to want to see her father. It also made sense for her to want to see Lo again. She invited Wolf and I over all the time. But why, all of a sudden, did we all need to be in the same room, especially given that quite a few of us didn't exactly get along?

"Dunno," I said, watching as Lo walked over to Richard Lyon like he wasn't one of the biggest dealers on the east coast. Then again, I had seen her walk up to a ruthless, heartless fucking skin trader like they had shared Sunday brunch every day for years.

"Bitches, man," Wolf said and I turned to find him smirking fondly at Summer.

"Got that right," I agreed, lifting my beer to him. "How was the run?" I asked, watching Lo throw her head back and laugh at something Richard said, her laugh a strange tinkling little sound that carried across the room.

"Hand me one," Reign said, walking up, gesturing to my beer.

I handed him one and, unable to help myself, smirked at him. "How fucking pussy whipped are you to allow this clusterfuck to happen, bro?"

Reign snorted, shaking his head at himself. "You've seen Summer get a bug up her ass about shit before. She starts using six syllable words and shit, day and night, never letting up."

"Other ways to take her mind off of it," I suggested, raising a brow. He knew what I meant.

"Man, I fuckin' *tried*. Ten minutes after, she's sitting up and starting again. Figured, what harm could it do?"

"Lo's got a gun strapped to her thigh," I pointed out.

"You got a gun in the small of your back. Wolf has one on his hip. *Summer*," he said pointedly, "has one inside her boot. Don't think we can judge."

"How many courses is this thing?" I asked, looking around at all the serving trays (yeah, serving trays... in my brother The Henchman leader's house) laid out on the kitchen counter, just waiting for food to be placed on them.

"Dinner and dessert," Reign said with a sigh. "Talked her down from four courses."

"Fuckin' serious?" Wolf asked, dangerously close to laughing.

"Serious about what?" Lo asked. I hadn't even seen her walk up, but there she was, at Reign's side.

The silence after her interruption was palpable and awkward with Reign recovering first, taking a swig of his beer and answering, "Summer wanted this to be a four course thing. Speaking of," he said, swiveling his head over his shoulder to where it looked like Summer and her father were having some sort of heated debate, "I gotta go see what's up." With that, he was gone.

Wolf looked at me with a silent shaking chuckle in his chest and said, "You're on your own." He grabbed a fresh beer and moved away, inclining his chin at Lo as he passed. "Woman," he said in his deep voice before he was gone.

Lo turned to watch him walk away, a strange small smile playing at her lips. When she turned back to me when Wolf was out of sight, she said, "I like him."

"Want me to hook that up?" I asked, taking a long swig of my beer. Jesus fuck if she would just hook up with one of the men, if she would just make it about loyalty, then I could stop fucking picturing her naked, riding me hard and fast, her tits jumping as she did, her head thrown back as she moaned my name...

Lo was giving me a sly smile. "As much as I like the strong and silent type," she started, taking a few steps forward so that her front was practically plastered against mine and for a horrifyingly hot moment, I thought she was going to kiss me. Then she reached behind me for a fresh beer and stepped back. It was then I realized I had been holding my breath and sucked in some air. "He's not meant for me."

"Meant for you?" I asked, smiling. "Baby, we aren't talking about forever. We're talking about tonight."

Unphased, she shrugged. "Not meant for that either. And I'm not your baby."

"Oh sweetheart," I said, smirking, getting up in her space until she took a step in retreat, "I can get you to the point where you're begging me to call you baby."

"Pretty confident in that, huh?" she asked with what I could only describe as a challenge in her eyes.

"Yep," I agreed with a nod.

She took her step back, making her press her tits into my chest and angle her head up to look me in the eye. "Never gonna fucking happen, Cash."

TWO

Lo

When I was eight years old and told my father that I wanted to be in the Marines just like him when I grew up, he told me that women in the military were nothing but a liability or a distraction and that it would be a cold day in hell he let any daughter of his be the reason a platoon of good men lost their lives.

When I was sixteen, I went into a convenience store after school. While I was looking through my junk food options, a man came in with a gun, demanding money. The man behind the counter, in his forties, foreign but in a way I couldn't describe, reached into the register but must have simultaneously reached for a gun. It was half raised in the air when the gunshot went off and I watched in absolute horror as the bullet wedged itself between the store owner's eyes with a spurt of impossibly red blood came out the back of the man's head, spraying all over the cigarette stand. His body hovered on his feet for a nauseating few seconds before he collapsed forward over the counter.

The robber, undeterred, reached into the register, stole the money, and took off.

I stood frozen as the wife of the store owner came in from the back having, no doubt, heard the gunshot. She stopped for the barest of seconds in the doorway, looking around until her eyes fell onto her husband. She flew at his body with a scream I could still hear when the night got too quiet, a scream that sounded like with him, a part of her died as well.

The police poured in; my father came; questioning was carried out. I answered in a strange numbness as I watched the wife have to be pried from her husband's dead body, her body shaking so hard from tears that she looked like she was having a seizure.

And I knew, in that moment I knew with a blinding sort of clarity, that I would never in my life ever know a love like that.

They were strange memories to have your mind constantly roll over, especially given that decades had passed. The fact of the matter was, those were two of the five biggest game-changing moments in my life that made me into the woman I had become. They were memories I worked hard to remember in excruciating technicolor detail, fearing that if I lost even a second of them, I would lose an integral part of myself.

They were the thoughts I had on my mind when the door to Reign and Summer's house opened and in walked Cash.

Cash, that was actually his real name, like Reign was his brother's real name. Power and money, they were the only things that mattered to their old man. Reign looked like their father, tall and muscular, dark hair, light green eyes. Fierce. Everything about the leader of The Henchmen MC was fierce, dark, and dangerous.

Cash, much to the detriment of every damn woman who crossed his path from the day his voice dropped, inherited his looks from their mother. He was every bit as tall as his brother, but where Reign's looks ran toward dark, Cash's ran toward light. He had his dirty blonde hair long on one side of his head and shaved to a peach fuzz up the other side. His eyes were a deep shade of green and his lips were almost perpetually turned up at the sides. Then, of course, there were the tattoos. I didn't even want to get into the tattoos. Oh, my *God*.

See, the problem with Cash was, he was likable. A man like him didn't cross your path and rub you the wrong way. He was laid-back, funny, flirtatious. If he was in the presence of a woman, you could tell he appreciated her and not just if she was hot shit (though he certainly... *appreciated* those ones all the more). It was almost as if you could just sense that he just genuinely *liked women* with all their contradictions and complexities. He wasn't the kind of man who bitched and moaned about us being emotional or needy or hard to get (because, to him, they never were). He just took women as they were.

And, fucking hell, it was like catnip.

Let's just say, it was no secret that Cash was a whore. Hell, no one could even blame him what with looking how he looked, walking like he walked (he simply... swaggered), talking like he talked (the silver-tongued devil), and riding around on his bike with his leather cut. Yeah. He could have any woman he wanted. And Cash wanted a lot of different women.

I didn't particularly have a problem with manwhores. If women want you and are happily giving of themselves to you, well, why *wouldn't* you indulge? He was youngish, he was hot, he was single. I didn't care how many women he dipped his wick into.

That being said, he wasn't getting near me.

He was hot. *I was affected*. That didn't mean I was stupid.

I had a few years on Cash. I'd been around the block. I knew my fair share of manwhores. I knew there was nothing there but hot sex and sore feelings to be had with men like him. Sure, at times, a woman needed some hot sex. The problem was, I was never the kind of woman who didn't sit up and think 'what if' and 'if only' when she woke up in a man's bed.

So, yeah, my body was practically electric when he was close enough to catch his smile or his laugh... but the fact of the matter was... it was *never gonna fucking happen.*

"Careful, beautiful, that sounds an awful lot like a challenge," he said his voice rumbling low and seductive and it ran through my system like a current.

"Consider it whatever you want, *handsome,* but let me tell you right now," I said, having to force myself to keep eye contact when his lips were giving me that devilish grin of his, "you will lose."

"Aw, Lo..." he started when the oven dinged loudly, making us both start and making me take two steps back before I even realized what I was doing.

"I need a big strong man to help me pull this ham out of the oven," Summer breezed in, giving me a knowing smile as she moved past me.

"Big, strong man, huh? Sounds like someone is calling my name," Cash said, turning to her, and I watched as his eyes softened.

Then we had dinner. It was strained at best at the beginning, with Summer trying to banter awkwardly and Cash or myself trying to jump in to save her. By the time coffee and dessert was served, things had gotten a little looser with Cash and Reign and, occasionally, Wolf, telling old war stories about the trouble they got into as kids. It was dinner conversation liberally dotted with 'fucks' and 'shits' and 'pussies', but at least it felt more natural.

Reign sat back in his chair, his arm going around the back of Summer's as his attention turned to her. I wasn't sure how she could stand to be the recipient of his intense brand of attention. I felt like squirming and his head was completely turned from me.

"So we did this asinine dinner party, babe," he said to her casually, his tone teasing. "And we never have to do it again, yeah?" he asked, sounding close to laughing as her cheeks heated slightly.

She knew as well as the rest of us what a disaster the whole night was.

Then she did the oddest thing, she turned completely in her chair, leaning past Reign and looking over the sink in the kitchen. My gaze followed hers to find her looking at the clock.

She worried her lower lip with her teeth for a second before sitting back and giving Reign a sweet smile. "Right," she agreed.

What the hell was that?

"Heading out," Wolf said, standing suddenly, his insane height making me suddenly feel like a little girl as I twisted my neck to look up at him. "Summer, good food," he said, giving her a tight-lipped smile. His gaze drifted over Richard who got a chin raise, then to me, who got a, "Woman," then finally to Cash and Reign. "Church." With that, he took his burly mountain-man-biker self across the house and out the front door.

His truck rumbled to life as I checked my phone to see if Janie texted me. She usually did, but sometimes if the plans were really concrete, she didn't bother; so I thanked Reign and Summer, asked if I could help with the cleanup, then made my way outside when I was shooed out of the kitchen.

It was cool outside and I instantly regretted the choice to go without a jacket as I stood in Reign's driveway, brows knitted, because Janie and the van were nowhere in sight. It wasn't like her. She always showed up on time, usually early. I reached into my pocket, hitting her number and listening to the ring.

"'s Janie, leave a message."

"Shit," I groaned, ending the call and hitting it again. Three more times. On the fourth, I shook the phone on a growl. "God damn it."

"Janie flaked on you?" Cash asked from behind me, making me jump. He shouldn't have been able to sneak up on me. I was being careless.

"She's probably just running late."

"Probably," he agreed, moving to stand next to me in his annoyingly warm-looking black leather jacket. He raised his arms up over his head, arching his back slightly on a groaning stretch that made his tee inch up from the waistband of his jeans and expose a delicious three inches of his tight abs that I found myself not able to look away from. I heard his low chuckle and realized he caught me staring. "Like what you see, honey?"

Oh, good Christ, with the endearments. Was there anything hotter than a guy who used them so readily and with such great variety?

"Eh," I said, shrugging a shoulder as I made pointed eye-contact.

He looked down at me, his eyes smiling at me like he knew I was bullshitting him and weighing if he was going to call me on it or not. Apparently he thought better of it because the next thing I knew, his hand moved out and his finger stroked down my bare goosebumped arm, giving me a shiver for an entirely different reason. "Little cold to be standing out here waiting on a ride," he observed, his thumb and forefinger snagging the edge of my t-shirt sleeve for a second before pulling away.

I pulled in a slow breath, hoping it would do something to slow my heart slamming in my chest. "I'll be fine," I said, feigning casualness when there was a very (and I mean *very*) persistent pulsating between my thighs.

"Lo," Cash said, his tone taking on a serious edge that made me turn my gaze back to him, brows drawn together. "I get that you're all independent and can handle your own shit, but what point could you be making by standing here in the cold?" he asked, and well, he had a point. "Ask me for a ride, Lo."

Of course the jerk couldn't just *offer* me a ride. No, he wanted me to have to ask for it.

I looked down at my phone, still nothing from Janie. I was starting to not only be frustrated, but get genuinely worried. Janie never didn't call or text back. I needed to get back to Hailstorm to see if anyone had heard from her.

I sighed, tucking my phone into my pocket. "Fine. Can you give me a ride?"

"Not gonna say please?" he asked, lips twitching.

"Forget it," I growled, moving past him to go back toward the house. I'd rather hitch a ride from Summer or Reign than deal with his nonsense.

"Lo, baby, rein in the fucking pride and get on my bike," he said, sounding every bit as exasperated as I felt.

I turned back to see him already moving down the driveway toward his bike, the gravel crunching under his big boots. I watched his lean, strong body move as he swaggered (God, it was so sexy) toward his bike, swinging his leg over, then finally looking up toward me, still standing dumbly on the front steps.

"Oh, fuck it," I murmured to myself, feeling a chill run through my body as I made my way toward his bike, putting a little extra oomph in my walk because he was staring me down.

"Don't have any helmets, darling," he said, tilting his head slightly when I got around him. "You're gonna have to trust me," he said, then the light hit his eyes again, a light I didn't trust, "and hold on tight."

Oh, shit.

I was totally going to have to hold on.

"Fine," I said, swinging a leg over the side of the bike and climbing onto the back, holding my body away from his as long as possible.

He chuckled and turned over the bike, then waited. My guess was he was waiting for me to hold on. When I didn't, he let the bike jerk forward until my arms flew out and grabbed the sides of his jacket. "How 'bout this, babe?" he asked, reaching for my hands and pulling them around his front and under (yes *under*) his tee, settling my freezing hands against his hot skin. I felt myself jolt at the contact, trying to pull away. "Relax," he murmured in such a low, soothing way that I automatically did. He released my hands and zipped up his jacket to further seal in the warmth. His hands moved to the handlebars and the bike burst into motion.

I wasn't unfamiliar with bikes. I didn't even dislike them, but something about being without a helmet at high speeds had me scooting forward, clamping my thighs into the outsides of his and pressing my hands tight into his toned stomach. Okay, that was complete and utter bullshit. I held on because he was hot and he called me beautiful in that whiskey-rich voice of his and I really wanted to know what he felt like inside of me, but I also knew that holding him while he drove me home was the closest I was ever going to get to him.

We pulled up to the gates of Hailstorm what felt like too short a time later, pausing for them to be unlocked before Cash just went ahead and rumbled through without being invited to do so.

We had almost made it to the main building when the first explosion went off, sending us and the bike flying through the air.

THREE

Cash

I was about to cut the engine, grab her, wrap her around my waist and carry her back to her bed, or a couch, or a goddamn wall, slam her up against it, and show her that it was, with fucking certainty, going to happen.

The next second, there was a flash, a sound loud enough to quiet the world, and I was suddenly flying through the air.

There was the barest of seconds to realize Lo was still wrapped around me before we crashed down on the ground several yards away.

Lo let out a groan at the contact as I cursed, trying to scramble upward, untangling my limbs from hers. Another explosion went off, making our bodies jolt at the sound. I pressed up on my forearm over her body, my free hand moving to the side of her face, touching just below a three inch gash down the side of her cheek. It was bleeding toward her ear, but it was shallow. If she treated it, it wouldn't even need stitches. "You okay?" I asked, feeling like I was yelling, but my ears had popped and I wasn't hearing right.

Her mouth didn't open, but her head nodded, her eyes hazy for a moment. Then, I watched the realization dawn on her: Hailstorm, her home, her compound full of her people, had been bombed. Her eyes went huge and she was suddenly moving upward, slamming her hands against my chest until I moved back, sitting my ass on my heels so she could get up and I could look around.

The good thing about Hailstorm, from an entirely logistical point of view, was it was made of fucking recycled shipping containers, meaning- it was all but indestructible. Fire-proof, wind-proof and, apparently, bomb-proof. There weren't even any residual fires blazing.

"Lo!" I called as she scrambled upward and started running. But she either didn't hear me, or didn't care, as she ran with a slight limp, favoring her left hip where the brunt of my lower body weight crashed down on her, and falling down beside the prone bodies of a group of her men.

Even from a distance, I could see they were alive, breathing. I stood slowly, turning and looking for anyone else hurt, taking off toward the side of one of the buildings where I saw what looked like long dark hair peeking out from a corner. My first thought was: Janie. Granted, I didn't know her much, but what I did know, I liked, and I felt my heart skip faster as I made my way to the body.

I fell down at her side, at once realizing first, that she was much sturdier in frame than Janie and, second, that she was also breathing. There was a nasty gash across her forehead where she had collided with the side of a solar panel stand.

"You alright?" I asked, brushing her hair out of the way as Lo flung herself down beside me.

"Gale? Shit, you're bleeding..."

"She's fine," I said, reassuring her though her voice was

calm, even, like she was down in the trenches of war all the time and blood didn't phase her.

"What the fuck is going on?" Lo asked herself, looking up around her grounds with intense eyes.

"Lo, you need to go get some triple antibiotic on your head if you're..."

"Yo, you're a Henchmen, right?" another voice asked and we both turned our heads to see a tall, good looking black man standing over us, a streak of blood over his white thermal, but looking otherwise unharmed.

"Yeah, why?" I asked, getting to my feet as Lo helped Gale up, watching us.

"Shit, man," the guy said, shaking his head.

"What is it?" I asked, feeling my entire body tighten.

He inclined his head at me, turned, and pointed down the hill. I followed his direction, looking, and seeing... fucking... fire at the place that had to be The Henchmen compound.

"Fuck!" I shouted, already running toward my bike, saying a silent prayer that she was still capable of running.

"Cash! Cash!" I was vaguely aware of Lo's voice calling me, and, damn if my name didn't sound good on her lips, but I was too busy pulling up my bike and trying to turn it over. "Cash, call them," Lo called, grabbing my arm in a vice-like grip and yanking hard until I turned to look at her. "Call them," she repeated, taking my hand, turning it, and slamming her cell into my palm.

I looked down at the pink case holding her cell, feeling my lips quirk up despite the situation at seeing a hint of the softness underneath all her sharp edges. "Right," I said, taking the phone and dialing the number for the compound. It rang four, five times, before I heard background noise and a curt growl.

"What?"

Repo. That was Repo. Thank Christ. If there was one person guaranteed to be at the compound (since he lived there and was young, single, and childless, and therefore all but married to the club) it was Repo.

"Repo. What's going on?"

"Cash? Fuck man," he said and I could hear shouts in the background. "It's fucking chaos."

"Is everyone around and accounted for?"

"Everyone was home but me, Jazz, and Shredder. You and the boss and Wolf alright?"

"Far as I know. Reign is home with Summer. Last I saw Wolf, he was on his way home. I'm up at Hailstorm," I supplied, looking down the hill at the fire that seemed suddenly less ravaging as it had a moment ago.

"They're fucked too," Repo observed as if he was looking off in the distance at me. "So was Lyon's place, the Mallick's bar, and Lex's McMansion."

"The fuck?" I asked, turning to look at Lo and her men who were watching me aptly. "Who the fuck would bomb all of the big players in town?" I asked, looking at Lo with a raised brow. She nodded her head at a few of her men who ran off toward the inner courtyard where a brick house stood, which was their command center. I'd been in there before when Reign, Wolf, and I first came to Hailstorm begging them to help us get Summer back.

"Dunno, man. But they just fucked with the wrong fucking people," Repo said with a sort of fierce determination that Reign really appreciated in him when he had been nothing but a probate to us. Even now, fully patched, he hadn't lost any of his youthful exuberance.

"How's the compound?"

"Fire got the shed out back," he said, the words weighty because that was the shed where we brought people who needed to... learn a lesson. It was old and way overdue for a tear down, but there was a sort of nostalgia attached to the damn thing and we never got around to it.

"That's it?"

"This place is a fortress," he reminded me with more than a little pride.

"Right. Is Reign in the loop?"

"He's on his way. You comin' in?"

I looked at Lo, still watching me, the cut on her face still bleeding half-heartedly. "Soon as I can. You'll tell my brother I'm alright."

"Right. See you when you get here."

"Break out the fucking whiskey," I said, running a hand over the shaved side of my head as the reality of the situation started to settle in. Things had just settled down in town. There hadn't been any real warring in a dog's age. Hell, the last shit that got stirred up was started by us. Since then, there had been relative peace, everyone minding their own fucking business.

But bombs went off at not one, but five of the biggest criminal organizations in the area. Someone was trying to send a message. That message seemed to be: you might be big and bad, but we're bigger and we're badder and we're coming for you. The fact that there wasn't any damage just meant it was a maneuver meant to scare us.

They were rattling our cage. Stupid fucks didn't know that all of us, every single one of us, even the Mallicks who didn't play dirty with any of the other organizations, were big fucking dogs and we were more than willing to come out snarling.

"Right, man."

I ended the call, holding the phone out toward Lo who took it, looking like she was about to say something. Her men ran back, one of them with a walkie near his ear.

"Lo," he said, shaking his head.

"What is it?"

"Lex," he said, letting that name settle in.

There were a lot of crime organizations around our parts.

The Henchmen were gun runners who generally didn't fuck with anyone unless they fucked with us. The Mallicks were a family of loan sharks (the dad, then five sons). Vicious, ruthless, but otherwise good, upstanding citizens who owned a dozen or so legitimate businesses that kept them busy, including their bar that was bombed. Then there was Summer's dad, Richard Lyon, who, while being a cocaine kingpin, somehow managed to run his empire with next to no bloodshed. Hailstorm had connections seemingly everywhere, alliances I never would (and didn't want to) understand, but they didn't hurt people for the hell of it (just for the paycheck apparently).

Now, Lex... Lex was a whole other fucking story. Lex was the closest thing to evil that walked the face of the Earth. He was a murdering, woman beating, sadistic rapist pig. The day someone took him out would be the day all the women in the area could breathe a sigh of relief. I prayed to fuck that his card was finally punched.

"What about Lex?" Lo asked, recovering before me, but her eyes had a strange sort of haunted I didn't understand.

"Well, all the places: here, their compound," he said, nodding his head at me, "Chaz's bar, Lyon's estate, it was all minimal damage. Lex's place? It was blown the fuck up, Lo."

"Interesting," Lo said, but a guard had gone down over her face. I didn't know her well, but I knew her enough to know that if she was putting a guard up, there was no way she was going to share with me why it was there. I had a feeling, though, that she and Lex Keith did not have the cordial kind of love/hate relationship she had with the awful human trash that was V. Lo hated Lex Keith with a fiery passion.

I found myself wanting to know why.

"We sending out feelers?" one of her men asked.

A brow raised and a smirk toyed at her lips. "Are you really asking me that?" she asked and the black guy, obviously more senior in some way than the others, nodded his head at the other guy who ran off to, I imagined, 'send out feelers'.

"You gonna keep us in the loop?" I asked, making Lo start like she had suddenly forgotten I was there.

"I'll meet you in command," she said to her man who nodded at her, then me, then walked off. "That depends," she said, closing some of the space between us.

"On what, babe?"

"On whether The Henchmen are going to share their information with us."

"I'll have to talk to Reign," I said, for the first time in my life regretting the fact that I had to defer decisions to someone else. In the past, I always liked that Reign was in charge, that he was the one to shoulder the burden. I had taken on that role once, for half a day, and I felt physically weighted by it. But standing in the yard of Hailstorm with their leader, asking me if me and my men would keep her informed, yeah, I wanted to be able to give her an answer. It made me feel beneath her to admit that I had to ask someone else for permission.

Lo nodded her head. "Let me know."

Christ, that felt like a kick to the balls.

I couldn't walk away feeling like I was beneath her. That shit just wouldn't play. Things needed to even out a bit.

Unfortunately, the only card I had to play was up my sleeve and a dirty way to win a game, but it was all I had.

I took a breath, closing the remaining few feet between us, my hand raising to move to stroke next to the cut on her cheek. Her entire body went stiff, her eyes went to mine, her lips parted. Oh, yeah, she wanted me. She might dislike me as much as I didn't like her, but her body was into me. I liked that in a sick sort of way.

"What are you doing, Cash?" she asked, attempting firm, but her tone came off a bit breathless.

"You need to stop being boss lady and go take care of this."

"It's nothing," she said, trying to jerk her head so I would drop my hand, but my fingers slid down her jaw to nab her chin instead.

"Gotta take care of yourself, gorgeous," I said, my thumb moving upward to rub the very edge of her lower lip. Her body softened slightly, her eyes going hazy. Meanwhile I was fucking hard as a stone just from touching her goddamn face. Whatever it was between us, whatever kind of attraction that we had going on, it either needed to be ignored completely or given into, because toying with it was going to give me the worst case of blue balls in history.

"Cash..." she murmured, her voice taking on a husky edge that I wanted to hear saying all sorts of dirty things in my ear while I fucked her.

My finger slid up, despite my better judgment, and stroked across the crease in her lips. Her body wavered toward mine and I felt myself leaning in, watching her brown eyes with an avid sort of fascination. The sound of a car rumbled up, making Lo spring away from me, her eyes wild, looking out at the road. I watched her hope crash as the car that showed up was a police cruiser, not whoever she had been expecting.

"Great," she grumbled as she made her way toward the gates that were still open from when we drove inside. I followed behind, watching the two cops climb out of the car- one younger, attractive, one older, stomach spilling over his waistband, looking very much uncomfortable at having to be at Hailstorm.

"Lo," the older cop said, nodding his head at her, surprising me that he actually knew who she was. From what I understood, no one but other criminals knew Lo by sight. She was a 'reputation only' kind of criminal. No one even knew she was a woman: hence her name, Lo, as in... on the 'down low'.

"Detective Collings," she said nodding at him. "Rookie," she said to the younger guy, giving him a smile that made him clear his throat.

"Seems you had a little trouble tonight," Collings observed.

"Seems like a lot of people had trouble tonight," Lo countered.

Collings nodded, looking over at me. "Reign's brother," he half-asked, half-declared.

I was proud to have Reign as a brother. That being said, it didn't exactly bolster a man's pride to be referred to as another man's brother.

"Cash," I supplied with a brow lift.

"Just over at your... compound," Collings said. "Seems no one has any idea who could be going around setting off bombs."

"Imagine that," I said, nodding.

Collings shook his head slightly, looking over at Lo. "Don't 'spose you have any information to share with us, Lo."

Lo gave him a soft, almost conspiratorial smile, "Do I ever have any information to share with you, Collings?"

"If that ain't the damn truth," Collings said, gesturing his younger officer toward the car. "Well, you got anything, you let us know, you hear?" he asked, looking at Lo, then at me.

"You're on my speed dial," I agreed with a grin that, surprisingly, made him chuckle.

"Right," he nodded, making his way back to his door and slipping inside his car.

"Old friend?" I asked Lo's profile as she watched them drive away.

"Something like that," she agreed, her eyes still on the road, scanning.

"Right," I said, rocking back on my heels, knowing the moment was gone. I needed to get back to the compound. "I have to get going," I said, making my way toward my bike and climbing on. Lo shook herself out of her stupor and made her way toward the side of my bike as well, watching me settle in. "So were you fucking with Collings or do you really have no idea who this was?" I asked, sensing something off about her, but not able to put my finger on it.

Lo took a breath, met my gaze hard, and said in a strong, firm voice, "I have no idea who set off the bombs, Cash."

I nodded, turned over my bike, and drove away.

FOUR

Lo

It was Janie.

Janie, my sweet little Jstorm.

She was the one setting off the bombs.

I knew it the moment Lex Keith's name was brought up. Everything fell into place. That was why she didn't pick me up from Reign's house. That was why all the other sites: Chaz's bar, The Henchmen compound, Lyon's place, and Hailstorm all had minimal, if any, actual damage. She was trying to create chaos. She wanted everyone to be scrambling to find explanations for every major criminal organization in the area being targeted.

Shit.

Shit. Shit. Shit. Shit. Shit.

I needed to find her.

I turned, going into the main shipping container, holding shoes and jackets, then through to the ones holding the living room and kitchen, through again until I got to the barracks. We could have made an attempt to all have our own personal space, blocking off rooms for one or two people. We certainly had the land to expand and shipping containers could be gotten on the cheap. But a large majority of my people were ex-military, they found barracks comfortable, familiar, somehow less stressful than trying to acclimate to normal living conditions.

There were only a few of us women in Hailstorm and while we took the sets of bunks at the furthest end of the room, we shared the space with the men. There was simply no reason not to.

I walked past the empty bunks, moving toward mine which was below Janie's with a growing sense of trepidation. I stopped by the ladder, climbing up two rungs and looking up. Her bed was made perfectly (as they all were), complete with hospital corners. But her books were missing. She always had a pile at the foot of her bed within easy reach when her nightmares that were actually memories came back too strong to let her sleep.

I hopped down, stooping down beside her trunk and flinging it open.

Empty.

"Goddamn it!" I yelled, slamming it shut, the sound echoing across the empty room.

All my men mattered to me, every last one. They all had their own horror stories; their own reasons they needed to disappear; their own reasons for not being able to leave the life of war and violence behind them. Many were vets, some just streetwise kids who got sucked in early and ran before they could be spit out dead before thirty. They all had little pieces of my heart.

But Janie had a huge chunk of it. Janie was like a little sister to me, or like the daughter I would never have. She was rough and tough and prickly and she wore her intelligence like a shield, but underneath it all was the little sixteen year old girl I came across one night, a girl I had taken in and raised for eight years.

She was... everything.

And she had just bombed five powerful organizations in the course of one night.

There would be repercussions.

People would want payment.

The worst of them would never forgive, the rest would never forget.

And because Janie was Hailstorm, we would never again know the same kind of alliances we had before. We would never be able to enjoy our drama-free reputation again.

But all that, well, it didn't matter. What mattered was Janie. What mattered was the fact that she had planned and orchestrated such an intricate plot and I had somehow not even known she was going off the deep end. That never should have been able to happen. I should have seen the signs. I should have been able to talk some reason into her.

And if Janie was gone, if she packed all her stuff and took off, then she was g-o-n-e. She had the skills to disappear. I *taught* her how to do that shit. I had coached her on getting off the grid, becoming someone new. She had stood by my side and watched me do it for other people. Christ, had she been planning it all along? Had she been standing up with me, taking every bit of knowledge I could throw around, and cataloging it for later?

A part of me didn't want to think I was that blind. The other part of me, though, knew she was perfectly capable of being that smart and calculated.

What the hell was I supposed to do?

"Lo?" Malcolm, an older man, mid-forties, tall, lean, fit, graying in an attractive way, with the sharpest ice blue eyes I had ever seen, ex-military, ex-private security, ex-PI, ex-everything, came up to me. "What's up?"

Malcolm had shown up at Hailstorm one day at the very beginning after having me screw up one of his PI cases, spitting mad and ready to beat 'that fucking Lo guy' into a bloody pulp.

Finding out I was Lo, well, his anger drained, he threw his head back and laughed, and a month later, he was living at Hailstorm and teaching me everything he knew. He was like a father figure to all of us (even though he was only a few years older than myself). And he knew me pretty damn well.

"I can't say yet, Malc," I admitted, knowing better than to even try to lie to him.

He nodded, accepting that, sitting down on a foot locker across from me. "Is it bad?"

I sat down too, looking down at my hands for a moment. Was it bad? It was the worst. It couldn't possibly get any worse.

"Yeah," I admitted, looking up at his face. He was attractive, unfairly so even at his age, a trait only men seemed to possess.

"Shit." He sighed. "Should we all be worried?"

"No," I said, firmly. "It isn't a threat. I am going to make sure it doesn't turn into one."

"Lo, you know I have immense respect for you. I know you're one of the best out there, darlin'," he said, giving me a charming smile, "but not even you should be wading into bad shit by yourself."

"I'm not in it alone," I said, half-lying, not aware I was stroking Janie's locker until Malcom's gaze settled there.

"Jstorm's all over this?" he asked, lips twitching up, revealing his soft spot for her.

Oh, yeah, she was all over it, just not in the way he thought.

"Yeah," I said quietly.

"You two together? You're a kickass team. But I'm not liking two women wading into bad shit alone either. Even two as badass as you two are," he added when he knew I was about to pounce on him. Sexism simply wasn't acceptable at Hailstorm. We women busted our asses to be taken just as seriously as the men, which often meant we had to work a lot harder than they did, but we earned the right to stand shoulder-to-shoulder with our male counterparts. "Just sayin'... you know..." he added, eyes looking darker, worried.

"I promise if it is looking dangerous, I will bring some men in on this."

"Good."

"I am going to be a little... in the wind dealing with this," I hedged. "I can trust you to hold down the fort?"

"Always, darlin'," he said, tone serious and I knew I could count on him. "I'll go round up the troops and fill them in. The usual."

"Thanks, Malc," I said, standing as he did and closing the distance to clamp him on the arm. I wasn't exactly a huggy kind of gal and he wouldn't be comfortable with his leader wrapping her arms around him anyway so it was as close to physical affection as we would get.

"Be safe, Lo," he said, making it sound less like a plea and more like a command.

"Always. I'll be in touch," I said, moving out of the barracks and quickly making my way to the line of vehicles we kept for common use.

I didn't pack. I didn't need to. I taught everyone to keep a bugout bag hidden somewhere close and then one far away in case they were ever in the need to get out of dodge. They knew it because I knew it. I had five bugout bags hidden in various places across the country. I never knew if shit would hit the fan in a way that not even the ferocious beast that was Hailstorm could fix. I always needed to be prepared.

I slipped in behind the wheel of a inconspicuous black hatchback and pulled out of Hailstorm with a lead-like sensation in my stomach.

I drove through town, slowing to check out the damage to Chaz's bar, seeing all five of the Mallick men and their father standing out front, arms crossed over their broad chests, looking hot and badass. Every last one of them was a black-haired, blue-eyed potential cover model. They also all looked quite vicious and pissed off as they had whatever kind of family meeting they were having. Out front of The Henchmen compound, bikes were lined up, making it seem like all hands were on deck. They were probably having church in wake of the bombings.

I took a turn out of my way, going up a hill a bit to check out the damage at Lex Keith's place.

It was bad. Whatever bombs Janie placed (and Janie was well known for her bomb work) were placed to cause maximum damage. The gate was blown open, for what, I wasn't sure. She wouldn't have needed to bomb the gates to get in. Was she not working alone? Jesus, did she team up with someone else without filling me in?

"What have you gotten yourself into, Janie?" I asked the car, watching the flames engulf Lex's mansion full of first edition copies of books he had never read and art he didn't understand.

A part of me, granted an ungracious, vengeful, borderline evil part of me, hoped he was slowly burning to death in there. The worst possible death for the worst possible person.

The other part of me, though, was pretty sure it wasn't possible to kill that evil bastard.

I did a quick K-turn and made my way back toward the other end of town, the bad end, the end even hardened gang members were a bit spooked to walk down alone at night. It had been a long, long time since I saw my old safe house.

Thirteen years ago, it was all I had in the world. I bought it with every last penny of stolen money I had on me, a steal really, but it was on the property directly across from a known and violent gang. So at twenty-four and female, it wasn't exactly a 'safe' place to be, but it was safer for me than what I needed to get away from. As time went on and I built up Hailstorm, there was really no reason to keep it aside from nostalgia. I could have made up a safe house anywhere. But I kept it.

I turned up the drive, checking out my mirrors to watch the guys across the street stand up on their stoop and watch me.

Crap.

It had been years. Leaders had likely come and went. New blood didn't recognize old faces. I stopped my car halfway up my drive, popped the trunk, and jumped out with the engine still running. I went to the trunk, trying my best to ignore the beating of my heart, reached in, and dragged out the two biggest guns that were stored inside.

I turned, arms raised, watching the mix of emotions run across their faces. Some, surprise. Others, fear. One, nothing. There was my leader.

"You guys hear of Hailstorm?" I asked, raising my voice to reach across the street.

"Yeah," the one I pegged as the leader answered, jerking his chin up and keeping eye contact. Cool as a freaking cucumber. He was a good choice for leadership.

"My name is Lo and if you step one mother fucking foot on this property, I will round up some of my men, come into your little... headquarters," I said, giving their dilapidated building a nod, "and personally chop off all of your dicks. You've heard my name?" I asked, seeing another small chin jerk. "Then you know I am perfectly fucking capable of following through with that threat. So, we cool?" I asked, keeping eye contact.

"Bitch, we cool," he said, giving me a small smile that might have been charming if he wasn't a heroin dealer and pimp. "Ain't gonna step a foot on your property."

"Good," I said, lowering the guns and stalking back to my car. It was a risky move to threaten a gang, alone, female. It could have gone a completely different way. But fact of the matter was, I couldn't bring my men into my safe house. That was a part of my life they didn't belong in. So I either needed to be up front with the local bad guys, or shrink away and find another place to crash.

I was always the type to nut-up, so that was what I did.

I threw the guns back into the trunk, got in the car, and drove the rest of the way toward the house.

Calling it a 'house' may have been generous. It was really no bigger than a large shed, made of crumbling white stucco and a peeling black roof. The windows had been barred before I moved in and I added a security door for extra peace of mind. All in all, it was locked down tight. Last time I had been there, I had connected a light to a timer and kept the power, water, and heat going despite never even visiting to see if the place was still standing.

I reached under my shirt, digging out the chain that held the only two keys I ever needed- one to a safety deposit box where I kept all my other keys, and the one to my old safe house.

I locked the car, despite knowing that it would do me no good in a neighborhood where there was a chance my tires, stereo, and transmission could be missing by morning, and made my way up the gravel walk.

I slipped the key into the lock, feeling a mix of emotions flood through my system. First, there was the nostalgia, the feeling of comfort, familiarity, especially knowing that literally every last thing inside would be as I had left it. Second, though, there was a weird uncertainty that had my stomach rolling so fast that I felt queasy. Pushing past it, I pressed the door open and reached inside for the light switch beside the door. I flicked and nothing happened.

The swirling in my stomach intensified as I took a step in, reaching for my cell to brighten my way to another light source. I swiped through my apps, looking for the flashlight as I kicked closed the front door.

But then something happened.

A light flicked on across the room.

The swirling feeling in my stomach turned into a

plummeting sensation.

"Hey, Willow," a voice called. My phone fell and I turned to run.

FIVE

Cash

"Point me in a direction, Prez," Repo said, fists clenched down by his sides. He had bulked up since he was patched-in, but was never a weakling to begin with. He kept his past locked down tight, but there was a darkness in his deep blue eyes and a scar that ran down the entire side of his cheek, cutting off at the sharp jut of his jaw. He'd seen some shit, done some shit before we even laid eyes on him. Match that with the fact that he had been beat to a pulp to try to save Summer once and then got up off his sick bed to come in, guns blazing, and help the rest of us get her out? Yeah, he was one of Reign's favorites.

"Don't have a direction to point you in yet, Repo," Reign said, taking a stool and shrugging his shoulders. "All I know is someone is puffing their chest. To hit us? That's personal. To hit us and, say, the Russians? That's about trying to take the gun trade in the area. But to hit us, Hailstorm, Lyon, the Mallicks, and Lex? That isn't nothing but a show of power, telling us all to watch our backs.

None of us have anything in common."

"Hailstorm helped us," Vin, an older member of the club, back from the days when our father ran shit, chimed in. "They helped you get Summer back. So did Lyon. And the Mallicks? Shane told us about that rat we had in the club."

Good points, all.

"But we have never gone anywhere near that fuckwad Lex," Reign said, looking up with his piercing light green eyes. "We haven't made any kind of stand against him, but I think it's pretty clear we want nothing to do with that rapist asshole."

Also a good point.

We had been in church for almost an hour and we had gotten nowhere. I imagined the Mallicks and Lyon and Hailstorm all having similarly fruitless meetings, a thought that made me feel marginally better.

"We need to reach out," I said, biting the inside my cheek and reaching for the bottle of whiskey and pouring a round. "I'll take Repo and go see the Mallicks. You can grab Summer and go see Lyon. I've already talked to Lo, but I will check in again."

"Who the fuck you wanna send to check in with Lex?" Reign asked, a cruel little smile on his lips.

"Wolf," I suggested with a shrug. Out of all of us, he would be the one most likely to keep his rage under control. He wasn't an easy fuck to rile. That being said, when he was riled, it took a small army to hold him back.

"Where the fuck *is* Wolf? Repo asked suddenly, looking around.

Reign and I straightened, looking around. "The fuck?" I asked, not seeing his face. How the fuck had I missed that?

"Did anyone call him?" Reign asked, looking at Repo for the answer.

"Sent out a mass text, man. But you know Wolf, he doesn't answer for shit."

That was true too.

"I'll drop over tomorrow after we see the Mallicks. You know him... he takes off into the woods to hunt or fish or some shit and we don't hear from him for days," I said, shrugging.

"Right," Reign agreed, nodding his head. "Well, I don't think there's any real threat to any of us individually so you all can go home, but be sharp, keep an eye out, check in. I want you all here by tomorrow afternoon to tell me if you have heard anything. Repo, Vin, Jazz, Shredder," he said, addressing the men who immediately straightened, "you guys good to stay here and hold shit down?"

"Always," Repo agreed first. Had he been anyone else, he'd be called a kiss-ass, but being the lethal fuck he was, he was just a loyal brother. Anyone who said any differently would regret the hell out of it.

"Alright," Reign said, standing. "Stay, drink, fuck, leave, I don't care," he said, giving his men a sly smile. "I got a woman at home who needs some... comforting."

With that, he was gone.

A moment later, his bike rumbled off.

"Want us to call some bitches?" Repo asked, sounding about as excited about the idea as I was, meaning, not at all. Usually, I was the one commanding we get some skirts in the clubhouse, but suddenly, I was just bone deep fucking tired. Taking one look at Repo, I saw the same exhaustion. He had, after all, been the one who needed to spring into action, round up the men, assess the grounds for threats, put out a fucking burning shed. He'd had a night. He wanted his bed. And, for once, he wanted it to sleep in. It was exactly what I wanted too.

"You do what you got to do. I got to get some sleep," I said, nodding at Repo who looked relieved to be able to follow my lead. "I got meetings and shit tomorrow. Don't want to be showing up hungover. This is serious shit."

The men nodded, but I saw one go right into his phone,

hitting digits. No doubt, he was calling bitches. Which was fine. They could have their fun.

I'd had enough excitement for one day.

SIX

Lo

I didn't even get four feet before I was snatched from behind, hauled off my feet, leaving me peddling air as I tried to reach behind me and claw at his face.

"You fucked up, Willow," he said close to my ear, sounding like his teeth were clamped together. "All this fucking time, taking careful steps, staying under the radar. You finally, finally fucked up."

He sounded excited about that fact. Hell, he *was* excited about that prospect. I knew that because I knew the bastard. I also knew that because I could feel his cock pressing at me through my jeans as I tried to swing my legs up then slam them back into him. My feet met thigh, but not with enough momentum to cause any kind of damage.

It could not be happening.

Fucking, fucking no.

I felt the hysteria rise up, frantic and useless, making my

head feel light and my throat feel tight. Every bit of self-defense training, every endless hour spend grappling in that very position just flew out of my head, leaving me clawing at his arms like some pedestrian caught on the street.

"Not even gonna ask where you fucked up, Wills? How unlike you," he growled, shoving me forward. The side of my face (along with the rest of my body) collided with the wall hard enough for my vision to go white for a second. But I wasn't granted the blissful oblivion of unconsciousness. What I got was a forearm pressed hard against the back of my neck and a hard, unyielding male body pushing mine harder into the wall.

"Let me go," I said, wishing my voice would come out stronger. "You have no fucking idea what you are doing."

"Oh, bitch, I know exactly what I am doing," his voice grumbled as his hand went up under the back of my tee, snaking around my belly, effectively making me wish I could claw the skin off so I could never have to feel his touch on it again. "Been a long, long time. Skin is still so soft," he said, low, almost seductive. I felt my stomach churn as his fingers toyed with the underside of my bra.

All I could think was: no.

Finding a bit of clarity, my foot slammed down on the top of his and I cocked an elbow, shoving it into his ribs, surprising him enough for his hand to drop from my neck and giving me space to turn. Before he even sucked in his breath, my fist landed true, hitting hard into his nose and I watched in satisfied disgust as blood started pouring out.

"Stupid cunt," he growled and lunged and I knew I was in for it.

I was trained. I was skilled.

That being said, I was still a woman and no matter how skilled you make yourself, no matter how good you become, you will always have a physical disadvantage against a man well over six-feet and built like a linebacker.

I never subscribed to sexism, but I also knew certain limitations came with my sex.

I just hoped I made it out alive as his arm cocked back and I felt the full force of a grown man's strength catch the side of my jaw, sending me flying. The explosion of pain radiated out from the strike point until the whole side of my face started to throb as I tried to push myself up off the floor, tried to gain my feet and my advantage of wiry quickness. But before I even had my upper body lifted up, his knees were at the sides of my hips, pinning me back down to the floor.

"You're never going to get away with this," I said, trying to beat back the old, familiar tug of genuine fear. It had been so long since I felt it, since I knew how fucked I truly was, how utterly devoid of hope, of rescue. I always had my men and women. I always had someone at my back. For the first time in more years than I cared to think about, I was completely and utterly alone.

"What? You gonna get your hacker friends to track me down? Get your sniper friends to take me out?" My eyes must have widened or my mouth opened, because his handsome, evil face turned out an ugly sneer. "Didn't think I'd know about them?" he asked, shaking his head. "Not as clever as you've always thought you were, Willow." He sat his ass back on his heels, watching me for a minute. I could have squirmed. I could have struck out, but the energy would have been wasted. It would be better to wait, to see where he planned to go from there, conserve my strength until I had a real shot. He clicked his tongue. "I guess I have to teach you a lesson, huh?"

I guess I have to teach you a lesson, huh?

Those ten words.

Fuck.

Those ten words had the nausea rising up my throat, threatening the very real likelihood of vomiting all over myself. But then he shifted his weight and I had a split second to register his fists rising before the pain started.

It felt like it went on forever, fists pounding into my jaw, my cheekbones, my stomach, his boots in my ribs, my back. There was no way to explain the pain of a beating, to describe how the sensations were all distinctly singular, but at the same time, how they all started to meld together, until it was all there was in the world: crippling, unthinkable pain that you prayed would hurt enough for your body to give up and let you pass out.

All I could hear was his grunting, his angry voice calling out, "bitch, slut, cunt, whore" with each blow. Then, some time later, I heard screaming. I wasn't even aware that it was coming from me until I felt the rough, rawness of my throat.

Then, suddenly, I heard the shots. At first, I heard them with genuine relief: it was over. He shot me. I was going to die. *Thank God.*

But then I felt only confusion as he sat back on his heels, his brows drawing together, like he was confused too.

"We're coming for you, mother fucker!" I heard shouted from outside.

Then suddenly, the weight was off of me. My head turned to the side to watch as he ran toward the door where, I imagined, he would try to take off into the old junkyard out back. I watched the door for a while. Five, ten minutes, I wasn't sure how long, but I was positive he was coming back. When longer passed and he didn't, I slowly tried to push myself up. The pain in my center was screaming out the very real likelihood of broken ribs and I felt the tears streaming hot and fast down my cheeks, burning into the open cuts I knew were spread across my face.

God fucking damn it.

"Fuck," I groaned, biting into my swollen lip as I felt the pain bring with it light-headedness and the threat of unconsciousness. I wasn't going to pass out. I was going to get my feet and I was going to get the fuck out of my safe house and I was going to...

I didn't know what I was going to do.

I couldn't go back to Hailstorm. I couldn't show up there looking how I knew I must have been looking. I couldn't answer their questions and bring them trouble. I needed to find another way to handle it. I needed...

"Shit," I cried out, not even caring how loud I was as I took slow, careful steps toward the door.

Okay. I had to *focus*.

First, I needed to get out of the house. I needed to get to my car. From there, I needed to get to a store and get elastic bandages, peroxide, triple antibiotic, and gauze. Then I needed to get to a gas station with an outside entrance to a bathroom and get cleaned up. From there... I had no fucking idea, but that was enough to keep be busy for a couple hours.

I pushed the front door open and stepped into my front lawn and froze.

There, standing on the sidewalk, staring at my house, was a group of the gang members from across the street.

Gunshots. There were gunshots. From outside. *No way.*

"We didn't step *one mother fucking foot* on your property," the leader called, waving his gun around carelessly.

"I was screaming," I heard myself say, my voice raspy and raw, but it was an accusation.

"Bitch," he said, shaking his head. "You got yourself roughed up. That sucks and all, but I wasn't putting my cock on the line in case that threat you delivered earlier meant *not even if I am screaming for help*."

I reached into my back pocket for my wallet, pulling out all the cash I had inside which must have been close to five-hundred bucks. "I need someone to get me some stuff from the store. The rest is yours to keep," I said, thinking it would likely be a better idea to not show up at some store looking how I looked. The leader jerked his chin toward one of his guys who stalked forward toward me and reached for the cash. "Peroxide, elastic bandages, triple antibiotic, and gauze."

"Got it," he said, wincing a little at the mess I knew my face was before he ran off.

"Ain't gonna ask what happened 'cause it ain't my business. But we see him again, you want a shout out?"

I moved over toward my car, opening the door and sitting inside, my legs in the driveway. "You see him again, I want fifty fucking bullets ripping his body apart," I said honestly. "You do that, you get a quarter of a mill from me the next day."

One of his brows went up before he gave me an small smile. "I might let my women sell themselves," he started oddly, "but I don't fucking put my hands on them."

"A pimp with morals," I said, attempting a smile, but it hurt too much. "Color me surprised."

"Just sayin'," he went on, not seeming the least bit offended, "that shit don't fly. We see him, they're identifying him by dental records."

I looked down at my hands, feeling weak for the first time in thirteen years. I didn't like it. It didn't sit right. "Kick the fucker's teeth in too," I mumbled, a little surprised at the vengeance in my voice. That wasn't me. I didn't go into things hot. I never let my feelings cloud a mission. That wasn't to say I didn't get angry, I didn't get bone-deep livid at some of the stuff I had seen, but I always took that and kept it locked up so I could be clear-headed.

"Here," I heard someone say, and I heard the rustling of a plastic bag and looked up to see the kid I sent to the store coming up, holding out the bag.

"Thanks," I said, taking the bag from him and carefully sliding my legs into the car. "Can one of you go grab my cell off the floor inside? I'll give you my number. You get him? You call me. I'll be by with the money once I make sure it's the right body."

"Slick got a picture," the leader told me. "We'll make sure we got the right guy before we kill him," he said, giving me an odd smile.

"Alright," I said, slipping my key into the ignition as someone came back with my cell. I rattled off the number, gave them a small nod, then got the fuck out of there.

It was nearing the latest part of the night, or earliest part of the morning, depending on whether you slept or not. The gas station was long abandoned and the guy behind the counter inside had his feet propped up, watching some rerun on the TV, his back to me. I pulled up to the bathroom and dragged myself inside. Taking as deep a breath as my aching ribs would allow, I looked up into the mirror.

"Jesus Christ," I mumbled, shaking my head at my reflection. I wasn't particularly a vain woman, but I knew there was going to be a scar or two. My left eye was swollen, but not to the point of closing. My right eye was blackened so bad it looked like it was the effect of poorly applied makeup. My nose, bleeding. My cheek, bruised and bleeding. My jaw, bruised. I reached down, lifting my shirt and tucking it up under my bra.

The bruising was just starting, a smattering of deep purple and blue. I sucked in a breath, trying to gauge if they were broken, cracked, or just bruised. I decided on cracked, eternally the optimist and ever the hater of hospitals, and started the long, slow, painful process of binding them up.

Finished, I pushed my shirt back down and set to cleaning my face. I watched my eyes in reflection, knowing what I had to do. And hating it. Maybe it was pride. Maybe it was shame. But whatever it was, made a coiling sensation tighten in my stomach.

"It's the only way," I said into the quiet of the room, my voice echoing back to me, trying to will myself to believe it.

CASH

I went into my car and waited for sunrise then I drove there with a pit in my stomach.

By the time I pulled up to the gate, I was ready to crawl out of my skin.

I tried to climb out of my car without wincing, failed, but walked up to the men outside the gate like I wasn't half-broken, like I could raise all kinds of hell if I needed to. Before I was even half-way there, one of the probates was running inside to, presumably, find someone with more authority to deal with me.

"Whoa whoa whoa... dunno what you are doing..." one of the probates started, obviously not knowing who I was.

"I need to talk to Reign."

"Listen, lady..." he started again.

"He owes me. I am calling it in."

"I don't know who you..."

"My name is Lo," I said, my voice getting loud. "I fucking saved Summer and Reign owes me. This is me calling it in!" I was shouting and I was too hurt, too tired, and too embarrassed to care.

I heard the crunching of shoes as the other guy came back with, I hoped, Reign.

"Lo?"

Oh, shit.

Anyone, literally fucking *anyone* but him...

I sucked in a breath, pulled my shoulders back, tucked my pride away, and turned.

SEVEN

Cash

I had barely gotten four hours of rest when someone was pounding on my fucking door at the compound.

"Someone better be fucking dead," I growled, climbing out of bed while pulling jeans up my legs. I swung open the door, eyes still adjusting to being awake. "What?" I asked the probate whose name I hadn't thought to ask yet.

"There's some woman at the gate saying she's calling in a favor Reign owes her."

I felt my lips quirk up. "Reign owes some chick a favor?" I asked, reaching for a tee out of my dresser, slipping into my shoes, then following him into the hall. "This I got to see."

"This is me calling it in!" a familiar voice screamed and I felt the lazy smirk turn into a full-on grin. Lo. Lo was calling in her favor. And I got to be the one to deal with her. Maybe that was good enough reason to lose a few hours of sleep.

"Lo?" I asked, my tone amused as I moved through the gate

the probate opened for me.

Her shoulders squared, no doubt less than thrilled to hear my voice, which only made my smile widen.

But then she turned to me fully and the smile fell away with what felt like a kick to my gut. Her gorgeous face was fucking... brutalized. Her eyes were swollen and blackened, bruises were darkening over her cheeks and jaw. There were cuts where fists must have landed multiple times. She winced as she took a step forward, making my eyes fall to her torso where you could see the unmistakable bulge of elastic wrappings through her tight t-shirt.

"What the fuck?" I heard myself hiss.

I knew Lo was a badass. She had a reputation that made most men's seem warm and fuzzy. She had done some shit in her life, she had ordered things done in her life, that most people couldn't fathom. She was trained, she was ruthless, and she was accustomed to being down in the trenches with her men. It stood to reason that she had gotten herself into sticky situations before, that she had gotten herself roughed up.

But... *fuck.*

It looked like someone had used her face as his own personal punching bag.

Now, if there's anything anyone knows about me: it was that I loved me some women. I loved them in all their pain-in-the-ass perfection. And to see that someone dared raised their hand to that perfection? Yeah... that shit would never fly with me.

"I'm calling it in, Cash," she said, raising her chin slightly.

"Honey, what happened to your face?" I asked, getting close.

"Call Reign," she said, ignoring my question.

"Lo, what happened to your face?" I pressed again, hand raising and brushing across her bruised jaw. She flinched and I felt the kick to my gut again.

"You *have* to help me," she said, her eyes looking almost glassy for a second. "Please call Reign." There was a hint of genuine desperation in her voice that was so very much unlike her that I knew there was no way I wasn't going to help her.

"Lo, let's get you out of here for a bit, okay?" I asked, reaching for her arm, glad when she didn't flinch away from my touch.

"I need to talk to Reign."

"I'll talk to Reign," I agreed as I led her back toward her little hatchback, but steering her toward the passenger door, opening it for her. "Get in," I said, my tone soft. When she attempted a brow raise and opened her mouth to object, I shook my head. "Get in the fucking car, babe." She huffed, but slowly lowered herself in. I moved around the hood, nodding at the probates. "Tell Repo I will text him about the Mallicks when I deal with this shit."

"Should we call the prez?"

"You keep this shit to your fucking selves until I say otherwise, understood?" I asked, my voice dipping low and threatening and it was so unlike the Cash they knew that they immediately straightened.

"Yeah, man. No problem."

"Won't say shit," the other agreed.

"See that you don't," I agreed, getting behind the driver's seat and adjusting it back. "Keys, Lo," I said, extending my hand to her.

"Where are we going?" she asked, handing them over without a fight.

"Can you get the belt on?" I asked instead, knowing she wouldn't like the answer to her question. Her arm cocked back but her breath hissed out of her mouth.

"I'm fine," she said, waving her hand.

I gave her a tight-lipped smile, leaning across her body to grab the belt, making our faces close. Her eyes immediately fell to her lap. It was so submissive that I started to imagine all the awful ways I could make the fucker who made her act like that way pay.

The belt clicked. "You alright?" I asked, not moving away.

"I'm fine," she said immediately, knee-jerk.

"Lo," I said and paused, waiting for her gaze to lift. It did, hesitantly. "Are you okay?"

Her eyes searched mine for a moment and her lip trembled slightly when she finally admitted, "No."

Shit.

"Well, we'll see what we can do about that, yeah?" I asked, winking at her, then moving back into my seat. She needed the space to pull herself together. She would never forgive herself if she broke down in front of me.

So I put the car into drive and I drove away while she took as deep of breaths as her ribs would allow and pulled it together.

I kept my mouth shut despite having a dozen questions I wanted to ask: Who had beat her? Did she know them? Was this linked to the bombings? Why wasn't she going to Hailstorm for help? What could I do to erase that haunted look in her eyes?

The list went on and on.

In the end, all I could do was drive. She didn't need my questions. She needed a bed to lie down on, some pain medicine, maybe a shot or two, and some sleep.

I could wait.

EIGHT

Lo

I wasn't going to cry. Hell to the no. That was *not* going to happen. It was certainly not going to happen in front of fucking Cash... no matter how nice he was being to me. Actually, the nice thing might have been why I was all teary-eyed in the first place. If he would just be his normal cocky, flirty, pain in the ass self, I probably would have just felt irritated and sexually frustrated. But, no, he had to go and be sweet. The bastard.

I blinked away the tears and worked through the hitch in my breathing, watching out the side window as we passed through the industrial side of town where The Henchmen clubhouse was located, through the part that was sketchy, but not scary, then into the 'burbs.

My eyes slanted toward him, my brows drawing together. Where the hell could he possibly be taking me in the suburbs? Then, like the beginning of some really awful sitcom, he pulled past a huge wooden sign boasting the name "Oliver Grove Townhouses" and we drove down a seemingly endless winding road of connected, identical half-homes.

By the time Cash pulled my car up in front of one that was no different from the others except for its empty flowerbeds, well, my mouth was hanging open.

"What are we doing here?" I asked, turning slightly to look at him, hearing one of the girls across the street playing a game of hopscotch (yes, hopscotch... I *did* say it was like a bad sitcom!) squealed loudly.

"Got a problem with my house, baby?" he asked, giving me a boyish smile as he unbelted himself and then me.

"You live *here*?" I asked, my tone a complete accusation.

As an answer, he just grinned bigger, getting out of the car and waving at the girls across the street.

"Cash!" they screamed like he was a long-absent, favorite uncle.

I gritted my teeth and climbed out of the car, careful to keep my face tilted away from the girls who, well, didn't need to see that kind of shit at their ages, and making my way slowly toward the house.

"Is that your *girlfriend*?" one of them said in that teasing girl tone and I felt myself wanting to smile, but it hurt too much.

"Hey, be cool," Cash said to them and they giggled.

"Is she pretty?" the more determined of the two pressed.

I winced, standing facing his front door, looking at my feet.

"The prettiest," he said, making my belly do a weird fluttery thing and I fought the urge to look over at him. "Next to you two," he added and there was more giggling. "Now get. I have to get my guest inside."

"Fiiiiine," they chorused and I could hear their feet taking off across the street.

"You're good with kids," I remarked, feeling awkward as he

slipped a key into his lock and opened the door.

"Lot of the men have kids," he said, shrugging off the compliment.

He stepped into his house, moving toward the kitchen that was situated just behind the living room of the open floor plan. Everything inside screamed "bachelor", from the empty wooden floors to the deep burnt orange color of the walls that were without any kind of art, to the worn and comfortable looking black leather couches facing the unnecessarily giant flatscreen. There were no throw pillows on the couches and no curtains on the windows, just woven wooden shades.

I turned toward the kitchen, watching him through the cutout in the wall, smelling fresh coffee brewing and it was almost enough to make me want to cry again. "Why do you live here?" I asked, needing to keep the conversation on safe topics.

Cash leaned his arms down on the counter and ducked his head to watch me. "Last fucking place in the world you would think to look for a one-percenter, ya know?" he asked with a devilish little grin and I felt a fluttering in an area decidedly lower than my stomach. God, but he was just a walking, talking, grinning temptation.

"Good plan," I mumbled when he just kept staring at me like he expected a response. I shifted my feet and he stood back up, moving around his kitchen.

"Coffee?"

"Yeah. One sugar."

He walked out a few minutes later, holding a coffee cup in one hand and gripping a bottle in his other. He handed me the coffee and I took it, sipping even though it was way too hot, just to have something to do. "What's that?" I asked as his hand uncurled to reveal a prescription bottle.

"Pain meds," he said, untwisting the cap of what looked to be a half-full bottle. "A few of us thought it would be fun to take our bikes off road. Drunk, obviously," he said, dropping two pills into his hand before twisting the bottle closed and slipping it into his jean pocket. "Sixteen stitches," he said with a smirk as he lifted up the side of his shirt to show a scar that ran up the side of his body. But I wasn't looking at the scar. What woman in her right mind would be looking at the scar when there were several deliciously perfect sculpted abs to ogle? "Hey Lo," he said, his voice teasing and my eyes guiltily flew upward. "See something you like, babe?"

Oh hell. Goddamn it all.

"A couple more hours in the gym could turn that six pack into an eight," I said, trying to sound casual, trying to not let on that while I had just been viciously beaten a few hours before and hadn't slept in well over twenty-four hours, that I was absolutely turned on.

"Sweetheart, do I look like a man who wastes his time in a gym?" he asked, dropping his shirt and holding out the pills toward me.

"Thanks, but no," I said, shaking my head. "I need to have my wits about me. I need..."

"Honey, you need to take these pills, go lie down in bed, and get some fuckin' rest. That is *all* you need to do right now."

"Cash, I really appreciate it, but I have to talk to Reign and get..."

I didn't get the rest out because, suddenly, he wasn't a safe four feet away from me anymore. He was all up in my personal space and his hand was lifted, his forefinger stroking over my lips gently. I swear that touch went straight to between my legs in a way that had a rush of wetness pooling there. My gaze flew up to his, finding his deep green eyes a little heavy-lidded, a little heated. In response, I felt my lips parting.

I realized my mistake a second later when I felt the pills slip inside as Cash smiled softly. "Swallow, baby."

Jesus Christ. That sounded sexual in all the right ways. I pressed my thighs closer together as I felt my eyes get heavier. Cash chuckled, a low, deep, rumbling sound that snapped me out of my daze and had me immediately sipping from my coffee and internally berating myself for being so freaking obvious about everything around him.

"Come on," he said, tugging a little at the hem of my tee before moving toward the staircase that led upstairs that had a knot tightening inside. Stairs. That was so going to hurt. But I wasn't going to be a baby about it and beg to stay on the couch instead. Cash was waiting two steps up when I finally got there. His head tilted to the side as he watched me. "How pissed would you be if I tried to help you right now?" he asked, sounding like he already knew the answer. I gave him a glare as I gripped the railing hard enough to make my fingers go white. "Thought so," he said, nodding and running up the stairs, leaving me to eke my way up alone.

I made the top landing what felt like an hour later, slumping slightly forward and deep breathing through the pain. Reassuring myself that the pain meds would kick in before I knew it, I pushed down the hall past the open door to the bathroom and to the only other door upstairs. I squished the knowledge that that meant I was going to be sleeping in the master bedroom, in Cash's bed, and forced myself to step into the doorway.

Well then.

That was how you did a bedroom.

The walls were a deep brown, all the trim and ceiling painted a soft beige. The mammoth California king bed was on top of a high dark (almost black) wood platform with matching headboard. There were extra pillows for overnight guests (of which, I was sure he had many) and the comforter was a crisp white seersucker material that made me want to bury underneath it and never come out.

"Kick outta those shoes," Cash said, back turned to me as he looked inside his closet. Dumbly, without any other option, I kicked out of my shoes. Cash turned, moving toward me, an oversize oatmeal-colored thermal bunched up in his hands. Without even explaining, he stopped in front of me and pushed it over my head, reaching for my hands and guiding them into the sleeves. I was too stunned to even think about brushing him away to do it myself. That was, until his hands pulled the material down my torso and his fingers moved to my button and zip.

"What are you doing?" I half gasped, half yelped, trying to brush his hands away.

But they stayed put and his gaze lifted to mine. "Baby, just let me fucking help you, okay?"

Knowing leaning down to push my pants down would be nothing short of excruciating and having someone willing to help me would save me a lot of pain and frustration, well, it didn't leave me room to argue.

Seeing my decision made, he ducked his head again and his hands slipped slightly into my waistband as he pushed the button through. The brush of his fingers against my belly had a slight tremble moving through my body and I prayed he didn't feel it. But then his gaze lifted to mine, questioning, searching, and I knew he had. He looked like he wanted to say something, but thought better of it, and ducked his head again. He pushed down the zip and his hands moved to my hips, grabbing my jeans and pulling them down carefully, watching as if not sure if there were any injuries anywhere else.

When he had my jeans down to my knees, his fingers brushed over my thighs that were somehow bruise-free. "Thank fuck," he murmured to himself.

"What?" I asked, watching the top of his head.

"Nothing," he said, shaking his head, and pulling my feet out of the legs. "Come on, sweetheart, let's get you in bed," he said, touching my hip and gently pushing me forward.

By the time I got myself under the blankets and into a position that didn't hurt, the drugs were making the throbbing and stabbing sensations completely dull and making my eyes get heavy. The blankets got pulled up under my chin and tucked gently under my shoulders. The bed depressed and my eyes fluttered open to see Cash sitting off the edge, looking down at me. His hand moved toward my face, hesitated, then stroked through my hair instead. Even half-numb from whatever heaven-sent drugs Cash had given me, I felt a tingle spread across my scalp.

"Can I ask you something?" he asked, his voice quiet. I made some kind of murmuring sound that he took for agreement and pressed on, "The fucker didn't rape you, did he?"

The word sent a jolt through my body and Cash's hand froze its stroking of my hair. "No," I said, the word firm, a little horrified.

"Didn't think so," he said to himself, brushing through my hair and I had to fight to keep my eyes open. "Sleep, baby."

"'Kay," I heard myself say and my eyes drifted closed easily.

Just before sleep claimed me, I heard a low chuckle. "I think I like you better all drugged-out complacent," he mumbled, but I was too tired to yell at him, so I didn't.

–

I woke up slowly, my body feeling sluggish, my brain feeling like it was wading through mud to get a thought to form properly. My eyes opened, squinting at the near-darkness of the only vaguely familiar room and I moved to bolt upward, disoriented. The stab through my ribs had me yelping loudly, as I lie back down and brushed a stray tear off my cheek.

"Fuck fuck fuck," I whimpered, the pain returning fast and furious, taking me by surprise and completely overwhelming me.

A light flicked on and I turned my head to see Cash leaning against the doorjamb. "Waking up is the worst," he said quietly, pausing before he moved into the room. "Drugs wear off?"

"Everything hurts," I admitted, surprising myself more than him. That wasn't something I did, sharing how I was feeling, not even when I was hurt. I didn't do that. It was admitting weakness.

At my words, his face fell slightly and I wished I could suck them back in and see the jovial, carefree Cash again. "I ordered food," he admitted, surprising me. "You want to take a shower first?"

God, how did he guess so right so easily?

"Yeah," I admitted, clenching my teeth and getting up out of bed.

"Easy," he said, reaching for me when I swayed on my feet. "You aren't gonna impress me by being all badass, so take your time."

I flashed my eyes at him though inside, I was grateful. I followed him into the hall and through to the bath and watched as he rummaged around in his linen closet and pulled out: two towels (yes, two, as if he knew I would need one to wrap my hair up in), a toothbrush in its packaging, a brush, a small basket full of first aid supplies, and a spare t-shirt that would work as a dress despite how tall I was.

"Clean up, get your face cared for, then call me up here and I'll wrap your ribs."

"It's fine. I can..."

"Sure you can," he agreed, but his lips were twitching, like he found my inability to accept help amusing. "But I can do it without hurting you and I can do it tighter so you don't wince every time you take a step. So call me or I'll just let myself in in ten minutes."

"Fine," I grumbled, avoiding my reflection in the mirror above his sink.

"Get your scrub on. I'll go wait for the food."

With that, he was gone and I went through the process of stripping off my clothes and unwrapping my bandages. I slipped out of my panties, turned the tap on hot, and poured hand soap on them. I wasn't a particularly high maintenance woman, but I absolutely refused to wear panties two days in a row without a wash. I went into the linen closet and found a blow dryer buried in the back and placed it on the counter. It would work for a makeshift clothes dryer.

I kept my face out of the water as I showered, slathering on soap and shampoo that smelled just like Cash and liking it a little too much. I dried, I dabbed antibiotic on my face, brushed my hair, blasted my panties with the blow dryer then slipped into them and got the tee over my head.

"Alright," I yelled as I scrubbed my teeth real quick.

Cash came in a minute later, going into the linen cabinet and getting fresh elastic bandages, leaving me to wonder how often he needed them. Normal people didn't keep a big supply of elastic bandages in their supply cabinets. I knew this because I had never even seen an elastic bandage until I needed one. But every bathroom closet at Hailstorm was stacked to the gills with them.

"Tee up," he said casually, pulling the paper wrapping off the bandages.

I took a shaky breath, trying to stifle the surge of insecurity I felt at that demand. It wasn't that I was *insecure*. Far from. I kept my body fit because my lifestyle and job demanded it, but that being said, I knew that keeping it fit kept it aesthetically appealing. I had toned legs with just enough of a womanly plump to them, same could be said for my ass. My stomach was flat, the slightest outline of abs could be seen on some days. My boobs had remained high and perky despite getting closer to forty than thirty and them being large to begin with. I had a good body.

But Cash seeing it... hell, that was enough to make a woman who never blushed, blush.

I grabbed the hem of my shirt and slowly pulled it up, unable to help myself from watching Cash for some kind of reaction. He kept his head lowered as he pulled off the little metal doohickey and started to unravel the bandage. His eyes rose slowly, landing on my hips and moving upward over my belly and stopping where my hands were holding the tee just under my breasts. His air rushed out of his chest, but he made no comment. He didn't ogle, he just slowly went to work.

"Okay," he said a while later, his hands moving to cover mine as he pulled the material of his tee down my body, covering me. "Did I hurt you?" he asked, finally looking me in the eye.

"No," my lips mumbled, my brain in no way part of the equation because suddenly, all I could think about was him lifting me up onto the counter, ripping off my panties, and burying inside me. Maybe it was because he had been so gentle with me, so careful. Or maybe it was because he had the respect for me to not make sexual comments when I was mostly naked in front of him as he wrapped me. Whatever it was, all I could think from the second he pressed the first inch of bandage to my skin, was how good his touch felt, how much better it would feel touching me places right above and right below where he was actually touching me.

"Good. Then let's feed you."

So then... he fed me.

NINE

Cash

Two of those pills knocked me on my ass for eight hours straight back when I took them. I figured that gave me just enough time to get to the clubhouse, grab Repo, see the Mallicks, then get back home and order food before she woke up. So I jotted down a note just in case she woke up and put it on the nightstand next to a spare gun, just in case trouble managed to find her, though there had been no tail the whole way to my place.

"What the fuck?" Repo asked when I pulled up to the compound, raising a brow at Lo's car. "Dude, I know you're like my superior and all that shit... but I'm not fucking going anywhere in that car."

I laughed, slamming the door and locking it. "We can take one of your projects then but I'm driving."

Repo gave me a grin then ran off toward the back of the property where he kept his half a dozen cars in various stages of repair and rebuild. That was how Repo blew off steam. That was how he channeled his dark moods when they came over him. The kicker was, he never wanted them when they were done. The second they were restored and running, he wanted them gone. He ended up making bank selling his finished projects.

I waited at the gates as he rumbled up in what looked like a '82 Firebird in a faded, God-awful yellow color. It was making a clanging sound that I knew was probably not a good sign, but Repo seemed completely unconcerned by. He pulled out the gates, leaving the engine running, and hopped out to run to the passenger side.

"Is this thing going to make it?" I asked as I sat down in the driver's side.

"It should," he said, shrugging like it didn't matter to him either way if it did or not.

"Right," I said, laughing and reaching for the stereo.

"Oh God, man... not more of that shit," he groaned, head on the rest, looking at the torn material on the ceiling.

"Shit?" I asked, one-handed connecting my iPod to his cassette tape adapter.

"That nineties and early two-thousands grunge, rock, alt shit," Repo, a very loyal metal fan winced.

I felt myself grin as I clicked on Nirvana and cranked it up. "Kids these days," I said, shaking my head at him despite there only being maybe a six or seven year difference in our ages.

We pulled up to Chaz's, the Mallick's bar, a few minutes later. Bikes were parked out front, Chaz's being for some reason a watering hole for the local weekend warriors. Apparently, a little bombing didn't shut down business.

"Are they as badass as their reputation?" Repo asked, looking at the bar, rocking back on his heels.

"I only know Shane and Reign knows him better than me, but... yeah," I said, reaching for the door and letting myself in.

The inside was sleek, almost upscale with slate gray walls

and floors stained so dark they were almost black which matched the bar to the right and all the tables and chairs inside. As I had expected, there was a table to the back with six black-haired (one with some whisps of gray) men with six sets of freakishly light blue eyes that belonged to the Mallick brothers : Ryan, Eli, Mark, Hunter, and Shane, as well as their father, Charles.

Beside me, I felt Repo stiffen when all their heads turned to us almost in unison.

"Henchmen?" I heard Hunter ask, brows drawing together. I knew him. He was the only Mallick son that wasn't in the business, wasn't a loanshark. He had gotten out a few years before, got himself hitched to some hellion named Fiona, had himself a couple of little girls, and worked with a tattoo gun. The rest though, still ruthless, calculating kneecap breakers.

"'Sup Cash?" Shane, the youngest and bulkiest of them asked, nodding his head at us and moving to stand.

"Just figured we would stop by and compare notes."

"Reign isn't stopping by for that?" Shane asked, brows drawing together and I knew they had a bit of a friendship going on since right before Reign met Summer. Well, since he told us one of his clients was one of our men and that man turned out to be a snitch.

"Reign is over at Lyon's," I said, shrugging. They knew the deal.

"We keep our noses out of other organizations around here, you know that," Ryan, the oldest, the more professional of all of them reminded me.

"Know that. Know we all also have enemies. Just wanted to see if we had any in common."

"You really think you, us, Hailstorm, Lyon, and Lex have a common enemy?" Chaz, their father asked and it took everything I had to keep the lazy grin on my face. He reminded me a lot of my father- fierce, commanding.

"Covering our bases. Talked to Hailstorm already. Came up with nothing."

"Guys want a round?" Shane asked, already waving a hand at the bartender.

"Whiskey," I answered.

"You?" Shane asked.

"Repo," Repo supplied. "And sure... vodka is fine."

"That your '82?" Mark asked, looking at me.

"His," I said, jerking my chin. "He gets bored with them when they're pretty again so if you're looking for a car..."

"Keep that in mind," Mark agreed, shutting up with a look from their father.

"You see Lex's?" Shane asked, leaning back in his chair.

"Not yet."

"Fire completely gutted the place."

I felt my brows drawing together, my smirk falling. I knew that his place got the worst of it, but I didn't think it was that bad. "Did the evil fuck make it out?"

Shane shrugged a big shoulder. "No one has any word on him. We know there were several casualties among his men, but no one knows or no one is talking about Lex's whereabouts."

"So we got shit," I said, throwing back my whiskey and handing the glass back to the waitress who brought it over, giving her a weak imitation of the smile I would normally give her, being all tits, ass, and long hair. She was so lush and, normally, I'd have been minutes away from burying deep in her pussy, no matter what was going on with the club. What the fuck was wrong with me?

"That about sums it up," Chaz agreed, giving me a 'what can 'ya do' shrug.

"You'll keep us in the loop if you come up with anything?"

Chaz nodded.

"Tell Reign that Lea *is* dragging my ass to whatever dinner party shit Summer has planned."

"Another fuckin' dinner party?" I asked, flat out grinning. "After the shitstorm that was her last one?" Shane sighed and I laughed. "You know, I never thought I'd see the day that two of the biggest dogs in town would be led around by their balls by some women."

"Should be happy," Shane said, smiling. "Got yourself less competition now. Just three of these fucks," he said, waving at his brothers. "And... who? Breaker and Shooter?"

I laughed at that until Repo cleared his throat. "Break and Shoot took off last night."

My smile died and I turned to Repo, eyes questioning. "What?"

"Shredder told me Rick told him that he saw them at Paine's shop, looking like they were sayin' goodbye then taking off with some dark-haired chick with a busted face."

"And you were sitting on this shit because?" I asked, feeling anger, strange and unsettling, build up inside.

"You can't honestly fucking think Break or Shoot would be in on this," Repo reasoned.

He was right. On a normal day, I would never think they would meddle in our, let alone everyone's, shit. Breaker and Shooter were contract muscle. They did jobs for whoever paid the right price. Breaker, well, he was good at breaking people. Shooter, well, was good at shooting. They were tight as brothers and generally kept to themselves business-wise. I'd shared more than a few nights of debauchery with Shooter- drinking too much, taking bets on which one of us would land the hottest chick in the room. I didn't know Breaker well, but Reign did. They were friends, as much as anyone outside of the club could be our friends. That being said, them taking off in the middle of the night when bombs were going off? That didn't sit right.

"Wasn't Breaker," Eli, the quietest, but also the most lethal of the brothers, spoke up confidently. "He's a hands-on kinda guy." His eyes met mine and held. "People recognize their own kind," he explained, looking down at his hands for a second. "You told me that Lex was beaten to death in an alley, then yeah, you can point at Breaker. But placing bombs? Too impersonal. Not his style."

"I'll get in contact, feel things out," I said, starting to feel bone-deep tired. There was fucking too much going on with the bombs, the accusations, whatever the fuck was going on with Lo... all of it. It needed to get it all the fuck sorted out so things could go back to normal- drinking, and riding, and women.

We walked back out to the car a few minutes later, Repo taking my glare with a defiant chin raise. "Think next time you share information with me before sending me in there and making me look dumb, yeah?"

He stopped at the passenger side of the car, arms spread out over the roof. "Don't blame me for you dropping the ball. There's bombs and you take off the next day and no one sees you for hours?"

"Careful, kid," I said, biting the inside of my cheek, trying to keep my head on straight. I was tired, I was confused, and I was in no position to get into a fight with one of the men, especially considering that he was absolutely fucking right. I should have been at the club. I should have been there setting things to right the second I knew there was a bombing, not fucking around at Hailstorm. I should have been gathering information, not undressing Lo.

"I'm not calling you out," he said, holding up his hands. "Just pointing some shit out before someone else starts saying them in less of a brotherly way."

"Cut me some slack this week, Repo. Got a lot of shit I'm dealing with." With that, and no further explanation, I drove us back to the compound. I showed my face for a while, talking to the members hanging around, making sure no one could say I wasn't there for them.

Finally, around dinner time, I got back in Lo's car and went back to my place to find her still passed out. So I ordered food and waited.

She must have woken up startled by the unfamiliar surroundings, flying up, forgetting about her ribs. The cry she let out had me running up the stairs, stalling outside the door to give her a second to pull herself together. If there was one thing Lo had in spades, aside from the best rack I had ever seen, it was pride. She would never forgive me for seeing her when she was upset.

Watching her slowly lift up my tee and bunch it under her tits... fuck, fuck me. I tried to keep my eyes down, to focus only on the nasty bruises across her ribs. But, well, I was a man after all and she had the fucking perfect body- long, strong legs, flat belly, flare of hips, and she had her hands just high enough for me to see the soft underside of her perfect tits. It took every damn bit of self-control I had to not let my fingers brush there.

She followed me downstairs a few minutes later, wearing nothing but my oversize tee and those black panties with the pink lace trim.

"I got a bit of everything," I said, unable to let any silence hang for too long. I was used to different types of women- women who liked to talk and bitch and fill the silences. Lo seemed perfectly content to not say anything at all and I wondered if that was just how she was- guarded, private, introspective or if it was from spending so much time around her men at Hailstorm.

She reached into the brown bag, pulling out white take-away containers, opening the tops, and setting them in the middle of the table. I watched as she took a plate and loaded up, feeling myself grin when she took enough to feed two growing teenage boys.

"What's your poison, Lo?" I asked, moving into the kitchen for drinks.

"Beer is fine if your taste is as good as your brother's," she said and I watched as she stared down at the dining table for a minute before deciding to move over to the living room and plopped herself down on the couch, reaching for the remote, making herself at home.

I gave her beer, made my plate, and sat down next to her, looking at the survivalist show she picked off of on-demand. "So are you going to tell me what favor you are calling in?"

"I want to talk to Reign," she said, staring pointedly at the TV.

"Honey," I said, sitting up and placing my plate on the coffee table, "I'm the one who got you somewhere safe, got you some medicine, let you sleep, wrapped you up, and fed you. You don't think you can tell me why I needed to do all that?"

"Cash it's..."

"Lo," I cut her off, shaking my head.

She sighed, putting her plate down, almost all eaten. She probably would have finished it if I hadn't distracted her. She took a breath before she turned to me. "Cash, I run a survivalist camp full of ex military who are really, really good at killing people in various ways. I didn't get to where I am today without making a shitton of enemies. Sometimes, not often, but sometimes, they pop up and create trouble."

"So that's all you're going to give me?"

"It's all I have to give. I was in my safe house. It was dark. I have a general description and the direction he took off in. The gang that runs that street are looking for him too."

"Seriously? I mean I know you keep a lot of shitty company, Lo, but a street gang?"

"They bought me medical supplies," she defended. "And they said if they got their hands on him, he'd be identifiable by dental records only."

"So that's why you keep the company of scum? Because

they can do dirty work for you?"

Her eyes narrowed at me. "I can do my own fucking dirty work, Cash."

I didn't doubt that and I didn't know why I was choosing that moment to pick a fight with her. She was hurt, physically but also her pride. I was being a fucking dick for no good reason. It didn't matter what I thought about how she operated her business. All that mattered was she was bloody and bruised and asking me for help.

"You give me a description, I'll put some feelers out, okay?"

Her chest deflated as she realized I was giving in. "Okay."

"How bad you hurting? You want more pills?"

"After this show," she said, sitting back casually and cradling her beer in her hands.

After the show, I shook two more pills into her hand then let her make her way up the stairs again. I tucked her into the bed and waited for her to fall asleep before I slid in behind her. I could have slept down on the couch, but I was trying really hard to convince myself that what I was doing was for her benefit- she'd have me close in case she needed anything in the middle of the night, or if she woke up in pain.

But the truth was, I just wanted to be close for my own reasons, reasons I didn't understand, and reasons I didn't plan on analyzing.

I just climbed in the empty side of the bed, curled up, and waited for sleep to claim me.

It was sometime in the middle of the night when I heard it: whimpering. I slowly surfaced, unsure what the sound was, still drowsy. As my eyes opened and I focused on the back of Lo, curled up away from me, awareness snapped me up.

CASH

"Honey?" I asked, my voice raspy from sleep. She didn't respond, just made more crying sounds. I reached out, grabbing her shoulder gently and pulling her back until she was flat on her back and I was on my side looking down at her. She was sleeping, dreaming. There were tears on her cheeks and her lips were trembling. "Baby, wake up," I said, my voice a little louder. My hand moved out, stroking her hair out of her face. The second my fingers touched her, her body stilled its writhing.

My hand drifted down the side of her neck, stroking the soft skin, down her arm, her side, over the bandages covering her ribs. Soon, the whimpering cries turned into muffled groans and I couldn't stop myself from touching her- over her bruised jaw, down the center of her chest, up the side of her leg.

Slowly, her eyes fluttered open and her brown eyes found mine in the dark.

"Cash?"

TEN

Lo

I was used to the nightmares. I couldn't remember the last time I had a night of completely dreamless sleep. I'd simply seen too many things, been through too much shit to be granted the serenity of a restful night. I accepted that as part of my life, as penance for the dark shit I had been involved in.

I woke up slowly, my skin feeling oddly tingly; my chest feeling tight. I felt the pulsating need between my thighs as the final hold of sleep let go and realized with a blinding kind of clarity that I was turned on. I was turned on in a bed that wasn't my own.

My eyes fluttered open to see the dark outline of a male body half-propped up over mine. It was then I felt a hand brushing across the very lowest point of my belly, toying with the waistband of my panties, his fingers brushing the exposed few inches beneath my bandages.

Holy shit.

Holy shit.

Cash was touching me.

"Cash?" I heard my voice ask, low and airless.

"You were crying," he said back, just as quietly.

"Cash what..."

"You were crying and when I touched you, you stopped."

Wow. Okay. I sucked in a breath, trying to calm the growing sense of need. "I'm not crying anymore."

His head shifted up and there was just enough moonlight slanting through the blinds for me to see his gaze was on my face. "Are you going to make me stop?"

Oh, God. I didn't want him to stop. But he needed to. Right?

"This is a bad..."

"Do you *want* me to stop, Lo?" he asked, his voice getting deeper and I felt it turn my insides to mush. "Don't analyze it, just answer. Do you want me to stop?"

"No," I said before I could stop myself. Then, again before I could stop it, I started, "Cash, everything hurt..."

"Not gonna' fuck you, babe," he said, with a little bit of regret in his voice. "But I promise that, in a few minutes, you won't be feeling any pain."

Well then. I kind of owed it to myself to get pain-free, right? At least, that was what I was going to choose to believe.

"Okay," I said, my breathing already shallow and fast and he wasn't even touching me anymore.

His body shifted slightly, lifting up, as his fingers whispered across the soft skin of my inner thighs. I felt my legs falling open, giving him more access, practically begging him to shift his touch upward and touch me where I really needed it. But his touch remained almost chaste, gentle, moving up to the lace of my panties around my thighs, then back down to my knees, then back up again.

Desire made every nerve ending feel overly sensitive, poised to respond to the barest of caresses. The material of my panties was wet and my hips were shifting around in frustration.

"Cash..." I whimpered. The end of his name caught on a hitch in my breath when his hand shifted and pressed down hard between my legs.

"Soaked," he said on a growl, his fingers shifting so his thumb pressed down on my clit, moving over it with slow, hard pressure side to side. My hand flew out, landing on his shoulder and digging my fingers in.

His thumb moved to start circling over the sensitive point and my ragged breathing turned to quiet groans as he drove me painfully slowly upward, promising oblivion but taking his sweet time to deliver. "Oh, *oh,*" I moaned, feeling myself start to crest. "No!" I cried out loudly as his hand moved away just in time.

"Shh," he shushed me, sounding amused. "I'm not done with you yet," he promised and I felt my pussy clench hard in anticipation.

I felt his weight shift, my eyes still unable to adjust to the darkness. "What are you..." I started and trailed off when his body settled and I felt his mouth close over my cleft through my panties. "Oh my God," I moaned, my hand slapping down on the top of his head, taking in the strange sensation of peach fuzz on one side and soft, long hair on the other. I sank my fingers into the long strands, twisting, and holding on as his tongue moved out and stroked the wet material over my too-sensitive clit.

His hand shifted to move between us and pulled my panties to the side to expose me and I didn't even get a chance to suck in a breath before I felt his tongue slide up my slick cleft and start lavishing over my clit. My orgasm built faster that time, my entire body tense, poised for the release. His other hand moved upward and I felt his finger slide inside me, slow, burying deep, stroking in and out until my moans became choked gasping, then curling upward and stroking over my G-spot.

My climax left me in a suspended nothingness for a long

moment before it finally broke through my system- a deep, fast pulsating around his finger as my thighs shook. My cry cut through the night as the waves kept coming, as his tongue and finger prolonged my release.

"Oh my God," I gasped as the aftershocks made my body tremble slightly.

Cash moved away slowly, pulling out of me, and pushing my panties back into place. His body shifted back to my side and he reached to pull the covers back over my body.

"Sleep, honey."

"Cash..." I started, not sure what I wanted to say, but knowing what just happened changed things and that meant we should probably discuss it.

"Sleep," he said again, moving over toward the far end of the bed and stretching out, leaving me little choice but to do what I was told.

–

I woke up in the early morning out of habit, and thanks to the fact that I spent almost the entire day before sleeping. My ribs objected to movement, but the stabbing was more of a dull ache and I realized maybe they were bruised and not cracked after all.

I went into the bathroom and went through my morning rituals until I felt mostly human again. Looking at my reflection, I took a deep breath. "What the fuck did you do?" I asked myself on a whisper. If I let myself think about it, I could still practically feel his tongue on me. So... yeah... I needed to not think about it.

It was stupid to think it mattered. I was a grown ass woman. Hooking up was hooking up. Sex was sex. That was the end of it. Lord knew, he had enough casual sex in his day for it to mean literally nothing that he had his face buried between my thighs just a few hours before.

The smell of coffee was the only thing that finally dragged me down the stairs and into the kitchen to where Cash was casually sitting on top of his counter in faded jeans and a white tee. A coffee cup was poised on his knee as he clicked away at his cell phone.

"Can I grab a cup?" I asked, moving toward the coffee machine where he had already set out a spare cup, a sugar bowl, and a spoon.

"Yeah, honey."

Oh, hell. He needed to stop calling me the cutesy names. I swear the word landed with a flutter in my nether-regions. The effect was strong enough to stop me mid-grab for the coffee pot.

"Sleep well?" he asked, as if it was perfectly normal for us to have conversations over coffee.

"Yeah. Those pills really throw you for a loop," I said, pouring my coffee, and turning to make my way out of the kitchen.

"Figured we would head up to Hailstorm today," he said, making my heart fly up into my throat and my body whirl around to face him, effectively spilling a third of my coffee onto the floor.

"Shit," I cursed, shaking the hot coffee off my hand.

"I got it," he said, hopping off the counter, somehow doing so without spilling any of *his* coffee, of course. He came toward me, paper towels at the ready and lowered himself down the floor at my feet. I knew I needed to take a step back, put some space between us, but my brain couldn't seem to get the message to my legs. Then, done scrubbing, his head cocked up to look at me and a devilish grin spread on his lips, making his face way too goddamn handsome. "I like this position," he said, one of his hands moving up toward the hem of my tee and inching it up.

He was an inch from my panties when I finally snapped myself out of it and swatted his hand away. "Hope you enjoyed last night because it's the last time you get anywhere near my pussy," I managed to choke out in what I hoped was a stern voice.

His smile didn't falter. If anything, it got all the more sinister. "I did enjoy last night. You got one sweet pussy for someone so fucking sour. But I can tell you one thing, as much as I enjoyed last night..." Oh, crap. I knew what was coming. "You enjoyed it a helluva lot more. Or was I imagining your pussy squeezing my finger as you came hard enough to wake up my neighbors?"

"Tell me something, *honey,*" I said, lowering my eyes at him, feeling embarrassment lead me steadily toward anger which was a much more comfortable emotion to be feeling around him. "Do you always molest half-asleep women who are taking refuge in your bed after getting the shit kicked out of them?"

Cash slowly got to his feet, not taking a single step backward and therefore was privy to the sensation of my hardened nipples (fucking traitors) brush his chest. "Nope. You're the first," he said with a casual shrug. The bastard was supposed to feel guilty even though I knew damn well I had consented. "So why don't you want to go to Hailstorm?"

I could tell from the lack of light in his eyes that he wasn't going to give in. He wasn't going to stop until he got an answer. I shook my head, looking off over his shoulder into the sprawling backyard that endless houses seemed to share. "Look... I didn't always have Hailstorm. And before them, I still had to survive in this life. I got into some shit. I got out of some shit. I don't want any of the dirt from my past thrown at them. Yeah, they'd be all too happy to wipe it off and help me handle it, but I don't want them involved."

I looked back to see him biting on the inside of his cheek, a habit I found myself wondering about. Was it a nervous tick? Was it anger? Was it something he did when he was mulling things over?

"Fair enough," he finally said, surprising me enough to jerk back. "Look... when shit went down with Summer, Reign didn't want to bring the club in on it. That wasn't their mess to clean up. I get it. So no Hailstorm. But you need to get some of your shit."

I felt myself nodding, moving a step back and hating that it always seemed to be me that was retreating. "I have a bag in a storage locker in town."

"Got a key or combination? I'll drop by and pick it up. I got some shit to handle today."

"I can get it."

"Nah. I think you're best staying put right now."

"You're not my father, Cash. You can't fucking ground me."

"No. But I can cuff you to a beam in the basement," he said, looking like he would enjoying doing just that a little bit too much. "You know... for your own safety," he grinned. "Not for any other more... sinister reasons. Totally wouldn't *molest* your very consenting pussy any more than I already have. Nope. Not me. I'd be a perfect gentleman about the whole thing."

"You can't be serious." No fucking way.

"Babydoll," he said, making me curl my lip slightly, "no one would ever accuse me of being serious. But let me tell you, about this... I am *dead fucking serious*. You are staying in this house and you are laying low until we figure this shit out." He paused, his cocky grin coming back. "Or at least until people out there," he waved toward the front door, "can look at you without wincing."

"Listen you cocky, condescending, c...."

"Like the alliteration thing you got going on, but I got shit to do so give me the combination or key and let me get on my way. Or keep wearing nothing but my tees. It's nice having the easy access," he said, moving forward at me and reaching behind me, slipping his hand up the back of my shirt then *under* my panties to squeeze my ass.

Pants.

I needed some fucking pants.

With suspenders.

Or a chastity belt.

"Center Street Storage, number seventy-eight. The combination is forty-two, thirteen, twenty-seven."

His hand did another small squeeze before it pulled completely away. "I find you stepped one foot out of my front door and make no mistake, you'll become intimately acquainted with the basement floor."

I felt my eyes rolling. "What? How are you even going to know? You have nanny cams around here?" I asked his back as he moved toward the front door, grabbing his jacket off a hook behind the door as he went.

"Nah. I live in the fucking suburbs. I got *neighbors,"* he said with a smirk as he went out the front door.

I grimaced at the closed door, knowing all-too-well how nosy neighbors could be. Hell, that was half of the reason I built Hailstorm up on a hill in the middle of nowhere. No one could get all up in my business.

I sighed, looking around his apartment. I was going to go stir crazy stuck in his place for God-knew how long. I went toward the living room, finding my cell on the coffee table and sitting down to call Janie. Again.

Six times later... still no answer.

I put my coffee down and shot her a text.

I know it was you, honey. I don't care. I just want to know you're okay. We can sort this out together. Call me. Anytime. I love you.

Then I made a call that had my stomach swirling so hard that I felt my coffee threatening to make another appearance as I forced myself to swallow hard.

"Morgue."

"It's Lo. Put Doc Fenton on."

There was a pause before another, deeper, sexier voice picked up. "Looking for a body again, Lo?"

God, I hoped to Christ not.

"Mid-twenties female, thin, covered in ink, long dark hair, blue eyes."

"Not the usual big bad then?" he asked and I heard papers flipping. "Nah, Lo. Out of luck this time."

"In luck," I clarified and I heard the sadness in my own voice.

"Oh," Fenton said, sounding almost concerned. "I'll keep an eye out for you, okay?"

"Yeah. I appreciate that."

"Be careful, Lo."

"Always," I agreed, hanging up.

She wasn't dead. Well, that wasn't exactly accurate. She wasn't at the morgue. But that was something at least. I'd known Janie for years. I knew her better than anyone else in the world. But, then again, I only knew her as well as she would allow me to know her. It was something she and I had in common. As much as she did know, there was a lot about me that she had no idea of- that no one did. One of those things was someone lying in wait for me to fuck up again so he could finish what he started in the safe house.

Maybe Cash was right in insisting I lay low.

"Ugh," I grimaced at even *thinking* that he was right about something.

It wasn't that I hated Cash. I didn't have the kind of animosity he seemed to harbor for me. If anything, I actually liked the bastard. He managed to belong to a bike gang and *not* be a chauvinistic pig. He was confident and endearing. He was charming. But underneath all of that, he was a cool, calm, collected, merciless, unshakable man. I'd seen him walk into a loathed skin trader's house and keep his very obvious rage under control and let me take the lead. Then when shit went down, he dove into the thick of it like he was raised in chaos, never once hesitating or second-guessing himself.

All of that, though, was exactly the problem.

I respected him.

On top of that, I was attracted to him.

And I was proving wholly incapable of fighting it.

That was simply unacceptable. I wasn't that kind of woman. I had always been able to keep myself under control. I always took the lead. I never let a man get the better of me. Well, at least it had been a long, long time since I had let that happen. But there was Cash, younger than me, less serious in all ways than me... and he was making me lose control. How the hell did that happen?

And, more importantly, how could I stop it from happening in the future?

ELEVEN

Cash

I dialed in the combination at her locker, more than a little curious about what she might have stored away, what little pieces of her I could pick up on. She kept herself locked down so tight and I found myself wanting to know more. But my excitement quickly got extinguished when I pushed the garage door up and found the entire unit empty except for the large Army green duffle bag in the center of the cement floor.

Who the hell rented a large storage unit to store a bag?

With a shrug, I hefted the considerable weight up and tucked it into the trunk of Lo's little car and hit the road again.

Reign had been texting me all morning, asking about the Mallicks at first while he was still tucked away at home with Summer. But then, when he got to the compound and found that Wolf still hadn't checked in, he was all up my ass about getting over there and checking on things. Wolf may have been a bit of a recluse, but he always showed his face around the clubhouse if something serious was going on.

So I drove out of the industrial part of town, through the shitty part, and further out to where it went woodsy and rural. Wolf lived up a hill that made climbing it by anything other than foot (or his monster-sized truck) all but impossible. I parked at the bottom and cursed him in new and inventive ways as I hauled it up the hill and through the woods to where it finally broke around a small log cabin that Wolf had taken years to build by his own two hands.

"You better be shacked up in here with some grade-A pussy if you're not showing up at church," I called through the door, not bothering to knock. The place was small, he would hear me if he was inside. When I heard nothing from inside, I turned and looked off into the seemingly endless woods with a growing sense of dread. "Oh you fuck. If I have to hunt you down..."

The door swung open behind me, making me whirl back around to find Wolf completely overtaking the doorway, his hand on the side of the door as if blocking my entrance. "Cash," he said, nodding his head at me.

"The fuck you doing up here when bombs are going off?"

"Anything I can do?" he asked, knowing damn well there wasn't, that we had it handled.

"That's not the point, Wolf. You don't miss church. Reign was worried. Now that he knows you aren't dead in one of your fucking tree stands or something, he's gonna be pissed."

"I'll deal with him," he said with a shrug.

He'd... *deal with him*? Wolf may have been our oldest friend, the little (but giant) quiet kid who used to stand lookout for me and Reign when we were getting ourselves into trouble, the guy who once took on half a bar of rival bikers when Reign refused to 'move out of their section'... but that personal history never changed the fact that he always treated Reign and the club with respect. He always showed, he always did his part, let his loyalty speak for itself seeing as the bastard never really said much of anything.

Something was up. And fuck if I didn't need one more goddamn complication in my life at that moment.

"What the fuck did *you* get yourself into now, man?"

"Nothin'," he said, but he wouldn't meet my eye; he was looking off over my shoulder.

"There are fucking bombs going off all over. No one has a goddamn idea who is setting them. Repo is up my ass about not being around enough and I can't be around because I got fuckin' Lo begging asylum at my house 'cause she got trouble and she won't involve Hailstorm in it..."

Shit. Fuck goddamn it. Me and my big mouth. No one was supposed to know anything about Lo, not even Wolf who would probably never string enough words together to tell anyone anyway.

"Lo?" a female voice asked from inside, making me quiet my internal battle and look at Wolf.

His head was thrown back, facing the sky, his eyes closed, like he thought someone just fucked something up.

I felt my smile quirk up, my sour mood lifting slightly. "I fuckin' knew you had a skirt in there," I chuckled, ducking under his hand before he could stop me and pushing inside his one-room house.

There was a small kitchenette to the left against the side wall, a little table beside it, a recliner in front of a massive TV, and his giant bed. That, and the door to the bathroom, was all he had inside his house, not that it would fit much more than that anyway.

My eyes went right to the bed where a girl was sitting cross-legged, a little busted up looking herself- white gauze wrapped up her arm, a bunch of scrapes down the side of one of her cheeks. Her long dark hair was pulled into a low ponytail and she was dressed in one of Wolf's white tees which, given that he was practically a giant and she was a tiny slip of a thing, completely swallowed up her body down to her knees.

"Jesus fucking Christ," I said, rolling my eyes.

Because she wasn't just any skirt.

She was Lo's fucking little protege.

She was the smart-as-a-whip, loud-mouthed, badass, tactical genius covered in ink with walls high enough around her to make Lo's walls look like a kid's playpen.

Janie.

Wolf moved inside, but left the door open and I took it as a none too subtle invitation for me to leave at any time.

"Well well well," I smiled, too amused for any of our good. "Look at this little development..."

"Cash," Wolf's deep voice warned, but I completely ignored it.

"She's not your usual type, man," I said, nodding at her. "But, hell, if you can put up with that smart mouth," I winked at Janie. I was fucking with her. I liked me a woman with a smart mouth, but she was always fun to get a rise out of, and that was just what I was getting as she moved herself up onto her knees on the center of the bed and glared at me.

"The operative word there being 'smart'," she started, moving toward the end of the bed and hopping off. "I know. It's a foreign concept to someone who barely has two brain cells to rub together and when he does, all they do is scream out 'pussy, pussy, pussy', but some of us actually have..."

"Retract the claws, kitten," I laughed, winking at her as I chucked her chin. "I was messing with you."

"Oh," she said, immediately deflating and I wouldn't be wrong to say she looked a little disappointed to miss out on a fight. She took a breath and looked up at me with those big blues of hers. "Why is Lo staying with you?"

"I dunno. Why you staying with Wolf?" I countered, worried

about the tongue-lashing Lo would give me if I shared her secret. Yeah, *me,* worried about a chick. What the fuck was happening? Her chin lifted defiantly and she stayed silent. And, as always, so did Wolf. "You alright, kid?" I asked, reaching out to touch the bandage. It was the barest of brushes over the gauze, but she shrieked and wrenched away. "The fuck..."

"Time to go," Wolf said, moving to step between me and Janie and it was clear that, for the first time, Wolf was standing against one of his brothers.

I bit into the inside of my cheek, rocking back on my heels for a second, trying to figure out if I should press the issue or not. In the end, it really wasn't my place, it was Reign's place and, frankly, when it came to chastising a man we had known our entire lives, yeah, I'd much rather my brother be the one to handle that shit.

"Alright," I said, putting my hands up and moving back a few steps. "But pick up your fucking phone and call Reign or you're gonna have a group of Henchmen up here asking questions and airing your laundry. Janie, kitten," I said, leaning past Wolf's body so I could see her (and it didn't escape me that she was watching Wolf's back with her brows drawn together in utter confusion). "Take care of that arm. I'll see you around."

I took the descent much more slowly than I had the ascent and, for once, it had nothing to do with the uneven footing. Or maybe everything to do with it, but in a much more figurative way.

It wasn't that I'd never had woman trouble before. But it had been a different kind of trouble. It was always: 'how do I get this woman into bed' trouble, or 'how do I break it to this woman that she ain't gonna be my old lady' trouble, or even 'how do I get this chick to stop slashing the tires on my bike' trouble.

I had never liked a woman just as intensely as I disliked her before. What the fuck did that say about me, that I could be so attracted to someone who did shit I thought was inexcusable? Yes, she was a challenge. Yes, that was always like fuckin' catnip to me. Still, it didn't make sense.

Maybe it was just desire. I could be that base and simple at times. If the woman was hot enough, I was willing to jump through hoops and look past a lot of crazy shit to get a taste of her.

And, having had a taste of Lo, well let's just say I wanted more. I wanted it all. I wanted to know what she felt like writhing beneath me. I wanted to know what my name sounded like being gasped from her lips as she came. I wanted to know how it felt to have her lips wrapped around my cock. I wanted to know if she was as wild and wanton as I imagined her to be. Did she dirty talk? Was she open to different positions? Could I get her to the point of no return, where she was willing to say, cry, beg for me to give her release? Could I get underneath her walls and peek at the woman underneath?

"Jesus Christ," I groaned, getting to the car, shaking my head at my reflection in the windows.

I needed to figure out what her problem was, fix it for her, and get her the hell out of my life before there was no turning back.

TWELVE

Lo

I heard the car a few hours later while I was elbow deep in cooking ingredients. To my surprise, and utter delight, Cash actually didn't have a bachelor's fridge (meaning full of meat and leftover takeout and wholly devoid of essentials like butter, eggs, or garlic). He was stocked to the gills and I couldn't help but wonder about him moving around his kitchen with the practiced ease he seemed to handle everything in his life, making meals.

Then, of course, I imagined him making meals for his women because, well, who went whole hog making a huge, multi-step meal for just themselves? Along with that thought came an intense and almost overpowering jolt of jealousy that was so unwelcome that I had to throw myself into something to distract myself or I would drive myself half-crazy about it.

Seeing as his house was almost freakishly tidy, I set my mind to cooking.

I was a fair cook, having spent endless hours making food

for my father when I was younger after my mother died. Him being a bit... *traditional* (read: chauvinistic) about women's roles in life, that meant it was my job to learn to handle the stove at the tender age of eleven. I had a fair amount of burn scars on my hands as testament to those first awkward, unsafe fumblings. Then, when I was on my own, living in the safe house, I never so much as hooked up my stove. If I couldn't make it in the microwave, I didn't eat it. I was sick of the task.

At Hailstorm, a bunch of the guys and even one or two of the women actually enjoyed the chore and even had more than a little skill at it, so they ended up being the ones who took turns feeding the rest of us.

I had been out of practice for the better part of twenty years but, well, it wasn't exactly something you could forget how to do and I was almost a little tickled to get to do it again... without a man expecting it to be done.

The door opened while I was chopping carrots for the stew I had starting to simmer on the top of the stove, the meat already cooking away in the broth and tomato mixture.

"What smells so good? You order in?" Cash asked and I could hear the sound of my bag hitting the floor in the living room and his boot-clad feet moving toward me. I didn't answer and when he moved into the doorway, he did a slow up-and-down inspection of me standing at his counter, wearing nothing but his tee, my hair in a messy knot at the top of my head, chopping away. "Are you... cooking for me?" he asked, a strange breathlessness in his tone that had my head snapping up to watch him directly, unsure where the inflection came from.

Uncertain what to say, I waved the knife casually around. "We needed to eat, right?" I asked, feeling a bit insecure about the whole thing.

"I've never had a woman cook for me before," he said, watching me with eyes that were too intense and completely devoid of his usual jocular lightness.

"It's not a big deal," I said, having to look away from him. There was something passing between us and it felt too intimate, too *something* I didn't quite understand.

I had barely had a chance to get another carrot out of the bag before I felt him move up behind me, as in *right behind me*, as in... his whole front was against my whole back and he was looking over my shoulder, his chin resting there casually like it was nothing new for us to stand together while I chopped vegetables, like we did it every night of our lives. His hand moved across my belly, pressing in slightly, and I swear the contact shot right between my thighs.

"It is to me," he said and my brain was racing a million different ways and I had to struggle to remember what he was responding to. Oh, right... me saying it wasn't a big deal. It was a big deal to him? Great. As if I didn't feel insecure enough about doing it.

"Don't get your hopes up. I'm not that great of a cook," I said, forcing my hands to focus on getting back into motion while I was pretty sure that the last thing I should have been allowed to handle at that moment was a sharpened object.

Cash's head shifted downward and then I felt his teeth sink into the exposed skin on my shoulder which his too-big shirt had slipped to the side to reveal. It was just the barest of bites, but holy hell, I *felt it.*

Then he moved away to stand next to the pot on the stove, arms behind him, grabbing the counter as he casually watched me work. And I *was* working, if for no other reason than to not have to look at him.

It was crazy that I was so turned on by him. True, he had given me some really good reasons to be turned on around him after the events of the night before. And, well, let me say one thing: a lot of men could fuck. A lot of men could climb on top of you, slip inside, and plow into you until weren't sure what your own name was anymore. But it took real skill, real understanding of women and how their bodies worked to get them off with oral. Sure, a lot of guys could manage it by sheer dumb luck. The clit was sensitive, you raked over it enough, eventually she's riding the waves. But Cash was in a whole league of his own. Cash ate me like he was a man in famine, like it was the only thing in the world that mattered to him, like it gave him what he needed to go on. He knew when the intensity was bordering on pain, and moved away. He knew when the motion was getting old, and changed directions. He paid attention. And, well, there was nothing like a man who paid attention to a woman's pleasure.

I had never came that hard from oral before. I had a sneaking suspicion that I never would again.

So, yeah, I was having trouble meeting his eye.

"Tell me something no one knows about you," he said out of the blue, making me narrowly miss slicing off the tip of my forefinger as I startled.

"What?"

"Tell me something no one knows about you."

"Why?

"Why not?"

"What are you twelve?"

"Christ, woman, would it kill you to answer the question? It's not like I am asking you what your favorite position is. Though," he said, his boyish smile creeping across his lips, "I wouldn't mind knowing that either."

I looked away, taking a deep breath. Tell him something no one else knew about me? It wasn't like it was a hard thing to figure out. Most people didn't know anything about me and positively no one knew everything.

"When I was seventeen," I started, shocking myself way more than him that I was willing to give him any of my secrets, "I really wanted to go to this show in town, but I was grounded. I snuck out when my dad was sleeping and had a blast. When I got home, I cut the lights on my car so he wouldn't see me pulling in. And, I kind of... tapped the bumper of my dad's truck because I couldn't see."

Cash's smile turned a little warm, a little too sweet. "He never found out?"

"Oh, he found out alright," I admitted, the bitter taste of the memory making me feel queasy, "about the sneaking out, not about the car. It was the only thing in my whole life that I could get past him. His truck was a real piece of shit, covered in dents and dings."

"Did you get in trouble?" he asked, still looking a little too pleased to get the information he wanted out of me.

He had *no* idea the kind of trouble I got into. "Yes," I said, with finality, and his smile fell. It was such a sad sight to behold, that I found my mouth opening again before I could stop it. "And... lotus."

His brows knitted together, trying to make that information make sense. "Lotus?"

I felt my own lips quirk up as I met his eyes, lifting my chin slightly. "My favorite position," I clarified and was rewarded with him throwing his head back and laughing. I was helpless to do anything but watch, a full smile spreading across my face, making the bruises smart, but it was worth the pain. "Your turn," I said, unable to stop myself.

He stopped laughing, but the smile remained, his head tilting to the side a little. "You have the sweetest pussy I have ever tasted."

The words hit with actual impact, making me take a step back, my face, no doubt, twisting in a mix of surprise and arousal. Who said things like that? In the kitchen? To someone they all but hated?

Apparently, fucking Cash did.

I swallowed hard, trying to pull myself together. "Classy," I tried, attempting to put a shield back up.

"Tight too," he went on, making the place in question, well, tighten.

"Cash..." I said, tone half-pleading as I shook my head at him.

"Yeah, I like it when you say my name. I'll like it even more when you say it when I have my cock inside you."

Oh, hell.

There was absolute chaos between my thighs at that idea.

"That's not going to happen, Cash," I said, remembering my words from Summer's dinner party that suddenly felt like it happened ages ago.

"It is," he said, shrugging a shoulder like it was inevitable, like my objections didn't hold any weight.

"No," I said, my tone as firm as I could make it, and seeing as I was raised by an ex-marine of a father and learned from the best, that was really freaking firm.

"Honey, why you fighting it so hard?"

"Why are you pushing it so hard? You don't even *like* me Cash."

Again, another shrug. "True."

Holy hell. He wasn't even going to try to deny it? He thought it would be a good idea to tell me he didn't like me and then expected me to still spread for him whenever he wanted?

"But what does that have to do with anything?"

He could not be serious. "It has to do with *everything*."

"Why?"

"Because I don't have sex with men who don't like me."

"Baby, just because I don't like you doesn't mean I wouldn't treat you real good. Do you need a refresher of last night?" he asked, giving me a sexy little smirk as he pushed away from the counter and made his way over toward me.

My hand raised instinctively, pressing the flat side of the knife against his chest to still his approach. "You try it, your balls will be part of that stew," I offered, pressing the knife a little harder against him.

"While I think you are perfectly capable of chopping a man's balls off, Lo, I know you're all bluster."

"Try me, Cash," I threatened.

"What was the dog park about?" he asked, once again throwing me off my game with his unusual change in conversation.

"What dog park?"

"When Reign, Wolf, and I came to Hailstorm to ask you for help with Summer and you took us to your command center... you had all kinds of shit on your walls: information on the local crime syndicates, plans for hits, mugshots of bail jumpers you guys were chasing down, and a fucking... flier for a dog park. What was the dog park about?"

"Why?"

"What? Are you twelve?" he asked, throwing my words back at me.

There was no reason not to answer, but I found myself not wanting to. Still, chances were, if I didn't, the conversation was probably going to turn sexual again and I needed for that not to happen.

I shrugged, pulling the knife from his chest. "We do a lot of different jobs. Like you said, hits for hire, catching skips, some private security, all that jazz. But sometimes we get wind of things and do stuff just because."

"What could you have gotten wind of at a dog park?"

"Six dogs died after having the water bowls poisoned with anti-freeze," I recalled easily. Janie had been so fucking furious about that case. She had worked day and night for weeks to come up with leads.

I remembered asking her one night as she downed her third

energy drink why that case in particular was affecting her so much. She looked up, exhaling a breath, her face looking unusually open and vulnerable and said in a quiet voice (which was also not like her. She tended to bitch and yell and scream), "No one should get away with hurting defenseless creatures."

I didn't ask what she meant. I didn't need to.

"You guys were trying to figure out who did it?"

"We *did* find out who did it," I clarified.

"Is he still breathing?" Cash asked, obviously having a really low opinion of me.

"Sure. Breathing nice and easy in a jail cell for the next fifteen years. Though, if he ever gets out, well, I don't doubt Janie might pay him a little visit."

"Janie?" Cash asked, looking almost guarded at the mention of her.

"She doesn't like when people pick on anyone or anything smaller than them."

"Who the fuck does?" was his knee-jerk response, like he really meant it, like it bothered him too. God, could he get any more endearing?

"So, um, did you have any trouble at the storage place?" Christ, that was dumb. What was wrong with me? I was a grown ass woman, I didn't mumble and stumble to find decent conversation.

"What the fuck you have in that bag? Bricks?"

"Books," I clarified immediately, more than a little surprised that he hadn't gone through it (and also extremely relieved). "You didn't look?"

"Of course not. So how long until dinner? Do I have long enough to run to the clubhouse and talk to my brother?"

"Sure." I mean... it was stew. It would, well, *stew* for as long as needed.

"Do you still want me to talk to Reign about your situation?"

My eyes shot up to his. Of course I did. That was the deal, wasn't it? But, somehow, I found myself saying instead, "Do you mind keeping this between us for the time being?"

He nodded, chucked me under the chin like a ten year old, and took off, leaving me utterly confused, still completely turned on, and having no idea what to do about either of those things.

So I made stew, and then I ate stew alone when he didn't come back as quickly as he made it sound like he would, then I went through my bag and got one of my books and curled up on the couch to read. I didn't, however, change into my own clothes. And I didn't stop to think about why... because I was pretty sure I already knew the reason.

By the time nine o'clock rolled around, the words on the pages seemed like they were swimming in front of my tired eyes and I bookmarked my page with one of the television remotes and curled up on the couch to watch mindless TV.

I didn't plan on sleeping, but that was exactly what I did.

I woke up sometime later to the feeling of someone lifting my legs, sliding under them, and then resting them on top of their jean-covered thighs. I didn't have to look to know it was Cash. No, instead, I kept my eyes closed, enjoying the feel of his warm hand on my bare skin as I pretended I was still asleep.

I heard the sound of his spoon scraping a bowl and knew he was eating. Then his weight shifted forward, his stomach pressing into my legs as he did so, to put his bowl on the coffee table.

I didn't know, however, that he had also picked up my book and pulled it open until his mouth opened to start reading, "'Declan ran his hand up her wet cleft..." My entire body jolted as my eyes flew open, mortification like nothing I had ever experienced before overwhelming my system.

I wasn't lying when I told Reign upon first meeting him that I was a sucker for a good love story. As such, I had a slight obsession with romance novels. And by 'slight obsession', I meant I devoured at least three a week... and they weren't the fade-to-black love scene kind. They were the down and dirty, explicit kind.

That was actually the reason I had decided to stop reading where I had: because the hero and heroine were *just* about to get it on for the first time and I wanted to be fully focused to be able to enjoy it.

And there was Cash, sitting on the couch next to me, my book in his hands with the half-naked man on the front, reading the sex scene.

Holy shit.

No. That could not be happening. No way in hell was the sexy as heck guy who went down on me the night before figuring out that I was a dirty little closet smut reader. No no no.

"Cash, give me that back," I demanded, sitting up as fast as my ribs would allow and making a grab for the book.

Cash simply lifted it out of my reach, smiling way too devilishly. "Nuh-uh. This sounds interesting." I reached for it again, but he swatted my hand again, holding the pages open with one hand and starting to read again. "'His tongue found the swollen, sensitive swell of her clit and started moving over it in slow, light circles until her hands fisted in the sheets and her hips were grinding up into him, begging for more...'"

I wanted to die. Right then and there, I wanted some undetectable blood clot to rush to my heart and just... end it because I simply could never face him again.

"Honey, relax," his voice said and my gaze lifted to find him looking down at me, no teasing humor on his face like I had expected. If anything, there almost seemed to be... heat.

"Please give me my book back," I tried, not caring how desperate my voice sounded. I *was* desperate.

"Do you like this book?"

Oh, hell. "Yes," I admitted, shaking my head at myself.

"Then why are you so embarrassed?"

"Cash..."

"'Cassidy let out a low moan, reaching down to grab Declan's head, pulling him up her body and wrapping her legs around him...'"

"Please stop reading."

"Are you getting hot, baby?" he asked, turning to look at me. My legs were pressed tightly together and I was more than a little shocked that I was able to be completely and utterly turned on and mortified at the same time. I had a sneaking suspicion that it had something to do with the fact that the sex scene was being read in the deep, smooth timbre of his voice. At my silence, he reached out, grabbed my hand and pulled it toward him. I had no idea what he was going to do until I felt my palm press up against the crotch of his jeans where, holy shit, he was hard and straining. "Who'd have thought a book could be as hot as porn?" he said, his lips quirked up.

His hand stayed on top of mine, pressing into his cock and my thumb automatically stroked over the head. Christ, I wanted him. I wanted him more than I had wanted someone in longer than I could remember. Cash's hand slid off of mine and both of his hands reached for my hips, gently pulling me toward him until I was straddling him.

"These are still hurting," he said, his hand flattening over the elastic bandages around my center.

"Yeah," I admitted, because they were.

"No way I can be inside of you without it hurting," he mused. "I don't want to hurt you."

Oh man.

Suddenly it wasn't just in my lady bits I felt him, it was in my chest, it was a fluttering, melting sensation that I was trying really hard to ignore.

Couldn't he be hot and sexy and a jerk? That would make

my life so much easier.

But no, he had to be hot and sexy and a sweetheart. Goddamn it.

The hand that wasn't on my ribs moved up and touched my lips softly. "These are still hurting too."

Oh, God. I wanted him to kiss me. No, strike that. I *needed* him to kiss me. I didn't care about it being a bad idea. I didn't care about having to regret it. And I damn sure didn't care about my sore lips.

"Kiss me, Cash," I said, my voice an airy whisper.

His eyes rose to mine and watched for a second before the hand on my ribs moved up to cup the back of my neck. The other stayed gently resting on my cheek. "Well, if you insist," he said with a cocky little grin before he pulled me toward him and his lips pressed down on mine.

It was soft, gentle, but it wasn't simply the promise of something *more*. It was consuming. It was strong, yet sweet and I felt it down to my toes, making them and everything in between feel tingly, making my soul feel lighter than it had in ages. My hands moved to rest on his shoulders for a moment before they went completely around the back of his neck, making our bodies meld together. My hips sank down and his hardness pressed up against my heat, but I didn't move against him, I didn't try to calm the pulsing desire there. All that mattered was the kiss, was the feeling of his lips on mine.

My mouth opened on a quiet sigh and his tongue slipped forward, tentatively toying with mine. It wasn't hesitation, like he was expecting me to pull away. It was teasing. It was him trying to get a response out of me no matter how softly he touched me, no matter how brief or light the touch. And it was... *working*.

His hand stroked down from my cheek to my neck, brushing gently over that sensitive skin and making a tremble vibrate through my body.

My hips stroked reflexively, making me break away from his lips as I felt his cock hit the sweet spot and a whimper escaped my lips.

Cash's eyes opened slowly, looking as heavy as mine felt. The hand at my neck started moving lower, over my clavicle, lower. His fingers brushed over my breast, his thumb stroking over my hardened nipple before his hand splayed and squeezed with just the right amount of pressure.

"You want this," he said, taking my nipple between his two fingers and rolling it.

He was right. I wanted that. I wanted that and so, so much more. I wanted everything. And I wanted him to be the one to give it to me.

"Yes," I said unnecessarily as he squeezed my nipple and had my hips dropped harder onto his, enjoying the pressure there.

"You gonna let me give it to you?"

Even not knowing what, exactly, he was asking, I felt my head nodding. "Yes."

"That's what I wanted to hear," he said with a small smile. His hand left my breast and moved downward, sliding down the center of my belly, getting to the triangle above my sex and pausing there, pressing hard for a moment before slipping suddenly downward and cupping my sex. I bit into my lip slightly, ignoring the pain in doing so, to stifle the groan that threatened to be loud enough to echo through his quiet house. His free hand moved upward and touched my lips as he pressed into my clit with his middle finger. "I want to hear you," he said and my teeth released my lip. "Good girl."

Normally, a man calling me a good girl, least of all a man *younger* than me, would be laughable, but when he did it, like with everything else he did, it was hot.

My hips shifted upward, giving him better access and he grunted in approval as his hand slid upward, slipping into the waistband of my panties and moving down to stroke through my wetness, letting it coat his fingers, his motions lazy and unhurried. I writhed into the sensation, the pressure becoming almost unbearable, inching toward the point of actual pain. Then, as if sensing the feelings creating chaos in my system, his finger pressed fully inside me. I felt myself tighten around him as I groaned, my hips moving against his hand, shamelessly seeking relief.

"You want more?"

"Yes," I said, arching my ass back so the palm of his hand pressed against my clit. He let out a low groan that sent a shiver through my insides as he slid another finger inside me. "Oh, God yes..." I whimpered, my eyes closing, head falling back as he finally started thrusting in and out of me.

"I know you're trying to imagine this is my cock," he said, curling his fingers inside of me, "but I want you to look at me." My eyes opened slowly, feeling weighted as I focused on his face. "You'll get my cock, honey. But right now, be with me here." His fingers stayed curled and started working over my G-spot, no longer soft, sweet, or slow, they were rapid and demanding and I felt my orgasm building quickly at the sudden change of pace. "So fucking tight," he groaned, leaning up slightly to take my mouth again, his lips as insistent and wild as his fingers. If there was pain, I was beyond experiencing it as his kiss seared into me, branded me in a way I hadn't known was possible, in a way that I was sure when all was said and done between me and Cash, I would still feel his lips on mine when I was lying in bed alone at night.

My breath hitched, his thumb pressed into my clit, and my world went white with the blinding pleasure. I cried out my release into his mouth, my fingers digging painfully into his back as my legs tensed up through the waves of pulsations.

"Cash," I gasped when I could draw a breath as the waves started to taper off, my body shuddering hard once.

"Fuck me," he said, moving away so he could look at my

face, his head shaking like he couldn't quite believe something. His hand moved up to rest on my cheek again as I struggled to get some semblance of control over myself.

That was intense. As in, I felt almost vulnerable from it, as in... I was almost a little teary-eyed and I needed to get it the fuck together. I was not, was absolutely not going to cry in front of him. No way. That would be humiliating. And, given the reading of my romance novel sex scene not long before, I was pretty sure I was at my mortification quotient for the day.

His fingers shifted upward slightly as if he could sense the battle I was fighting as if, oh fuck, he could see the water in my eyes.

I needed to get. it. together.

"You can take your fingers out of me now," I said, trying for casual and being pretty sure I nailed it.

"What if I don't want to?" Cash teased, his lips twitching, but there was a depth in his eyes that I didn't trust.

"You're going to do it anyway," I said, brows raising and I jerked my hips backward until his fingers slid away. He took his time removing his fingers from my panties. When he finally did, I slid off his lap and snatched my book where he left it on the arm of the chair, "If you don't mind, I am going to go finish myself off," I said with what I could only call an unfriendly sneer. I couldn't be weak, not around Cash, not around any man. I needed to get alone and get myself calmed down. If that meant I needed to bruise his ego a little in the process, well, that was unfortunately just going to have to be alright with me.

"Finish yourself off?" he asked, twisting his head around to look at me. And then, to my absolute horror (and maybe absolute delight) he raised his glistening fingers to his mouth and slipped them inside, licking my taste off. "Honey," he said, sliding them out, giving me a grin, "I have it on pretty good authority that I finished you off just fine."

"One orgasm, Cash?" I started, not adding that it was one all-consuming, life-changing orgasm. "What is this... amateur hour? I expected better from a man with a reputation like yours." Then I took up off the stairs fast enough for me to want to cry out in pain in doing so, but not fast enough to look like I was running away. Which was exactly what I was doing. I was running- away from Cash, away from the twisted mix of feelings I had toward him, away from the rush of feelings he brought out of me. I was fucking running.

THIRTEEN

Cash

The woman was going to fucking kill me. Death by utter fucking confusion and the most severe case of blue balls known to man. All I had to do was look at her and I was hard. One kiss and I was ready to forsake all other women. She was what I wanted. If I were honest, she was who I had been thinking about every time I sank inside another woman since I met her a year before. She had been invading my thoughts way before I suddenly found her in my house.

I adjusted my jeans to get more comfortable, well, as comfortable as I could be with a raging hard-on, listening to her slam the bathroom door upstairs and turn on the water.

She didn't need a shower. She needed a couple of minutes away from me to put her walls back into place because with the orgasm I had just given her, they had come crashing down, leaving nothing in front of me but the most beautiful sight I had ever seen in my entire God-forsaken life: the real Lo.

As soon as the tremors stopped shaking through her body, her eyes found my face and all I saw in hers was raw, almost painful vulnerability. It was so shocking I almost couldn't believe it belonged to her. She was always so strong, so unflappable. But, I guessed, that was why she had all those walls, all those guards: to keep anyone from seeing the woman underneath, a woman that had been through something, who had endured, who had survived by locking it all away so no one could ever use it against her.

I wanted to know what she had been through. I wanted to know her story. And seeing as, many times, I barely stuck around long enough to learn a chick's last name, that was really fucking terrifying. The problem was amplified by the fact that it didn't make any sense.

Why her? Why the only woman I had come across in years, hell a lifetime, that I didn't like? Why would she be the one who was different?

I had just jumped off the couch to storm up the stairs and get some kind of clue as to what was going on in her head, when there was a knock at my door. I, unlike my brother, didn't hide the fact that I had my own place. Guys from the club, women I fucked, they all showed up from time to time, usually without calling. It was nothing out of the norm.

Opening the door and finding Wolf, however, was.

"What are you doing here?" I asked, brows drawing together.

"Got some shit..." he started and trailed off with a shake of his head.

"Yeah, man," I said, letting out a humorless laugh. "I got some shit too. Want a drink?"

Wolf inclined his chin and stepped inside, following me to the kitchen where I poured us each some whiskey. We each threw back the first round, needing the burn to settle inside, needing it to loosen up the words we weren't ready to share yet.

"You gonna talk about it?" I asked, pouring us each a second round.

"Are you?" he countered and I shook my head, looking down at my boots. If only it were that easy. Besides, what could I say?

Wolf made a grunting noise, staring off out the darkened window as I heard footsteps on the stairs. Shit. How had I not heard the water shut off? Before I could even call out a warning, Lo stepped into the doorway in yet another of my tees, this one a little tighter, a little shorter, white. You didn't even have to look hard to see the little pointed peaks of her nipples through the thin material.

Lo stopped short, her red-rimmed eyes going wide. Focusing on those eyes, on the fact that she had been upstairs crying in the shower, I missed the look as it spread across Wolf's face. I didn't miss, however, the low, lethal, chilling growling noise that came from somewhere deep in his chest. It drew my attention away from Lo, finally finding his face and seeing the kind of blind rage there that scared men much greater than me to their bones. He was looking at Lo's face, her bruises and cuts, her tear-stained cheeks, her swollen eyelids.

The sound came back louder, making Lo take a step back, watching Wolf like she might need to spring into action at any time. But Wolf wasn't looking at her. No, he was looking at me and there was nothing but accusation and a bitter kind of hatred there. Shocked, I felt myself straightening as his lips thinned out.

"Wolf what's..."

"A woman?" his deep voice boomed loudly, making Lo jump slightly, her eyes moving around to, I imagined, locate a weapon.

"A woman?" I repeated, at a complete loss.

"Her. Fucking. Face." Each word was its own sentence. Each word got louder and louder until the dog next door started barking manically.

Jesus Christ.

He thought I did it. He thought I busted up her face.

"Seriously?" I felt myself asking, feeling anger- foreign, very unlike me, bubbling up under my skin, making me feel like I wanted to claw it off. "You don't fucking know me better than..."

I didn't get the rest out because suddenly he wasn't across the room from me anymore. He was right in front of me and his fist was cocked backward. I'd been hit plenty in my life before. It came with the job. It came with being a member of a biker gang. It came with fucking whatever skirt I wanted despite her relationship status. I could take a punch. That being said, Wolf in full rage-mode was like being hit by the Hulk.

"Wolf, no!" I heard Lo screech, making Wolf start, his arm still cocked, as he twisted his head to look at her.

"Shouldn't fucking hit you," he ground out, the words barely coming out from how hard he was clenching his jaw.

"Wolf, Cash didn't hit me," Lo said calmly, reassuringly. It was the same tone someone used when talking to a scared child or a skittish dog. Low, almost melodic. Wolf's hand fell, but his body was still tight, practically pulsing with rage. "Cash would never hit a woman," she said with so much conviction that my eyes stopped watching Wolf for a sign that he might pounce and moved to look at Lo. As if sensing my inspection, though her gaze was fully focused on the bearded, light-eyed, rage monster in my kitchen, she went on, "He's an asshole and all, but he wouldn't do that."

Wolf huffed out his breath, slowly relaxing. It was a sight to see- how he went from inhumanely angry to the cool, collected, calm man he always was so effortlessly.

"Sure?" he asked her, his haunting honey-colored eyes unblinking on hers.

"Yes, I'm sure. This," she said, waving a hand at her face, "had nothing to do with him. Do I seem like the kind of woman who would stay in the house with a man who beat her?" she asked, her tone oddly sharp.

"Lotta' women do," he shrugged, putting down his full glass of whiskey and turning back to look at me. "Gotta go."

"No," I said, shaking my head. "Stay. You wanted to talk about something. Let's talk about it. If it is about J..."

"No," he cut in, the word almost angry again and I quickly shut up. I guessed Janie was a touchy subject, but who was I to judge? Lo was a touchy subject for me too.

"Then just stay. Have a drink. Lo made food..."

"Club," he said instead, and it was a dismissal. "Lo," he said, nodding his head at her as she moved out of his way.

With that, I heard his boots across my floor and the front door slamming before his truck roared to life out front.

"He's, ah," Lo started, with a head shake, "a really intense guy, huh?"

"That would be putting it mildly," I agreed with a smile, throwing back my round.

"What was with that reaction?"

"He doesn't like men who put their hands on women."

"History there?" Lo asked wisely.

"Yeah," I nodded, not giving her any more than that. It wasn't a secret among The Henchmen. Wolf's sordid past was common knowledge. That being said, it was private. It was for the brothers to know and the brothers only.

"You gonna share that or what?" she said, nodding at me as I poured more whiskey into my glass.

I reached up into the cabinet for another glass and poured her a round. "So are all those walls back into place?" I asked as I handed her the glass.

Her hand retreated for the barest of seconds before she grabbed it out of my hand and threw it back. "I don't know what you're talking about."

"No? Then why have you been crying?"

Lo's eyes got small as she took a breath. "I don't know what you're talking about."

I felt the ironic smile pull at my lips. "You want to keep your private shit private, say that. Don't lie to me, baby."

"Nothing to keep private," she said with a casual shoulder-shrug. "And like I told you before, I'm not your baby."

"And like I told *you* before, I can have you begging for me to call you that."

"I think you greatly overestimate your skills there, Cash."

That was the wrong fucking thing to say.

I put my glass down on the counter with a loud clank, reached inside to pull out an ice cube, and moved toward her.

"What are you..." she started, but I wasn't in the mood for explanations. I was in the mood to prove to her that she couldn't use that lame-ass argument anymore. So before she could open her mouth to object, I grabbed the front of her tee and yanked it up hard, popping her head out of the top and pulling the material down her arms slightly, pinning them to her body, seeing that she hadn't bothered to re-wrap her ribs or dig out one of her bras or fresh panties, leaving her gloriously naked before me. "Cash..."

"Yep. You're going to be screaming that in a minute," I promised, a smirk toying with my lips before I lifted my hand and ran the ice cube down the side of her neck, making a shiver course through her body. I wasn't going to take it slow. I wasn't going to ease her into it. I wasn't going to do anything but drive her to the brink of utter oblivion as fast as was fucking possible. I wanted her creaming. I wanted her crying out loud enough for the neighbors to blush. I wanted her to *beg*.

I slid the ice cube over her chest then found her nipple and circled it, enjoying the hiss of breath out of her lungs. Her eyes were huge, surprised, turned on. I worked the one nipple until it was as tight and pointed as it could get before I moved toward the other which was already half-hardened in desire. Her body convulsed as I moved the ice toward the center of her chest, watching as the muscles just under the surface of her skin tensed at the sensation, making her body pull away initially before sinking into the feeling. I ran it across her hips, side to side, giving her a sly smile as I lowered myself down on my knees in front of her.

When I looked up, her eyes were glued to mine, expectant, but more importantly, open. I pulled the ice away from her skin, watching her breathing make her chest and belly expand and contract for a moment before I slowly slipped the cube into my mouth, pushing it to peek out of my lips slightly and holding it there with my tongue. Understanding and the slightest hint of uncertainty registered on her features before I grabbed her knee and slipped her leg over my shoulder. Before she would even draw a breath to object, I moved forward and ran the ice up her cleft. Her body shook so hard I thought her legs were going to give out, making me grab her hips and slam her against the wall behind her, holding her there as I teased the ice around the hood of her clit.

A strangled whimper escaped her lips as her thighs tightened. Finally, slowly and with the barest bit of pressure, I pushed the ice cube against her clit and listened to her breath catch on a shocked moan. I slipped the ice back into my mouth, moving it to the side so my tongue could slip out and work over her in fast circles, letting the warmth on her cold clit drive her toward the brink of orgasm faster than she could have thought possible. I slipped the ice back out, pressed it against her again and listened as she cried out my name. Close. She was so close.

Again, I cheeked the ice and pulled slightly back, smiling at the frustrated whimper she let out. "Am I overestimating my skills, Lo?" I asked, my tone not teasing. I was dead fucking serious about that shit.

"N... no," she ground out, her hips gyrating slightly and I let my fingers trail up her inner thigh, teasing the crease where it met her sex, but not giving her any kind of release.

"I'm the fucking best you've ever had, aren't I?" I asked, not needing to ask. I knew I was. And it wasn't arrogance; it was just stone cold fact.

"Yes," she whimpered.

"And what do you want me to call you?" I asked, my fingers tracing across her slick lips, moving up toward her clit, but not touching it.

Her eyes flashed for a second and I saw the guarded Lo trying to put her defenses back up. In response, I pushed my thumb into her tight pussy, feeling it quiver slightly, just seconds away from tightening and pulsating as she cried through a mind-numbing orgasm.

"B... baby..." she cried out.

"There it is," I agreed with a smile, slipping the ice out and pressing it against her clit. But just for a split second before I cheeked it while simultaneously slipping my thumb out of her pussy. I pushed her leg off my shoulder and stood quickly. In a sick, unfair way, enjoying the look of utter shock and unfulfilled desire on her face. "Now you know what the fuck I am capable of, what my *reputation* with women has afforded me. Now you want my cock, Lo," I said with an uncharacteristic cruel smirk, "you're gonna have to *ask for it*. I'm done with this shit," I said, moving past her and taking off toward my basement to tear into the punching bag until I could think clearly again.

Because I meant what I said- I was so fucking done with that shit, with the 'one minute she wants me, the next she doesn't' shit, with the 'soft and sweet Lo making me dinner and letting me touch her sweet pussy as she cried out my name, then almost cried over the intensity turning into the guarded, snippy, she-wolf Lo with no explanation of the switch'.

I was done.

She wanted me? Well the ball was in her court.

CASH

I pounded into the bag until I quieted the voice inside that was praying she picked up a racket to play.

Because that shit just made no sense.

FOURTEEN

Lo

The second I heard the basement door close, I let my legs give out from under me, sliding down onto the floor, knees to my chest. I wrapped my arms around my legs and tried to deep-breathe through the desire that was no longer bordering on, but had firmly landed in, pain. It hurt. It literally hurt I was so turned on.

"Fuck," I cursed quietly, closing my eyes tight against the memory of what I had done. I had given him what little power I had left. I had admitted he was good. I told him he was the best that I had ever had. I had said I wanted him to call me baby.

Then he had taken that power along with what had promised to be the orgasm of a lifetime... and walked away with it.

I expected the anger to start building, to flood my system with something familiar, something comfortable that I could latch onto, something I could wrap around myself with its empty kind of security. But it didn't come. All I felt was the soul-crushing unfulfilled desire and a sadness that felt so deep, I could swear that I could drown in it.

It wasn't that it was new. The sadness, it was always there buried deep, wanting to be dealt with, wanting me to acknowledge it so it would finally go away. But I never did, so it never did.

Somehow, it felt worse than I remembered. It wasn't just a swirling, uncomfortable thing. No, it felt sore. *I* felt sore. I felt like every ounce of happiness, of grit and determination, of hardly won strength got ripped away and left in the wake nothing but pain. It was the kind of pain that started in your soul and heart and radiated outward until you felt it in your bones, in your muscles, in every exposed inch of skin, in every lifeless strand of hair. It was the kind of pain that made you feel like a giant open wound.

The tears stung at the back of my eyes and I didn't bother fighting them. What was the use? What had all the fighting actually gotten me over the years?

I felt my body jolt at those thoughts.

"Freedom," I told myself quietly. That was what fighting had gotten me- free. It got me a life with colleagues who were like family to me. It got me the chance to build a life that I didn't wake up into every single day wishing to die. It got me security. It got me the confidence to stand up for myself. It got me respect.

And that, well, it was *everything*.

I absolutely fucking refused to fall back into the sadness, to let it surround me until my arms were too tired to keep my head above water anymore. I wasn't that woman anymore. I was never going to be her again.

I was going to get the fuck off of his kitchen floor, dry my eyes, get my own goddamn clothes on, and take my control back.

Fuck him and his games and his demands. Fuck him and his knee-weakening smile and his heart-pounding endearments. Fuck him and his unwanted attraction to me.

CASH

He wanted someone to hate?

Well... fucking... fine.

I would give him someone to hate.

It didn't matter. *He* didn't matter. Who was he anyway? Just a biker. A hard-drinking, casual-sex-having, takes-himself- too-casually, too-good-looking -for- his- own- good, child-man.

I stifled the voice that whispered that in just a couple days, he had elicited a bigger range of emotional responses from me than any man had since I was a teenager. That could easily be explained by the fact that I just got my ass handed to me and was achy and alone without my support system behind me.

Well, that was all about to get fixed.

I pulled myself up off of the floor, swatting my cheeks in what I could only call disgust and stomped over to my duffle bag, hefting it up and slamming it down on the dining table. I rifled inside, pushing three more paperback romances out of the way and grabbing a pair of thick, moss green cargo pants, a bra, and a tan tank top, leaving the thick matching moss green shirt hung off the back of a chair as I slipped newly sock-clad feet into boots. Standing, I felt almost like myself again. The smarting in my ribs was enough to have me wincing when I moved too fast, but that was getting better too. Another two days, I could get back to training.

Unable to do anything that physical, I hauled the laptop out of the bag along with the notebook and pen I stored away, and sat down to get to work. True, I couldn't be at Hailstorm, but that didn't mean I couldn't log into our systems and see what was going on, try to see if I could find any traces of Janie/Jstorm in the deep web. She liked to spend a lot of time in those murky, awful depths, looking for causes for us to champion or sometimes simply to release viruses into real scumbag's systems when she could. Always a maker of chaos and righter of wrongs. That was my strong, yet fragile Janie.

CASH

One floor beneath me, the chain to the punching bag was swinging mercilessly and I felt myself nodding as I searched through the internet. Good. I was glad he was in a mood. I hoped his balls felt like they were going to explode.

An hour later, hitting a dead end with Janie, I finally took a deep breath and typed in the name I didn't even want to think of: Damian Crane.

His face popped up along with a couple articles. No social media accounts, not that I had been expecting any. He was never the type of man to put his personal shit out there. His last known address was still the one I was familiar with. His registered car was the silver SUV he had bought new six years before.

Nothing, literally nothing to go on.

"Ugh!" I growled at the screen, clicking out of one of the open internet tabs, leaving me staring at a picture of Damian in his black and red jacket with medals hanging off the left side of his chest, big golden buttons down the center, white and black hat on his head, typical Marine deadness to his eyes.

"A little... frustrated?" Cash's teasing voice asked and my head jerked up to where he was leaning in the kitchen doorway.

Christ. How hadn't I heard him climbing up the stairs?

He looked different. Sweaty, sure. The wetness was making his shirt cling to his chest and stomach and the long side of his hair was drenched and slicked slightly back from his face. It wasn't just the exercise-flushed skin or the sweat though. All the traces of genuine anger and confusion and challenge I had seen in his kitchen before were gone. It was the usual Cash standing in front of me- casual, easy-going, playful smirk on his lips.

"Don't flatter yourself. It has nothing to do with you," I said in as hollow a tone as I could muster.

"Sure it doesn't," he said, giving me the power of his full smile and I had to force one of my brows to lift. Unaffected, he twisted open the top of the water bottle he was holding and brought it to his lips. I did not... absolutely did not watch his Adam's apple as he swallowed. Nope. Not me. I was a strong, sexually experienced woman who did not go all ga-ga over a fucking Adam's apple. "What?" he asked, looking me up and down and waving a hand at my body, "no guns?"

"Do you really think it would be wise for me to have a weapon on me when I'm around you?" I shot back, giving him my own smirk.

He look down at his feet for a second, shaking his head. "I like this Lo, baby. But I think I like the vulnerable one better."

"There's only one of me," I said with force behind my words. I wanted it to be true. It *had* to be true.

"Honey," he said, rounding the dining table and leaning back against it right beside my chair, "there's at least two of you. And the crazy part? I don't think anyone knows either one."

God, he was so right. "What? Have you been going to night classes? Psych 101? You don't know what you're talking about."

His smile got a little softer and his hand reached out, touching my chin gently. "I'm gonna figure you out sooner or later. Just so you know. And I'm sure you'll be pissed at me for getting under those shields, but too fuckin' bad."

I swallowed hard because nothing about his words suggested there was anything but determination there. "What happened to hating me?"

His fingers stroked out over my cheek. "You know what I think?" he asked, almost as if waiting for an answer. I didn't and, well, I found myself wanting to know so I shook my head. "I think you want me to hate you. I think that's easier for you to accept. So I'm not going to do that anymore." Oh, hell. Great. That was just great. And he wasn't done either. "I am going to give you something no one has ever given you before."

I didn't want to ask. I really didn't. But I couldn't help myself. "What's that?"

"A chance."

Thrown, my head jerked a little, his hand falling from my face. "A chance for what?"

"To show yourself to me."

I closed my eyes against the rush of warmth at his words. I wanted that. I wanted that chance. I wanted someone who gave a shit enough to be patient, to let me slowly battle my comfort zones. God, how I wanted that.

But that person could not be Cash.

Because Cash would eventually fuck me and be done with me like every woman who came before. Unlike them, though, I would never fully recover. And I had enough damage that was stitched together with sheer power of will and a hefty thread of denial.

"That's not going to happen, Cash." Why did my voice sound so sad?

"Maybe... maybe not. We'll see."

I took a breath, shaking my head. "I'll be out of your hair as soon as my ribs feel better. Another day or two and I should be able to handle my own shit again."

He shrugged my comment away like it changed nothing and pushed off the table. Before I could think to react, he was standing behind me, bent over my shoulder and looking at the picture open on my laptop.

"He looks like an asshole," Cash said with a casual chuckle. "Did he drown a bunch of bunnies or something?" he went on, completely oblivious to how my body had tensed, how every cell in my body was poised to attack or run if he overstepped the invisible line I kept around the subject. "Who is Damian Crane, babe?"

FIFTEEN

Lo

I remembered my wedding night with what was the genuine definition of 'bittersweet'. I was eighteen and way too young to enter into that kind of arrangement, signing my future away to the boy next door. But that being said, it was my only way out. It was the only end in sight. It was the only way to get away from my father. So six weeks after the birthday finally making me legally able to no longer be the property of one man, I walked up to the Justice of the Peace and became the property of another.

I was young, idealistic, nose hopelessly buried in romance novels I bought at the drugstore with the money leftover from buying the groceries for the week- a thing my father allowed only because he felt they were a good way for me to learn to take care of my future husband.

My father liked my husband because, well, he was in the Marines. That was all it took for my dad- be a brother. It didn't matter where your stance was on political issues or social beliefs. If you were a fellow Devil Dog, you were alright in his book.

I had been a virgin, again... young and idealistic about what that meant. I had learned from my books that it would hurt, I would cry, I would bleed, but my partner would totally be able to make me break apart in ecstasy despite of all of that.

What a bitter disappointment to get back to his, then *our,* apartment, have him all but rip my pretty white summer dress off of me, leaving me too shell shocked, humiliated, and insecure to ask him to take it slow. So his big hands closed over my breasts, grabbing, pinching my nipples too hard, but I didn't object. He pressed me backward through the apartment until the backs of my legs hit the bed and I fell onto it. His big body climbed over mine, his lips trailing down my neck, taking my nipples into his mouth and sucking.

I started to feel a twinge of desire then, just a strange fluttering of need between my thighs. As if sensing it, his hand moved there and stoked through my lips, sinking a finger inside after a minute. "Wet," he groaned against my neck and I could feel him reaching between us to undo his pants and free himself.

The desire quickly got replaced with genuine fear as I felt the head of his dick press against me, feeling too big. But before I could even draw a breath to consider that, he was inside me, not slow and gentle, not inch by inch, one thrust and he was buried to the hilt. I let out a scream at the kind of pain I couldn't describe stabbing at the contact of our bodies.

The only bit of relief I got was the fact that after less than a minute or two of rough thrusting (and accompanying pain), he let out a groan and came inside me.

He was breathing into my neck as I tried to blink the tears away.

All I could think was- it was nothing like I had read, like I had fantasized about. If that was what sex was, I couldn't imagine why anyone wanted to do it. Let alone write books about it.

He pushed himself up and looked down at me, giving me a white-toothed smile and the pain felt like a dull ache as I looked at him- my husband, the boy I had known since I was six years old, the man I had entrusted with my future.

"You're mine now," he said and I felt a flutter in my belly. It sounded like something one of my fictional heroes would say to their women- always alpha and possessive. In that moment, I felt my smile spread to match his and everything felt right in the world.

I had no idea what the reality of belonging to Damian Crane meant. If I had, I would have waited for him to fall into a sex-lulled sleep, slipped back into my clothes, and ran like hell as far and as fast as I could.

It was alright at first. He was demanding, at times, even more so than my father had been. But I was a wife, not a daughter. My duties were amplified. I cooked, I cleaned, I did our laundry, I paid the bills. Then at night, I would lay on my back or get onto all fours and he would fuck me. That was what it was too- fucking. We didn't have sex. We damn sure never made love. And to even say "we" was inappropriate. *We* didn't do anything. He fucked. I laid there. I took it. After the first two or three times, it stopped hurting. The lack of pain, however, didn't help the fact that it did nothing for me. Nothing. I was a newlywed woman who didn't know what an orgasm felt like.

It wasn't long before the name-calling started. At first, I thought it was Damian's version of dirty talk. *Bitch. Slut. Cunt. Whore.* I should have known that wasn't what it was because each time he said it, I winced because I heard the malice underneath. I heard it, but I refused to acknowledge it.

Besides, having sex that did nothing for you while being called names, well, that wasn't that bad. What was bad was when he was too lazy to fuck me. That was when I learned that the loving, passionate way women went down on their heroes in my books was going to be as far from my reality as the sex itself was. Because when Damian wanted my mouth, he wanted it hard and he wanted it deep. He wanted it so that I was gagging all over him, his cock buried in my throat, my mascara running down my face, his cum coming out of my nose. He wanted it brutal. And that was how I started to feel afterward in the bathroom as I cried silently, wiping my face, brushing my teeth, trying to swallow past the razor-blade sensation of my throat- brutalized.

But he was my husband.

That was my job.

It never even crossed my mind to refuse him.

Then, like some prayer answered, he was deployed. I felt so guilty even thinking that- that I was happy that he was being shipped off to do God-knew what, maybe to never return. But that was what I felt- happiness.

He was gone and while I was still a kept woman, his little barefoot wife, I had more freedom too. I went out with girls I went to school with and had lost touch. I took a couple cheap classes at the night school. If I didn't want to wash the dishes every night, I didn't. If I didn't want to wear makeup the way he liked it (mascara, red lips)... I didn't bother. They were small things, but at twenty years old and having never known even a taste of independence, I reveled in each tiny victory.

Then he was coming home again.

I tried (and failed) to be glad for it, to have my husband back. Granted, he was rough with me in bed and he made a lot of demands on me... but he was still the boy I used to make mud pies with, who I first kissed when I was fifteen, who told me I was the prettiest girl in town. And sometimes, he could still be that sweet. I would catch him watching me as I did something stupid like ironing and ask him what he was thinking and he would say things like... 'the best thing that ever happened to me' or 'I still can't believe you're mine'. They were words that made little flutterings move through my belly. They were things that made the never-ending work tolerable.

He let himself in the apartment slamming the door, making me yelp and turn, dropping the glass I was drying. I was supposed to pick him up from the airport. I was supposed to get pretty and go greet him like a good wife, let him squeeze me too tight, kiss me too intimate for a public place. That was what was supposed to happen. But not for another two hours.

"What the fuck did you do, Willow?" he growled, dropping his bag and stomping toward where I stood frozen, barefoot in the kitchen, surrounded by shards of glass.

"I... I wasn't expecting you. You scared me," I said, taking a deep breath.

"You fucking sayin' it's my fault you broke a glass? Who pays for that shit, Willow? Huh? Who!"

He'd never yelled at me before. Been a little gruff, a little unnecessarily forceful in his tone? Sure. But he had never outright yelled. I felt my body jolt away from the sound, fear uncurling like a snake in my belly, jaws unhinged, ready to swallow me up from the inside.

"I'm sorry, Damian. I didn't mean to..."

"No. You're not sorry. Not yet. But you're going to be."

I didn't even register that I should be terrified when he reached down and started to unfasten his belt. In my world, that didn't pose a threat. If anything, I thought he was going to make me suck him off or fuck him or something. And, well, who could blame him for wanting that as soon as he was home after so long without it?

"Throw the rest of that in the sink, bitch."

Bitch? *Bitch?*I threw the rest of the glass in the sink, my hands suddenly trembling. "I'm so glad you're hom..."

"Shut the fuck up. I know what you've been up to." Oh, shit. Shit shit shit. He knew about the classes and the friends. Alright.

That was okay. I could smooth that all over. I just needed to talk to him and say... "Fucking everything with a cock," he accused, taking his belt and folding it in half, gripping the end tight.

"What? Damian, no! I've only ever been with yo..."

"Don't you fucking lie to me you dirty slut! I know you've been giving away my cunt to every man you could."

Suddenly, my eyes went to the belt and I understood. Oh, God, I understood. The feeling I felt then was hard to describe. Fear, yes, but it was different than any fear I had ever known before because it was mingled with something else. It was mingled with the knowledge that unlike a random mugging on the street, that this would not be the only time. If my husband was going to beat me, he was going to keep beating me. There would be no end in sight. The nausea rose up in my throat and I had to swallow hard through it to keep it down.

"I'm gonna show you what happens when my woman steps out on me. I guess I have to teach you a lesson, huh?"

His arm lifted, cocked back, and all that was after that was the searing, indescribable pain of leather biting into my skin. It was simply... blinding. All consuming. It was all there was in the world, the pain. I lost my footing early, slamming down on all fours on the floor, feeling the glass cutting into my palms and my legs as I tried to scramble away, tears pouring down my face. But on my hands and knees, I was in the perfect position for him to whip my skirt up, rip my panties off, and apply the belt to the bare, unprotected skin of my ass. The sick came up then, leaving me gagging all over the kitchen floor as the belt broke into the already raised welts on my skin.

"You belong to *me*," he growled, getting down behind me and I knew what was next. Somehow, I preferred it. I didn't even bother to say no. If it took the belt away, I would let him fuck me until my legs gave out. The belt moved upward and I felt him slide it around my neck, tightening it into a collar and pulling until I couldn't even try to gasp for breath. It was then that he pushed inside of me.

After, he left me on the floor to cry. And, lord, how I cried. I had never cried like that before in my life- loud, loud enough to alert the neighbors if they hadn't already heard me screaming through my beating, and uncontrolled, my entire body convulsing hard with the sobs that I felt would never end.

He came out when I was quieter, still crying and I was pretty sure I would never stop crying, picked me up, and carried me to the bathroom where he dropped me on my ass in the tub, chuckling when I screamed at the pressure against the open wounds across my back and bottom. I watched in horror as he moved toward the medicine cabinet and grabbed alcohol, tweezers, triple antibiotic, and gauze. He came back toward me, not bothering to look at my face as he unscrewed the cap and poured the alcohol all down my legs and over my palms, ignoring my cries of pain.

"Next time you'll act right, Wills," he chided as he pulled out the tweezers and went to work pulling the glass out of my skin. Once finished, he applied the antibiotic liberally and wrapped me up before pushing me onto my stomach and seeing to the cuts on my back.

See the thing was... it wasn't regret. Him taking care of me? It wasn't out of regret or out of concern for my well being. He took care of my wounds because he didn't want there to be any reason for me to ever have to go to the hospital, to ever get a chance to tell anyone what was going on.

He left me in the tub when he was finished cleaning me up. I didn't cry. I suddenly found myself out of tears. All I felt was sad. So incredibly sad.

My husband had beat me.

I was a battered woman.

I was a cliché.

But there was nothing I could do about it.

I did what every trapped, abused woman did at first- I stayed.

I stayed and I got beat in different ways, depending on my offense. Sometimes it was bare-handed spanking. Sometimes it was the belt again. Later, it was his bare fists slamming into my face, into my sides.

It was my twenty-fourth birthday when I decided I couldn't take it anymore. The night before, Damian thought the shorts I wore to the market were too revealing and when I got home, I was called my new names: *bitch, slut, cunt, whore.* Then he pulled off the shorts in question and he beat my ass until I wet myself.

And. I. Was. Done.

The actual word 'done' took on a whole new meaning as I sat in the bathtub where he always dealt with the aftermath of his anger on my skin and I twirled the knife around in my hand, trying to get to the point where I knew I could do it- sink it into my wrist and drag it up my arm, slicing open the vein and making it impossible for them to fix me, to give me back to him.

I was never going to belong to him again. Never. He was never going to get a chance to lay his hands on me again. He was never going to be able to be the reason I cried at night.

If that meant my only way out was to slice myself open and take myself out of the world, then so be it.

The only problem was... Damian came home from work early. Damian came home from work and I flew out of that tub, tucking the knife behind my back when he threw the bathroom door open without knocking. There was no such thing as privacy in my life. He had once stood there and watched me pull out a tampon and nothing had ever felt more mortifying.

"Why isn't dinner ready?" he demanded, ready for a fight already.

It was three in the afternoon, that was why dinner wasn't

ready. Well, that and the fact that I didn't plan to live to see dinner when I got up in the morning.

"Answer me, bitch!" he roared, closing in on me.

I don't know where the urge came from, where it had been buried all the other times he had come at me, why it hadn't surfaced before. Wherever it had been hiding, it was showing itself then, an all-consuming burst of self-preservation. I felt the handle of the knife in my hand and I squeezed it hard, feeling a calmness settle over me as I did.

"Answer me, cunt."

"No," I said, taking a step forward instead of in retreat like he had come to expect from me.

The confused look on his face was seared into my memory. It was the only time I let his face pop into my head, when I was trying to remember that dumbfounded look.

"What the fuck did you just say to me, bitch?"

"I said no," I shot back, my jaw clenched tight as I kept talking. "You should be familiar with it. You've heard me scream it out every time you've beaten me the past four years, you son of a bitch."

His brows went up, but the rage I had been expecting didn't surface. If anything, he almost looked calm, amused. A evil smirk toyed with his lips. "I guess I have to teach you a lesson, huh?"

He reached for me then and with reflexes I didn't know I had, my arm came up and I stabbed the knife straight through his outstretched palm. I should have been horrified, sickened, frozen on the spot at the sight of the blade sticking out of both ends of his hand. But, in reality, all I felt was pleasure, down to my toes, it was positively arousing.

With a smile, I ripped it back out, Damian's scream echoing off the bathroom tile and bouncing back at me.

"You stupid..."

He didn't get the rest out because then I was stabbing. Fast, frequent, unrelenting. All I saw was red- blood everywhere. All I heard were his screams and groans and curses.

By the time my vision cleared, Damian was on the floor, clutching his hand to his side, his clothes saturated with blood. He was still breathing, but my knife was lodged in one of his ribs and I couldn't pull it back out.

Horrified, but still determined as ever to be done, I flew out of the bathroom, rubbing my bloodstained hands over the comforter of the bed as I grabbed as much as I could and threw it into a bag. That included his gun and the twenty five thousand dollars cash he kept under the floorboards under our bed because he was convinced the banks were going to fail.

With that and not a glance backward, I left him.

Also, more importantly, I left that woman behind too. The victim. I was done with her. I was never, *fucking ever* going to be her again.

And I never was.

SIXTEEN

Cash

The funny thing about my anger, it's like one of those sparklers kids play with on the fourth of July. It burns bright and brilliant for a matter of minutes then fizzles out to nothing at all. I had never been the type who could use their pissed-off-edness to fuel a revenge plot. I didn't hold grudges.

It was simply never the way I operated. I blamed my father. I blamed the fact that he never seemed to be anything but angry. From the day my mother died, even more so. It was like he blamed the world for her loss and he was all too happy to take that rage out on anyone who so much as stepped on his toes.

Even as a kid, I knew I didn't want to be that way. I knew it wasn't right, it didn't fit my personality. Reign had moments when it did suit him, when it did fit him. But as president of a gun running bike gang full of testosterone-driven men... well... he needed to be able to tap into that on occasion, to hold professional grudges. It was part of what made him good at what he did.

Being second in command, well, it left me more freedom to let that shit go. I didn't need to hang on to it, so I didn't.

All I needed was a good fight, a good fuck, or a good workout and the rage always slipped away, not leaving a trace, like it had never been there to begin with.

That was me.

That, apparently, was not Lo.

Which, well, I had already guessed at on my own, but walking up the stairs to see her in her clothes like they were a shield, working hard, looking like her intimidating self (which I found sexy as hell, but that was beside the point)... I knew she was going to do whatever it took to hold onto the anger she felt at me. It wasn't just anger that I left her high and dry either. It was something else, something she wasn't letting me see.

In the end, though, it didn't matter how much she wanted to hold onto it. Eventually, she would give in. And I'd be there. I'd be there and I'd get some answers and I'd get to know who Lo was after all.

When I asked her who the fuck the Damian Crane guy was, it was like I set a bomb off in my house, it was like she was holding herself off from shooting right out of her skin.

"Bad guy, huh?" I asked, going for casual, trying to take that look off her face, that look of absolute, bone-deep fear. Whoever the fuck Damian Crane was, he wasn't just a bad guy. He wasn't just a job. He was a ghost, one of her ghosts.

Finally, finally I had something to go on. Later. Alone.

"It's cool, don't tell me. Not my business. Now why don't you close all that shit down and get your plump ass up in my bed?"

"Plump?" was her immediate reaction, as it was any woman's who didn't realize plump was a damn good thing.

"Yeah, plump. Round. Thick. Bite-able."

She made a strange snorting noise. "What happened to having to ask for your cock?" she asked, closing her laptop, giving me one of her famous brow raises.

"Oh, darlin', you're still going to have to ask for that. But it wasn't what I had in mind."

"That's what you always have in mind," she said, but the bitterness had left her tone and all I heard was teasing.

"True enough," I shrugged, not offended. It *was* true. "But right now, I was thinking- movie and sleep."

"Movie and sleep?" she parroted, looking at me like I suggested an orgy and ritual animal sacrifice.

"Yeah. Movie is your choice. Just not any of those shit vampire / werewolf love story things."

"I *like* those vampire / werewolf love story things," she countered with a smile that almost made me take a step back it was so genuine, open.

"Of course you do," I smiled back, grabbing one of her romance novels out of her bag and gently tapping her on her forehead with it.

With that, I turned up toward the stairs.

"What are you doing with my book?" she called, but she was walking up with me.

"I dunno. I might find myself in need of some... literary pornography later," I laughed.

"Gross. Give me my book back," she said, reaching for it as she climbed the stairs and for the first time, she didn't need to use the rail to help herself up.

"What? You're allowed to use it to get you all warmed up to trip the switch but I'm not..."

"Trip the switch?" she asked, standing beside the bed and grinning.

"Yeah, you know... trip the switch, polish the pearl, diddle the skittle, double click the mouse, circle the wagon..." I trailed off to the sound of her laughter. It was like I remembered it, feminine, tinkling.

"You're ridiculous," she said, shaking her head.

"You love it," I shot back, reaching behind my back and hauling off my shirt. I tried not to smile when her mouth parted slightly and her breathing got a little less even. She was right- I was a cocky fuck. As such, I knew I had a good body. Not huge, I was never the type of man who needed to have muscles so big they couldn't put their arms down to their sides, but I kept shit tight. I reached for my pants as I kicked out of my boots.

My hands had just pushed them off my hips when she swallowed hard. "What are you doing?"

"Shower babe," I said, moving past her toward the hall again. I was just about to round the curve of the wall and be out of view when I pushed my boxer briefs down and gave her a view of my ass. I didn't have to look to know she was watching. I smiled the rest of the way until I got into the shower, reached down, and dealt with the epic case of blue balls she had me dealing with.

I walked back with a towel slung low on my hips to find her in the bed, changed into one of my tees. I was sure she had something to sleep in inside her bag, but she chose my clothes instead. Whether she realized it or not, it meant something.

"So what movie are we watching?" I asked, going to my closet and finding a pair of black sweats. I turned slightly to the side, ripped off the towel, and slipped into the pants.

"Ah... what?" she asked, shaking her head when the silence dragged on.

"Movie, Lo," I clarified with a knowing smirk.

"Oh, right. Um. I don't know. Something without violence. I get enough of that shit in my life."

I nodded, clicked through the on-demand choices, picked the most recent stupid comedy, and put it on. I climbed into my side of the bed, stretching an arm across the back of the pillows.

She half-watched the movie and I could feel her gaze falling on me more than occasionally. "You gonna come over here or what, gorgeous?" I asked, slanting my face toward her, ruffling a bit of her hair with my hand that was resting above her pillow. There was only the barest of seconds before her body shifted and curled into my side. My arm slid down and wrapped around her back, holding her against me. "There you go," I murmured, leaning down to kiss the top of her hair.

"Don't ruin it," she shot back, but the malice wasn't in her words anymore.

"No. Wouldn't want that. So," I went right on, unable to help myself, "you like my naked body, huh?" A half-exhale, half-snort escaped her. "I don't blame you. It's pretty fucking amazing. They should build statues of me." At that, I got her tinkling laugh again and I smiled. "Know what?"

"No... what?" she asked without hesitation.

"They should build statues of yours too."

Her head tilted upward and her eyes rolled. "Oh please. I'm closing in on my forties. No one is building statues of my body."

"Best tits I've ever seen."

She smiled, shaking her head. "And considering the sheer amount of tits your eyes have been privy to..."

"Exactly," I agreed, reaching my free hand down to boop her nose.

Her brows drew together like she was trying to figure something out. "You're in a good mood."

"I'm always in a good mood."

"You weren't like... two hours ago."

"And that was two hours ago so why the fuck we talkin' about it now?"

Her lips pursed slightly and she nodded. "Good point."

"So are we watching this movie or what?" I asked and her head settled back onto my chest.

"Sure. If you can shut up for a while," she said, her words warm and teasing.

"No promises."

"You're still talking."

"So are you."

We fell asleep sometime before the credits actually rolled.

I woke up to her kissing down my chest, the sleep drawing back like a fog against the sensation.

"Baby..." I heard my voice murmur, already husky, already turned on.

Her body shifted and her legs landed on either side of my body. Her lips trailed slowly down the center of my stomach, her soft hair tickling over my skin. My hand moved down, gathering her hair to one side of her neck so I could watch her as her tongue slipped out to trace the skin directly above the waistband of my pants.

"Lo, baby, if this is some kind of payback..." I started, one of my hands curling into a fist as her teeth nipped into my skin.

At my words, she shifted again, moving upward to look down at me. Her hips shifted downward and stroked across my cock and both of our mouths opened on a groan.

"Not payback," she said, her eyes heavy.

Thank fuck.

"How are these?" I asked, pressing my hand into her ribs.

"I'll be fine," she said, brushing against my cock again.

My hands rested on her hips for a second, guiding her movements, driving us both upward before I bunched up the material of her tee and started sliding it upward. I sat up close to her body so I could pull it free and my hands moved up to cup her face and pull it to mine.

It wasn't soft and sweet like the last kiss, we were beyond that. The kiss was rough and wild, full of the desire we had both been trying to deny. Her tongue pressed into my mouth and my hands slid down from her face to her breasts, teasing over her nipples until they were hard in my hands. My arm slid up and around her back, holding her to me as I shifted our weight and gently moved her onto the mattress, my weight balanced half-off of her. I lifted up and smiled down at her.

"What?" she asked, looking cautious.

"You haven't asked yet," I reminded her, smirking.

She laughed, rolling her eyes. "Shut up and fuck me, Cash."

Well then. Okay.

SEVENTEEN

Lo

I didn't expect gentle.

I didn't think he was capable. Well, that wasn't true. He had been very gentle with me before, but I kind of figured that it was because I was in so much pain. I always imagined he fucked like he lived: fast and carefree. Not hard and rough and dominating, because that wasn't his personality. Giving, energetic, inventive, maybe a little kinky at times. Just not... soft.

But that was exactly what he was giving me.

His lips explored mine until every inch of my skin felt like it was buzzing, electric. "Cash..." I groaned as his lips trailed down the side of my neck, unhurried, happy to take his time to explore despite the fact that he had already seen my body. His lips closed over my nipple, making a shiver run through my body as his tongue flicked over the sensitive point. My back arched as the wetness pooled between my thighs. God, I wanted him. But at the same time, I found myself utterly, bone-deep terrified.

"Cash..."

"Shh," he murmured, moving across my chest to lavish over my other nipple. His hand slid downward and slipped between my thighs to slide up my sex. His finger stroked whisper-light over my clit, just enough to make my body tense, but not enough to allow release. He wanted to drag it out.

He wanted, *oh God,* to make love to me.

There had been men after Damian. Not for a long time. A few years. I needed to get myself back together- physically, emotionally. But there were men. I wanted to reclaim that part of my life, to show myself that I could enjoy my body. I did too, I learned how to relax and enjoy, to have an orgasm. That being said, it was always sex. Sometimes it was pure fucking. It was never, ever making love.

This was.

And instead of feeling the warm, swirling comfort I always thought I would feel, all I felt was fear. All I felt was the soul-deep understanding that I would never rise from his bed feeling the same way I felt sliding in. I would feel different. I would be different.

That shit was terrifying.

"Honey relax," he murmured, shifting downward, licking the skin above my bandages then, sweet lord, kissing down the bandages, moving over to my sore ribs and planting the tenderest of kisses there. He shifted to the side and kissed up the inside of my thigh, over the triangle of my sex, down the other thigh.

"Cash..."

His head titled up, watching me with heavy lidded eyes.

I reached downward, grabbing his shoulders and pulling him back over me. His arms planted on my sides, but he allowed more of his weight to press into me, a weight I found myself craving as my hands slid up and down his back. His lips found mine again and I shifted my legs wider so he could settle fully between. His body shifted and his cock pressed against my heat, drawing a moan from me and a deep rumbling in the chest from him.

"Now Cash..." I demanded, desperate. I needed him. I needed him in a way I wasn't familiar with.

He shifted, digging into the bedside table and pulling out a condom which he put on with practiced ease and speed. He settled back against me, rubbing his cock between my folds until I was writhing. His eyes were intense on mine, like he was seeing me for the first time. And, in a way, he was. He was seeing beneath the shields, he was seeing the me underneath it all.

His cock pushed up against my entrance and paused while he kissed me, slow, deep. When he finally did press inside, it was painfully slow. I felt every inch fill and spread me.

My legs shifted, feet to the mattress, knees pressed tight into his body, pulling him deep.

"*Fuck* baby," he groaned, buried to the hilt.

My hands dug into his back, the pressure deep in my belly becoming impossible to ignore. I needed him to *move.* I needed some relief from the undeniable, clawing need.

"Cash, please..." I begged, beyond caring about seeming needy. I *was* needy.

He withdrew halfway and then just as slowly as before, he pressed back in. Over and over, making every muscle in my body tense, making the ache only build.

I had a vice like grip on his back, my legs wrapped around his hips, my hips grinding up into his with each impossibly slow thrust.

"Faster," I demanded, whimpering as he buried deep and arched up slightly, making his cock hit an unknown sweet spot and his pelvis press into my clit.

His lips lowered to mine and his mouth caught my moans. "Not this time," he said into my ear.

"I can't..." I objected on a frustrated whimper.

"Yes you can. You can come for me just like this. Just relax and let it happen."

He was right. I was overthinking it.

"Does that feel good?" he asked, pressing back in.

"Yes," I groaned, feeling the climax getting closer.

"You're so fucking tight," he groaned, closing his eyes for a second.

He was just as far gone as I was, just as anxious for release. Somehow, that knowledge help drive me up where I needed to be. He pushed forward again and I felt the waves of ecstasy wash over me, by entire body shaking, my voice calling out his name as my fingers scratched across his back.

"Christ, baby," he groaned, pushing through my orgasm until he felt my body stop the pulsating, then he buried deep and came, growling out my name.

I held onto him after which was totally not like me, but I couldn't help myself. I wrapped him up with legs and arms and held on like I never wanted to let go. A part of me didn't. Cash's breath was in my neck, slowly returning to normal, his face resting over my heart which felt like it never would.

"Let me up baby," he said quietly, kissing between my breasts. When I didn't move to do what he requested, he chuckled slightly. "I gotta deal with this condom then I'll come right back."

I grumbled, but released him, the slight ache between my thighs as he slid away reminding me it had been a while since I had a man. He got up and walked gloriously naked into the hall. I watched, shamelessly until he was out of sight before curling up on my side and trying not to think.

But, hell, I was me and I was thinking.

I was especially thinking about the crack I felt in the shield covering my heart. It was small, just a hairline fracture, but it was enough.

"Trying to push me away already?" he asked, making me start as he climbed in behind me, cocking his legs up under mine and wrapping an arm around my belly.

"What are you talking about?"

"Curled up away from me," he murmured into my neck.

"It's more comfortable to sleep like this," I protested.

"With busted ribs?" he countered. And he was right- my ribs were throbbing a little.

"Go to sleep, Cash."

"Let me in, Lo."

"I thought I already did," I said, attempting cheeky. Cheeky was better than what I was really feeling.

"Cute," he said back.

"I thought so."

"Baby..."

"Let it go, Cash. I'm tired."

There was a long pause before he sighed. "Alright."

Truth was, I was anything but tired. In fact, he fell asleep holding me a few minutes later and I stayed awake for hours, staring at the wall, trying to not freak out, trying to not analyze every possible thing that could happen. Like I could wake up and he could be cold and dismissive, he could be done with me. But... would that be the worst thing? That was usually what I wanted- easy, uncomplicated. Hell, sometimes it was me sneaking out in the middle of the night to avoid the awkward conversation in the morning. I was never the flowers and candy and promise rings kind of girl. That wasn't the life I led. If I woke up and he was through with me, well, all the better.

–

CASH

I woke up to his cock pressing against my lips from behind.

"You're already wet," he informed me unnecessarily. I guessed he wasn't done with me quite yet. "Think your ribs can take it if I fuck you like this?"

Hell yes. I didn't even care if it did hurt; I just wanted him.

"Mmhmm," I murmured, pressing my ass back into him.

"You're killing me, honey," he groaned.

"What are you going to do about it then?" I asked, smiling at the wall.

He chuckled, turning to get a condom. "I guess I'll fuck you now then," he said and, without anything further, he slammed in hard and deep.

"Fuck," I cried out, pushing back, feeling his cock press against my G-spot as he pulsed his hips slightly.

"Hard and fast, he said, biting into my ear as his hand slid down my belly and cupped my sex, sliding over my clit. "Sure you can take it?"

"All talk," I teased, my voice breathy as he tapped my clit relentlessly.

His chuckle was the last thing I consciously focused on before he was slamming into me. Hard and fast, just like he promised. My entire body jolted with each thrust. His cock hit my G-spot and his finger was on my clit. It was only a matter of maybe two or three minutes before I felt the tight gripping sensation of my orgasm budding.

"Oh my God," I groaned, pushing back into him, shameless, uninhibited.

"Come," he demanded, his other hand going to my breast and squeezing hard. Then it shot through my system, frantic, almost blinding in its intensity. "Fuck that feels good," he groaned, still thrusting and as I came down and he was still fucking me, I realized we weren't done.

"Cash... I can't..."

"You will," he said, withdrawing suddenly and rolling onto his back.

"What are you doing?" I asked, forcing my come-drunk limbs to move so I could face him.

"You're going to ride me. Normal cowgirl or reverse, your choice," he told me, all smiles with his hands resting behind his head.

"You can't be serious."

"Saddle up," he smirked, patting his hipbone.

And, well, was there really any way to refuse a man like him? Looking as self-satisfied as he looked? Offering to let me pick the position like he'd be equally happy no matter what I chose.

In the end, I threw one leg over his body, going full-on cowgirl because I wanted to watch his face as I rode him. One of his hands released his head and moved down his body to grab his cock and hold it up for me to slide onto. And I did, glorying every thick inch.

"Beautiful," he said when he was buried deep, looking up at me with my head thrown back. My head tilted down and I studied him with heavy-lidded eyes and realized with absolute clarity that he was trouble. He was the one, the one who was capable of getting in and putting down roots. "Stop thinking," he demanded, his hand drifting casually up and down my thigh.

I smiled down at him. "Good idea," I agreed, taking the lead and driving us both to completion, covered in sweat, panting, loud.

I collapsed onto his chest, my head buried under his neck. His arms were draped casually around my back. My body was jumping slightly in aftershocks, my leg muscles trembling from the strain, but there was nothing in the world that could tear me away from him in that moment.

"Did you know Wolf and Janie are fucking?"

Okay.

There was one thing that could tear me away from him, and it did. I flew upward, falling onto my ass beside him, throwing my hair out of my face. "What?" I heard myself screech.

"I'll take that as a no," he smiled lazily, turning on his side toward me and stroking his hand over my breast, the nipple hardening immediately.

"What the fuck do you mean they are fucking?"

Cash's brows drew together at my tone. "After you passed out from the pain meds, I ran over to Wolf's. He's been MIA and everyone was getting worried. Apparently, he was holed up with Janie."

He was holed up with Janie.

That made no sense.

"Did he tell you that?"

"No. I saw her myself. Talked to her. If anything, Wolf seemed pissed to be interrupted. Though," he said, pressing his hand between my legs and brushing through my wetness, "I get that."

"How do you know they are fucking?" I asked, swatting his hand away.

Janie didn't sleep around. That wasn't her way. She didn't do casual. She wasn't exactly social. She was standoffish. She didn't go out of her way to meet or connect with men. Not that I blamed her. She just wasn't interested.

"She was on his bed in his shirt... and nothing else."

Holy shit.

Okay. That was good. She was okay. She was still in town. Cash was still in the dark about her setting the bombs. Which, I hoped, meant everyone else was clueless as well.

"Was she alright?" I asked, unable to stop the desperate emotion from leaking into my voice.

Cash's brows drew together. "You saw how Wolf reacted when he thought I hit you. No way in hell would he ever hurt her."

"Cash..." I pleaded, needing more.

"She was fine, Lo. A little banged up but..."

"Banged up?" I yelled, my eyes bugging out, my heart slamming in my chest.

"Nothing. Just a couple scratches on her face, a bandage on her arm. Looked like she maybe fell and got some cuts is all. She was fine, baby."

"You were just *sitting* on this?" I exploded, slamming my hands into his chest. Unprepared, he fell back onto the mattress, watching me like I had lost my mind.

"What the hell, Lo?"

"She's hurt and you don't tell me? She's in one of The Henchmen's houses and *you don't tell me?*"

He sat back up, shaking his head at me. "I thought you knew. She's your girl. Thought you were tight."

"We *were* tight until she didn't pick me up from Reign's and fucking *disappeared!*"

Shit. Shit shit shit. I hadn't meant to say that.

"What?" he asked, like he hadn't heard me. Of course he heard me. I had been screaming. "What do you mean she disappeared?"

My gaze fell to my knees, unsure how the hell I could get out of this.

"Lo?"

"She didn't pick me up and she didn't come back to Hailstorm either. No one has heard from her. I've called. I've texted."

"Maybe she just wanted a break. She eats, sleeps, and breathes Hailstorm. I know you probably think Wolf is..."

"Unhinged?" I supplied.

"But he's a good guy. If she's with him and not answering,

she's got to be happy."

If she was alone with any man, in his house, half-naked... she was anything but happy. She was... I didn't even want to think about it.

"I need to see her."

"Christ, babe. I don't think I was even supposed to tell you I saw her. I can't be bringing you there."

"Look, I get your loyalty. What you feel for Wolf... that's what I feel for Janie. You have to bring me to her."

Something happened then that was so shocking, I felt it in the uncomfortable swirling in my stomach- a guard came down over his face, locking calm, jocular, cocky Cash away, leaving nothing behind. Just a biker. A faceless Henchmen.

"Sorry, Lo. Can't." Even his voice didn't sound like him.

So that was the way it was.

Well, that was to be expected in a way I guess. Brotherhood before everything, especially 'bitches'. That was how an MC worked. What part of me had gotten confident enough to think that I would change it, that my asking would somehow outweigh that?

I felt the crack in my heart start to seal over and I could only describe it as excruciating.

Stupid, stupid me.

"Right," I said through gritted teeth, moving off the bed with rigid purpose.

"Lo, don't do this..." his voice pleaded, his hand reaching out and closing around my wrist.

I turned back, my other hand moving over his hand, grabbing, and twisting hard. "I didn't do this," I countered, dropping his hand and enjoying it a little when he had to rub it with his other hand, "you did."

With that, I grabbed my clothes off the floor and made a dart for the bathroom. I slammed the door and locked it.

"Idiot," I hissed at my reflection, barely bothering to register that the cuts had scabbed over and the bruises had gone from the graphic blue and purple to a faded yellow and green.

I turned on the water, unwrapped my ribs, and stepped under the spray, staying there until the tap ran cold. Showered and dressed and convinced I was ready to be a cold, indifferent bitch if I needed to be, I went downstairs to, well, look for a fight.

All I was greeted with was fresh brewed coffee with a sticky note attached to the pot. "Nice try. But you haven't pushed me away yet. Be back later. Shit to do – Cash."

He just expected me to stick around for him? Well he was going to be sorely disappointed when I wasn't there, wasn't he?

It wasn't all spite. I genuinely needed to get out. I had logged into the Hailstorm system and got the information on the properties belonging to Henchmen members. Now that I found Wolf's place, I needed to go there and check on Janie for myself. Fuck Cash and his reluctance to share the information. I didn't need him. I didn't need any man and that was the way it should be.

I picked up my cell and called a cab seeing as Cash stole my car yet again. I gave it a couple minutes before making my way toward the door and pulling it open.

"You made another mistake, Wills," Damian's voice met me, making my entire body run cold as I turned my head to see him leaning against the side of Cash's house. "You're never going to learn, are you?"

The shock made my reaction slow and he was off the house and shoving me in to Cash's living room before I could draw a breath. All I could think as I slammed hard into the couch and heard him kick closed the door, was what Cash was going to think when he saw chaos and blood all over his house.

Even facing my worst fears, he was on my mind.

Goddamn it.

EIGHTEEN

Cash

Damian Crane was a goddamn hero.

I felt an unfamiliar knot tighten in my stomach as I read through the articles about his service, how he saved countless lives, how he came home after duty only to be stabbed twelve times in his own bathroom.

"What the fuck are you up to now, Lo?" I asked the inside of her car as I flicked through the websites on my phone, trying to find something out, trying to get any piece of dirt I could find to untie the knot, to make it so that Lo wasn't on the hunt for a fucking American hero.

There was nothing.

He was a Marine. And when he finally came back home, he worked at a private security firm. There was nothing to suggest criminal activity. Nothing to suggest he was anything other than a model citizen.

There was only one article mentioning his family- his dead father who was also a Marine, his mother who was battling dementia, and his wife Willow.

For the fuck of it, I typed 'Willow Crane' into the search bar.

What came up made the knot disappear, but only because I felt like I got a swift kick to the goddamn guts. Because what came up was a bunch of pictures of a young, gorgeous, soft Lo. There was no mistaking her- the long blonde hair, the strong legs, the great rack, the brown eyes. The only difference was the eyes didn't have the mask down over them, blocking out all emotion. No, Willow Crane's eyes were so sad, so haunted as she stood next to her husband that I almost couldn't believe it was the same woman.

"Jesus Christ," I murmured as memories flashed into my mind, one in particular.

Wolf was in the kitchen, freaking out because he thought I hit Lo and Lo had said something in a tone that was way too sharp, way too defensive. *Do I seem like the kind of woman who would stay in the house with a man who beat her?*

"Fuck," I growled, zooming in on the picture. If you looked really closely, you could see the bruises on her arm, just above the elbow, peeking out from under her sleeves. "Damn it."

She married Damian Crane. And the asshole beat her.

It went so against the Lo I knew, the woman she had made herself, that it was hard to imagine. But looking at her picture, she looked so young, so much softer in the body without all the hours of training she did at Hailstorm. She looked... soft and... sweet. No way did she stand a chance against the giant, hulking mass that was her husband who had been trained how to do combat by the best special operations team our government had to offer.

I clicked back through the articles, finding the one about the stabbing- twelve knife wounds. Overkill. A crime of passion. I knew with a kind of absolute certainty that I didn't usually possess, that Willow Crane had been the one to do it. And, in doing so, she stopped being Willow Crane and started being Lo.

What the fuck did I do with that kind of information? Approach Lo? Ask her about it? Risk her shutting down on me?

It really didn't take much thinking to realize he had been the one who had beat her a few days before. That was why she wasn't involving Hailstorm. She didn't want them to know about her past, to know she used to be a battered woman. She didn't want anyone to hear that and think of her as weak. Never mind the fact that she stabbed that fucker twelve times and got away, built a life where no one could ever hurt her again; never mind that she was the strongest woman I had ever met and that was really saying something since I knew exactly what kind of torture Summer had been subject to. Summer had three months of that. Lo had years of enduring beatings and... fuck... I didn't want to think about the other things that might have happened to her.

It was then that I decided to do something that she would never forgive me for because it wasn't my place to do so. But, at the same time, I needed help... and they were the only ones who could help me.

I needed to find the mother fucker and then I needed to teach him what I thought about a man who put his hands on the woman who trusted him to take care of her.

To do that, well, I fucking needed to bring in Hailstorm on the plan.

I drove there thinking of all the ways I was royally fucking things up with Lo. Then I wondered why the fuck it mattered. She was a woman I was fucking. She wasn't *my* woman. Hell, I never *had* a woman that I would call mine. That wasn't what I did.

But for some reason, betraying her, it was bothering me... even if it was for her own good.

"I know you were here the other night, man, but can't say you're a welcome guest," the guy at the gate told me on a shrug.

"Don't have time to have a pissing contest with you. Get me

who is in charge. It's about Lo and it's fucking important."

At that, his face betrayed him- he looked concerned. He closed the door to his little booth and picked up a phone. Not two minutes later, an older man with graying hair walked out. He had the silver fox thing about him I hoped I had at his age. Bet he still got all the pussy he wanted.

"Malcolm," he said, nodding his head at me.

"Cash," I said, getting out of my car and making my way to the gate.

"This is about Lo?" he asked, lowering his voice a little.

"Yeah."

"You know where she is?"

"My house," I said and every muscle in his body tightened. "She's in trouble, Malc," I said, keeping my voice low so only he heard me. "She's gonna hate me for coming here, but I need your help to get her out of trouble."

He nodded his head at the guy in the booth who pressed the button to open the gate. "I knew something was up," he told me as I fell into step with him as he led me toward the command center so we could talk without being overheard. Hailstorm always had people everywhere. "Alright," he said, closing the door to the brick building with reinforced walls and bullet resistant windows (Hailstorm was a fucking fortress) and leaning back against it, his arms crossed over his chest. "What's going on?"

"Do you know Lo's real name?" I asked, not knowing if she shared more with her higher-ups than she did with most people.

"Wasn't my place to ask," he said simply.

"Her name is Willow Crane," I said, pulling my phone out from my pocket and showing him the picture I found earlier. He looked at young Lo, his face softening. "That is her husband, Damian Crane- Marine, American hero, wife beater..."

Malcolm's face snapped up and I saw a mix of sadness and anger in his eyes. "What?"

"Yeah, man. For years until she finally got sick of it and stabbed him twelve times and left his half-dead ass behind."

"Half-dead?" Malcolm asked, looking disappointed.

I nodded. "She showed up at the compound a couple days ago. She was... beaten. Her face, man," I said, looking down at my shoes for a second.

"Fuck," he cursed back.

"And her ribs," I added. "As you guys know, she helped us out a while back. She was calling in a favor..."

"Because she didn't want us to know about this?"

"Yeah."

"Now we need to work together and find this bastard."

"Yeah," I agreed again. "I don't have the resources you guys do to locate him. But let me get one thing straight, man," I said and his brow raised. "When we find that mother fucker, he's mine."

"Only if you make him hurt," Malcolm said, pushing off the door, looking fierce.

"That's the plan."

"Alright. Let's get to work," he said, moving over toward the computers and sitting down. "Wish to hell Jstorm was still around."

"Jstorm?" I asked, taking the seat next to him despite not having a damn clue how to work any of their software.

"Janie. She's the best at this shit."

"Well, we will have to make do," I said, not sharing what I knew about Janie. The situation was messed up enough as it was.

It was the middle of the afternoon and Malcolm was beside me letting off a string of curses that would have made a truck driver blush as he clicked and typed, doing God-knew what.

"Nothing?"

"Not nothing. I know his place, his work. But he's on vacation from what I can gather. No one has seen him. Even tapped into the facial recognition software they have on the streets around here... nothing is catching him."

"Fuck," I said, shaking my head and standing. I needed to go, to do something. I couldn't sit around all day feeling utterly useless. "I got to go. Lo is going to be wondering where I am." That was a lie, she was probably happy as hell that I was gone. "I'll give you my number and you can keep in touch." Malcolm swiveled his chair to me, a weird grin on his face. "What?"

"I have your number. We have *all* of your numbers."

"Oh... right," I laughed, rubbing the back of my neck. They knew everything.

"Congrats on your clean STD screen last month," he added with a huge smile. "With all the tail you get..."

"That's not fucking creepy at all," I laughed.

"We need to know everyone's dirty secrets," he shrugged.

"Right, well... keep me updated."

"Will do," Malcolm said, swiveling back to the computer and not bothering to walk me out.

I was glad for the privacy as I looked around the grounds, looking at the life Lo had built for herself and for her people. It was pretty fucking amazing what she had done for herself in just over ten years.

"Is Lo alright?" the guy at the gate asked, unable to help himself.

"She's fine. She'll be even better in about... thirty minutes," I said, giving him a sly smile that left him slack-jawed as I pulled away.

I pushed back the frustration and the guilt as I drove into my development. I needed to...

Every single thought flew out of my head as I pulled into my driveway to find my door thrown open. Don't ask me how I knew, but I knew. Technically, there could have been any number of reasons the door was open, but in that moment, I knew she was gone. I barely got the car into park as I flew out and up my front path and into... utter fucking chaos.

CASH

My dining room table was slammed against the wall, the chairs overturned, porcelain from a coffee cup splintered everywhere. And there was blood. Smeared across one of the walls, drops on the carpet.

"Fuck!" I growled, picking up one of the overturned chairs and throwing it across the room, not getting an ounce of satisfaction from it breaking apart.

I turned back toward the living room and spotted Lo's gun half lodged underneath the couch. She had gotten to it at some point. I went to it, hoping in an altogether too hopeless way that maybe she had gotten a shot off, but that hope drained when I opened it and found all bullets still inside.

On a frustrated yell, I grabbed Lo's phone off the floor, hoping I could find Hailstorm's number and fill them in. I stepped out onto my front path, not able to stomach the thought of being in my house with her blood on my walls.

"Mr. Cash!" I heard from the side and groaned. The last thing I needed was to talk to one of my neighbors right then. "Mr. Cash," Ernie, the sixty-something year old widow that lived across the street next to the girls' family called as he shuffled over to me in his tan slacks, green checkered shirt, and brown belt... looking every bit the old man.

"Ernie, I have to..."

"I know you're a busy man. And this is probably none of my business..." he hedged.

I sighed inwardly. "What isn't your business?"

"Well... there was a man here earlier..."

Immediately, I straightened and went from half-listening to completely fucking apt. I ripped my phone out of my pocket, again drawing up the picture of Willow and Damian. "This him?" I asked, a little too roughly.

He took his time getting his glasses from around his neck onto his nose and pulling my phone up to his face. "Yes. Yes, I'd have to say that is the man I saw." He pushed the phone back at me. "I know it's not my place, but well, I would want to know if I were in your place, son..."

"Know what? I asked, trying to draw forth a little patience.

"Your girlfriend... she, ah, well my boy... there's no easy way to say this. She left with that man."

"How long ago?" I asked, not wanting to ask if she left willingly, not willing to bring up that can of worms and force old Ernie to call the police.

"Well, I was just finishing lunch. Maybe around noon?" He paused. "Sorry to have to be the one to tell you about this, son."

"Happen to get a make on his car?"

Ernie looked surprised for a moment before his chest puffed out slightly. "Better than that. I got the license plate number. You know... you can never be too careful when you see strange cars in the area."

It was right then that I thought a thought I never imagined I would: Thank fucking God for nosy neighbors.

Ernie rattled off the number and gave me a sympathetic clamp on the shoulder before heading back to his house to stare out the window some more. I swiped through Lo's contacts as I got back into the car and backed out of the driveway.

"Malcolm," his voice met my ear and I felt a slight amount of relief that I had someone to share the information with.

"It's Cash," I said immediately.

"Where's Lo? Why are you on her phone?"

"She's gone. He got her while I was there." There was no use easing him into it. Besides, he struck me as the kind of man who handled emergency situations with a practiced kind of ease. "I have a plate and model number. Maybe you can catch it on your cameras."

I rattled off the information and he gave me a clipped, "On it," before he disconnected.

CASH

I drove, realizing I had nowhere to drive to so I drove to the compound, tearing through the main area, completely ignoring anyone who talked to me and stomping down the steps to the basement, going through two locked security doors to get to the gun safe.

"The fuck you doing?" Repo asked from behind me as I put a gun in the waistband of my jeans.

"Not club business," I said, trying to brush past him and shocked when his hands landed on my shoulders and shoved me back against the wall. "The fuck..."

"Everything is club business," he countered.

"Don't do this, Repo," I warned, in no mood for his brotherhood shit. I knew the club meant fucking everything to him, but he was overstepping a line.

"Don't put personal shit over your loyalties."

"Like Reign did?" I exploded, shoving him back.

"Different situation and you know it," he countered.

"Same fucking thing, man. And I don't have the time to fucking fill you in. So back the fuck off and let me handle my shit."

"Cash, man..." he said, clearly taking a step back, but not wanting to let it drop.

"Back," I said, emphasizing with a shove, "off." With that... I stormed back up the stairs and took off toward my bike.

My phone buzzed in my pocket and I picked it up. "Malc?"

"Got an address. We're on our way but you're closer."

"Give it to me," I demanded, already on my bike.

He gave it to me and I sped off, full of a sensation I had never understood before: heart in your throat.

She was okay.

She *had* to be okay.

NINETEEN

Lo

The funny thing about the space of years is, it doesn't exist, not really. When your past comes crashing into your present, it didn't bring with it the foggy haze of time. The kind of dread I used to feel spreading through my whole body sprang through my system as Damian closed in on me. Suddenly, I wasn't the woman who pulled herself up from her bootstraps, a woman who built a career cutting men off at the knees who dared use his power for evil, a woman who never backed down from a fight, a woman who never ever cowered. I was just little Willow Crane; I was just a girl raised to be submissive; I was the young woman who learned to never so much as step a toe out of line out of fear of retribution.

I rubbed my side as I tried to push myself up, as I tried to remember my training, get my wits about me. I still had a chance so long as I was in Cash's house, so long as I wasn't taken to a second location.

"Shoulda known you'd shack yourself up with some man. Trading pussy that belongs to me for protection."

That was when the anger kicked in, heady, so strong I finally understood the term 'seeing red', because my vision was tinted in it.

"That's where you fucked up, Damian," I growled, getting to my feet, ignoring the slight shooting pain up my side. In response, I got a brow raise. "I don't need a man to protect me," I said and flew at him.

Somewhere in the back of my mind, I knew I was screwed. I knew our training was about matched and he had the advantage of six inches in height and a solid hundred pounds of merciless muscle. I also didn't have the flinch factor- the fact that most men who found themselves in a fight against a woman, no matter how big and bad they were, would hesitate, would flinch. It gave me the chance to challenge, to get the better of them. I had five years of proof that Damian didn't flinch.

So, yeah. I was screwed.

But damn if I was going to cower, to let myself get beat by him again.

I was going to put every bit of myself into the fight. I was going to make him hurt.

I got a hook to his ribs and a knee to his groin before he got me, flinging me hard at the wall and I watched in a fascinated kind of horror as my blood dripped down Cash's dining room wall.

"So you gave him my pussy just because you're a slut, is that it?" He growled, grabbing me by the ends of my hair, twirling, and twisting.

I pressed my lips together, refusing to give him the satisfaction of my cries, then, "Newsflash, Damian... it's *my* pussy and I've been sharing it with any man I want for the past thirteen years. And guess what? They, unlike you, could actually make me come."

"Stupid cunt!" Then I was slammed against the wall hard enough for my vision to waver in darkness for a second. The crack was accompanied by an immediate and skull-splitting migraine.

Despite it (and quite frankly sure it couldn't possibly hurt any more than it already did), I threw my head back, cracking him in the mouth and swung out from him and made a grab for my bag, rummaging around until I found my gun and pulled it out. I swung around, arm raised, to have my wrist grabbed and twisted until it cracked and he grabbed the gun and tossed it.

Shit.

That was really my only chance.

"I should drag you upstairs to his bed and fuck you there until he gets home."

I sneered. "He'd kill you," I said simply, knowing to my marrow that it was the truth.

"Please... some weakass biker..."

"You've obviously never seen him in action. He'd take you." It was mostly bluster. I honestly had no idea who would win if they were matched up. They both had their strengths. Cash might have the advantage of not letting his rage get to him, of battling cold. But other than that...

"Don't worry. He's gonna get what's coming to him," he grinned and I felt sick satisfaction seeing the blood staining his teeth.

Fuck.

I didn't consider that. I didn't think I was putting Cash in any kind of danger. There was no way I could let him get hurt because of me. He had been nothing but good to me and I had done my best to be a bitch.

That was what he was going to remember about me.

I had no delusions about my future- it wasn't going to be a very *long* future. I was going to die, slowly, painfully. And that was going to happen soon.

I would never get another chance to let Cash see a better side of me.

All he would have to remember me by was my snippy-ness and the sex. Hell, he would probably find another chick in an afternoon and forget about the sex too.

There was nothing I could do about that now.

Hopefully he found something decent to remember me by.

"Now you're going to be a good girl and go to my car with me."

Ha. Fat chance.

"Like hell," I smirked, charging at him.

From there... it was just blow after blow, the shocking jarring of my fist colliding with his bones, and the almost blinding pain of his fists in my face or busted ribs. It didn't take much for me to get pinned. Two, three minutes tops and I was trapped under his weight, his body pressing so hard into my chest and abdomen that I couldn't draw a proper breath.

"It's gonna take some time to break this spirit of yours," he grunted, grabbing my hands when I reached up to claw down his face and pinning them over my head. "But, trust me, wife, I am looking forward to it." He shifted both of my wrists into one of his palms and brought the other hand down to my throat. "Starting now," he said, pressing down and cutting off what little air supply I had. "We're gonna keep doing this until you agree to get up and walk to my car like the obedient little bitch you used to be."

If he was going for cooperation, he was going about it the wrong way, reminding me of how powerless I used to be under his control.

As such, he got six times, six times of completely cutting off my air supply until my face went tingly and numb and I felt oblivion start to pull at me, only to have him pull away at the last possible second and force my consciousness back.

"Fine," I gasped, the sensation of razor blades down my

throat with each swallow. What was the point of resisting? Cash hadn't been gone that long; he could be gone for hours more. The chances of him charging in and helping me were slim to none and the way things were going, I'd have been too weak to pitch in in a fight and it would just be Cash and Damian. Both had reason to want to kill each other. Either could win. I couldn't put him in that situation. It was better to do what Damian wanted.

So I did.

"Fucking stubborn little cunt," he said, getting off my body and reaching down to haul me onto my feet. I wavered and, in absolute horror, had to reach out to Damian's chest to steady myself, making him chuckle. His arm went around my shoulders, hauling my front against his side as he led me awkwardly outside toward his truck.

But he didn't lead me to the trunk, watching at a house across the street like he had somehow made someone watching though I couldn't see anyone. He pushed me into the passenger seat and belted me. I didn't even see the cuffs that were draped around the seatbelt until I felt one of the bracelets snap around my wrist.

"What's the matter, Damian? You afraid I might hurt you while you're driving?"

"Shut the fuck up or I'll knock your ass out, Wills," he said, closing the other bracelet and slamming the door.

All I could think as we drove and then pulled in and stopped at our destination was- it was supposed to be mine. The city I had been calling home since I ran far the hell away from Damian thirteen years before, it was supposed to be mine. It wasn't supposed to be tainted by him. But with the deft, comfortable way he drove the streets and the fact that he obviously owned the building he was taking me too, well, it suggested I had been sharing Navesink Bank with him for a good, long while. How long had he been watching me? Weeks? Months? God... years? That thought had a sick feeling coating my tongue as I watched him hop out of his side of the car in front of a building I had driven by almost every day of my life since I moved- an old, what I thought was abandoned, carpet store.

Maybe I should have known better. The windows were intact; the small patch of lawn out front was mowed; there were no broken bottles or used condoms littering the parking lot. I just never had any reason to notice those things before.

Thirteen years with no word, well, it would give anyone a false sense of security.

"You're going to really like what I have been working on here," Damian said, a smirk on his face that I suddenly wondered how I never recognized as evil when we were young. Maybe, though, it hadn't been there then. Maybe he had been teasing and sweet as I remembered. Maybe the shit he had gone through overseas, maybe it did something to him, warped him. I had seen countless cases of that with the men and women who showed up at Hailstorm over the years, ready to offer their skills only to have to be expelled because of uncontrollable outbursts or a purely sadistic nature.

I took in plenty of people with their own issues- PTSD nightmares, an inability to connect with 'normal' people, men too scared to go home and taint their families with their dark souls.

I'd seen it.

But Damian, well, he was the worst of the worst.

I couldn't imagine how the government released these men and women onto the general populous. There's no way he could have passed an in-depth psych evaluation.

Hell, I always made sure the people I booted got put away and got care. I guess I fucking cared more than the government did.

"I'm sure I'll be just tickled," I said, rolling my eyes, one that was unmistakably swollen yet again as he unlocked one of my wrists and slid off my belt. The cuff stayed hanging off my left arm as he used it to drag me around the back of the building where he stopped at a door to punch in a pass code.

Inside was simply an abandoned storefront. There was a service desk and racks that the carpets stood in on the sides of the room. The floor was littered with dust and dirt. The unbroken windows were grimy with years of filth.

Damian tugged the cuff and led me into the back storage room, then to a door, and down. Of course... the basement. How stereotypically cliché. The temperature dropped a good ten degrees once we hit the bottom that was still blanketed in darkness. He wanted to be able to watch my reaction. God, he was such a sick fuck. I felt my cuff go slack for a second before he wrapped it around the railing and I heard him shuffling away from me in the dark.

I was determined to show nothing, no shock, no fear, nothing.

The light clicked on and I found myself in a genuine, indescribable awe.

Because it wasn't the torture chamber I had been expecting with chains on the walls and a display of weapons on a table or whatever the hell sick fucks with a screw loose came up with to hurt someone.

No, this was an entirely different kind of torture chamber.

It was an exact fucking replica of our old apartment. He had it down to the same tiles on the backsplash in the kitchen. He had the same fucking comforter on the bed, sans the blood stains from the last time I had seen it. There was even the tub I had sat in and contemplated taking my own life.

Jesus Christ.

"Welcome home, Willow," he said, giving me a white-toothed smile that I wanted to scratch off his face.

"You're fucking crazier than I thought," I said, shaking my head at the array of perfume bottles on the dresser beside the bed.

It had been thirteen years, but I knew that every last one of them was exactly where I had left them.

"That language has got to go," he said casually, walking toward the center of the room. "Women shouldn't talk that way."

"Don't like hearing my language then maybe you shouldn't have fucking kidnapped me."

"You're my wife," he said, rolling his eyes as he reached down for something in the center of the floor, something I had missed before, literally the only thing in the whole space that was out of place: a U-shaped metal bar attached to the cement floor with a very long, very heavy looking chain with an ankle cuff.

Oh, mother fucker.

"I divorced you ten years ago, Damian," I reminded him. It was a day I celebrated alone each year, eating a ton of cookie dough ice cream and going to the shooting range, like I did the day I was finally free of him.

"I never agreed to that."

That was true. He never did. But, then again, that really didn't matter. Contested divorces were granted all the time. No matter what your spouse wanted, you had a right to get shot of their sorry asses. "And yet somehow, I still don't belong to you."

His eyes lowered, hating being wrong, hating having his property taken from him. "You belonged to me from the second I got into that pussy of yours for the first time," he growled, stalking over to me and slamming me backward so I fell back onto the steps, cursing as the edge of one caught me in my lower back, and making the cuff bite into the skin of my wrist as it pulled tight. He was on me before I could try to kick out a leg, grabbing my ankle and slapping the cuff on. The weight immediately made my leg slam down onto the step. "And I got all the time in the world to remind you of that again," he said, kneeling down next to me, grabbing my chin and forcing it up. "It won't be a pleasant process for you."

"What else is new? From the second I accepted your ring, you brought me nothing but fucking misery you useless piece of shit."

He clucked his tongue, letting go of my chin, but only to cock his arm and backhand me across the face. He stood up, releasing my wrist from the cuff, then taking off up the steps. "Oh and don't get up any hopes of escape. That chain will let you get a third the way up the steps and there's no way you'd fit through the windows, not even with the weight you've lost. You're going to be here for a good long time, Wills."

The door at the landing slammed and I pushed myself up, wincing at the pain in my back, trying to will away the tears I felt stinging my eyes. I could do a lot of things: yell, scream, fight, spit fire. But I would not, under any circumstances, waste any more tears on him.

I looked around, taking deep breaths to calm the hysterical anxiety building inside. Because, I noticed as I looked around, he was right- there was no escape. There was no way I could get away. My only hope was for rescue and given that I hadn't been able to figure out Damian owned the store, no one else was going to be able to either.

Suddenly, I had the memory of my father visiting the apartment one afternoon when Damian was at work. It had been a week since the last time he beat me, but the emotional impact of it had lasted longer than the bruises and seeing my father, a man who had kept me in his own kind of prison my whole life, had somehow seemed like a chance for rescue.

"Dad... he beats me," I said, my voice a quiver and his head snapped to me, eyes wide.

"What?"

"He... beats me. With his hands. With a belt..."

It was one of the few times in my life I remembered him looking stricken. His gaze quickly fell to the floor, looking at his boots. "Why?"

"Because he thinks I need to be punished."

"For?"

It was that moment that I felt hope die. I closed my eyes and shook my head. "Any little thing," I admitted though I knew it was pointless; he wasn't going to save me.

"Can't say it's not his place. He's your husband. Your behavior is a reflection of him. He needs to find ways to make sure you stay in line. As your father, I don't like hearing that. But you aren't a little girl anymore. You're a married woman and it's your job to follow your husband's rules and deal with the consequences of breaking them."

"Okay."

I never asked for help again. Not even from the sheriff who raised a brow at the bruises on my wrists while we were in line at the check-out at the grocery store. Not even when he caught my eye afterward and asked me if I was alright. There was simply no spirit, no fight left in me at that point.

It was pointless, hopeless.

That was exactly the feeling I had in that moment, sitting on the stairs in my new prison, seeing no escape, knowing there was no one coming to save me. I guess thirteen years of freedom was all that I was going to get. I had some good times. I took out some bad guys. I saved some good ones. I'd had sex. I'd drank. I'd made friends. I'd traveled. All in all, it wasn't bad. I fit into thirteen years what most people didn't manage in a lifetime. And thank god, because those memories were going to be the only thing that got me through.

I knew that some day, some time, he would screw up. He would get comfortable. He would think he had succeeded in breaking my spirit. Then I would have a chance. The lock on my ankle, big and ugly as it was, it was absolutely pick-able. I could get it off with enough attempts. And, well, I had nothing but time.

Then I just needed to wait for a time he stumbled, he turned his back on me when I was too close. I could take him down if he didn't see me coming. Get him unconscious and then, well, do whatever the hell was necessary to make sure he didn't come after me again.

I got up off the stairs and made the rest of the way down, cringing at the weight of the shackle. It was going to rip apart the skin underneath, no matter how thick a layer of clothing I wore. It was going to rub and weigh and make it raw.

Oh, the joys of captivity.

I moved around slowly, trying to drag the shackled leg as much as possible so the cuff didn't move, looking in the cabinets, trying to see what options I had for self-defense or to pick the lock. Only plastic utensils, of course. He wasn't *that* stupid. The cabinets were full of paper plates and bowls, disposable cups. There was one pot and one skillet in a drawer next to the stove. The refrigerator was fully stocked, so at least I wasn't going to slowly starve to death on top of everything else. The water in the kitchen and bathroom worked. There was nothing in the medicine cabinet but gauze, bandages, and triple antibiotic. He didn't even keep the rubbing alcohol in there anymore, I guessed worried I might have seen that as an easy out- though death by rubbing alcohol was practically unheard-of.

Hell, if I wanted to end it, all I needed to do was fill up the tub, or stop drinking for a few days, or wrap my ankle chain around my neck. All much more fool-proof solutions to self-conclusion than drinking some bathroom antiseptic that would probably just make me vomit uncontrollably and maybe have a seizure... then survive. I was pretty sure I was going to be enduring enough torture by Damian's hands... I wasn't going to be inflicting it on myself as well

I walked over to the bed, a bed I was praying like hell I wasn't going to be having to share with Damian, and sat down on the side that used to be mine. I opened the nightstand, finding a necklace that used to belong to my mother and two of the paperback romances I had been reading before I got the hell out of there.

With a shrug and a resigned sigh, I pulled one out and climbed up in bed. If I was going to be physically captive, at least I had a mental escape.

Later, I fell asleep. And I dreamed of Cash saving me.

TWENTY

Cash

The son of a bitch owned a carpet store in town. How the fuck that didn't show up on Lo's radar was completely beyond me. I was sure she had been keeping tabs on him. She was too diligent not to. But she missed it. For years.

I pushed my bike way over the speed limit, road safety being the absolute fucking last thing on my mind. All that mattered was getting to her as quickly as possible, before that whackjob husband of hers managed to do any more damage than he had back at my place. If he put his hands on her... if he forced her to...

I forced that thought away as I turned into the industrial part of town, where Shane Mallick had a warehouse he had converted into a huge house for him and his woman, and tried to calm the pounding of my heart.

There was nothing about the carpet store that suggested it could be livable, but no way was I leaving without checking it out. The side door was steel-bar enforced and attached to a security system. On a frustrated sigh, I moved to the front of the building, picking up one of the penny bricks that made up an abandoned front flowerbed and tossed it through one of the front panels of glass, not waiting for it all to fall out before climbing through.

Just as I suspected... nothing.

"Damn it!" I yelled as I tore through the front and back rooms, looking for something, anything.

There was nothing. No doors, nothing but a few dusty shelving units and wall stands for the carpets. Fucking empty.

"There's fucking nothing here," I growled into the phone, cutting off Malcolm's greeting.

"What do you mean there's nothing there?"

"I mean it's just a fucking empty carpet store. There's nothing and no one inside, Malc. She's not here."

"She has to be there," he insisted and I heard an edge of desperation in his tone.

"You're welcome to fucking come here and look, man, but there ain't shit." I kicked the side of the service desk, enjoying the stab of pain up my foot. "What the fuck are we going to do now? Where else can we look?"

There was a long pause before, "I don't know."

"What do you mean you don't know? You have to know. You guys know fucking everything."

"He's a ghost, man. He even pays his bills in cash. There's nothing to go on. I tried."

I tore out of the busted window, going to my bike and sitting on it for a long minute. I was in no shape to drive. I needed a direction to go in. I needed skulls to crack together. I needed some fucking... hope.

She couldn't just be... gone.

But the fact of the matter was- she could. She could very well be long gone. This Damian fuck obviously kept a lot of cash on hand. He could easily get out of town. He could take Lo and disappear and no one would ever see her again. The Henchmen tried to keep their noses out of everyone else's business, but that didn't mean we didn't know things, that we didn't know just how the other low lives handled certain situations, how they managed to up and completely fall off the face of the Earth when trouble caught up with them. And this Damian guy had years to do nothing but plan on what he was going to do when he got his hands on his wife again.

"Mother fucker," I growled into the phone, not even realizing I still had it pressed to my ear.

"We're going to find her," Malcolm's voice said, holding an authoritative edge that only managed to make me snort.

"You don't know that, man."

"Cash, I fucking know it. Because this is, from this moment on, the fucking only case Hailstorm is working. Every man and woman will be putting their time and skills into locating her. We will find her. We never fail."

"Yeah, sure."

"I wish fucking Jstorm was around..."

"Jstorm?" I repeated, looking up at the store with a churning in my stomach.

"Janie," he corrected.

"Janie?" I repeated. "Why?"

"Because she's the best at this. She can find anyone's trail online. She's some kind of internet prodigy. It's incredible."

I didn't even bother to respond or say goodbye. I shoved the phone in my pocket and drove off toward Wolf's. It was about damn time I found a way to contribute. I had felt like a useless bystander all day.

"Not now," Wolf growled at me, blocking the door.

It wasn't even a conscious thought that had me reaching behind my back, grabbing the gun, and raising it at him, at my brother, at a man I trusted my life to, a man who I loved as much as my own blood.

"Seriously?" Wolf asked, not even flinching. His brow rose slowly as he watched me with those freaky honey-colored eyes of his.

"I need Janie's help."

"No."

I pulled off the safety. "This is not a discussion. Lo is in the hands of some fucking psychopath and no one, not even those freaks at that camp of hers can find her. So I need *Janie's fucking help.*"

Before Wolf could open his mouth to object again, for whatever the fuck reason he had to do such a thing, the door behind him was wrenched fully open to reveal Janie standing there, yet again in one of Wolf's tees.

"Who has her?"

"Damian Crane," I answered immediately. "Her husband."

"Ex," Janie answered automatically.

"What?"

"Ex-husband. She had a contested divorce that finalized a decade ago. He's her ex-husband."

"How do you know this shit?"

Janie looked away over my shoulder for a minute, biting into her bottom lip, looking almost... guilty. "When I can't sleep, which is often," she started, "I go online. I look into stuff. When I was first at Hailstorm, I looked into the people. So... I know her name is Willow Swift. When she was eighteen, she married Damian Crane. They were married until she was twenty-seven though, obviously, she was not with him that whole time because she was building up Hailstorm at the time and no one there had ever so much as heard his name. I don't know why she wasn't..."

"He beat her," I supplied and Janie's whole body jerked backward as if I had struck her. Her blue eyes, already big, got rounder and her mouth fell open.

"What?" she asked on a horrified whisper.

"I found a picture. There were bruises on her arm. That, coupled with the article that said he was stabbed twelve times in his apartment..."

"Oh my God..."

"Enough," Wolf said, giving me a hard look before turning his focus on Janie, his entire face softening.

"He has her, Janie..." I said, my voice of plea.

"I need a computer," she said, her head jerking up. "Right now," she said, her voice more firm, but still shaking slightly as she focused her attention on Wolf.

"'Kay," he said on a shrug and moved inside.

Janie and I both followed. "How long?"

"Hours. I don't know. I was at Hailstorm trying to get their help in locating him before he found her again."

"Again?"

"That's why she was begging asylum at my place, kid. He got to her and he busted her up. Her face... her ribs... it was bad. He did a number. She went to The Henchmen. I just so happened to be there so I took her home. I took care of her. And then..."

Janie was watching me with an odd look on her face, her eyes sharp, like she could see right through me. "And then?" she prompted as we heard Wolf rustling around in a closet.

"And then when I got home, my place was trashed. Her blood was on the walls. My neighbor gave me a make and plate of his truck. I called Malcolm and got him on it."

"They got nothing?" she asked, looking almost... offended at that.

"Nothing useful. He said every other case is closed until you guys find her."

"Well... duh," Janie said, straightening as Wolf walked back toward us, a laptop box in his hands. As in... he had never taken it out of said box. A smile teased up the sides of Janie's lips. "You're ridiculous," she said to him, but it was almost... warm. She took the box and made short work of getting the unused laptop up and running.

"She's your woman," Wolf said, leaning against the counter in the kitchen, pinning me with his eyes.

It was then that it finally hit me, with the kind of clarity that made me feel dumb as hell for not realizing it earlier. He was right. She was. It didn't matter that it didn't make sense, that I spent so much time disliking her and her practices, that she didn't always show me her full self. She never showed Malcolm and Janie and the rest of her people her full self either, and she was still theirs, they still loved her.

Loved?

What the fuck?

I didn't *love* her.

That wasn't me. I didn't do that shit. I didn't fall in love.

But that didn't change the fact that he was right, that she was mine. She had been mine since the second I walked into Reign's house and caught sight of her again. She was mine every time she pushed me away, every time she showed me glimpses of what was underneath, every time she laughed and smiled at me, every time she moaned out my name. She was fucking *mine.* And I was going to kill the mother fucker who dared think he could put his hands on what belonged to me.

"Yeah," I agreed, nodding.

Wolf nodded back. "I get that."

My brows drew together as I turned to look at him and found his gaze fixed on Janie. So that was the way it was. She was his. Damn. How the fuck did something like that happen?

"You'll get him," Wolf said, clamping a hand down on my shoulder and squeezing.

"Yeah," I agreed, a little spirit returning to my voice.

"Carpet store?" Janie called out and I almost laughed

because it had taken Malcolm hours to find that information out and Janie/Jstorm had managed it in minutes.

"Been there. Nothing."

Janie made some kind of growling noise and then all I heard was her fingers viciously stabbing the buttons on the keypad.

"Reign?" Wolf asked a few minutes later.

Here's the thing about knowing someone as weird as Wolf for as long as I had known him- you get to understand their oddities. Like the way Wolf never seemed to manage a full sentence, yet I totally understood his meaning. Had I filled in my brother on all the shit that was going on?

"No. But... Repo knows some of it and I'm sure that shit will trickle back sooner rather than later."

"Loyal."

"Yeah." That would be the word to describe Repo alright. Meanwhile me and Wolf, the two highest up in rank aside from Reign were running around getting into all kinds of shit without even filling him in and holing up with women and not checking in like we were supposed to when fucking bombs were going off for no damn good reason.

"As much as I *love* to sit here listening to you two hens clucking like a couple chicks," Janie said, the furious tapping not so much as hesitating as she spoke. "I am going to need some coffee and silence."

Wolf grunted and turned to make the coffee while very loud, very piercing metal music came screaming from the laptop speakers. Apparently, Janie's kind of silence was different than a normal person's.

I moved toward a chair propped up against the wall in the back of the room and sat down, trying to not let my mind race over the worse-case scenarios and failing until, despite me thinking it was in no way possible, I fell asleep.

CASH

I woke up to Janie yelling out, "What about the basement?"

I jolted up in the chair, blinking at the light that was suddenly streaming in through the windows, wondering absentmindedly how much time had passed, and how the fuck I had managed to fall asleep when I was so worried.

"What?" I asked, rubbing at my eyes as I sat forward, spotting Wolf sitting across from Janie at the table, holding a steaming coffee cup between his hands.

"The basement," she said again, sounding exasperated.

"What basement?"

"The one at the carpet store."

What?

"Kid, there wasn't a basement. No doors to a staircase. Nothing."

"Then what is this?" she asked, swinging the laptop around and stabbing her finger at the screen.

I bolted off my chair and knelt down beside her, looking at what was the city plans for the building. And, holy fuck, there was a basement. "No..."

"Yeah. There's a basement. He must have hidden the..."

I didn't hear the rest of that conversation as I flew out of the house, cursing Wolf seven ways to Sunday for living out in the middle of bumfuck nowhere.

"Yo," Wolf called, but I didn't slow down. He would catch up and I couldn't afford to lose a second. "Here," he said, slamming my cell into my hand. I took it, looking over at him with drawn-together brows. "Charged it," he shrugged.

"Tell Janie to call Malcolm and get them all to..."

"Already is," he said, and he suddenly wasn't by my side anymore.

I glanced back to see him turning back to his house... and his woman.

CASH

I turned forward again and flew down the rest of the hill and got on my bike... to go get my woman.

And kill the mother fucker who took her from me.

TWENTY-ONE

Lo

I woke up slowly, lulled by a warm swirling feeling inside that I couldn't quite name, but it made me feel safe and comfortable and... happy. I kept my eyes closed, trying to hold on to the last dregs of my dreams, wanting to forever feel that sweetness.

I felt my lips curl upward just a second before I heard a voice that reminded me that nothing in my life was sweet dreams, that it was always bitter nightmares.

"Calling out another man's name in my house?" Damian growled and I felt a heaviness settle in my belly. Dread, it was dread. Because I knew that tone. "Such a disappointing wife. Always fucking complaining, always nagging..." I never complained. I certainly never nagged. "Always lying there like a dead fucking fish when I was inside you."

"Maybe because you had no fucking idea how to please a woman, Damian," I said, shrugging a shoulder.

"Not my fault you can't come."

At that, I couldn't choke back the laughter. I should have; I should have found a way to keep it to myself, to not ask for any beatings, but I just... couldn't. "Oh, I can come, Damian. Just not with that pathetic machine-gun fucking you were always so fond o..."

I didn't get the rest out, mainly because his hands were at my throat and pressing, hard. Not hard enough for the air supply to get completely cut off. No, he was good, It was just hard enough to hurt like a mother fucker and be scary as hell.

"Maybe you just need a refresher," he threatened, his hand moving from my throat to press hard between my legs. Every bit of me was screaming out *no* at the contact and before his fingers could crook and rake over me again, I cocked back my legs and slammed them forward with everything in me. Caught off guard, he flew off the end of the bed, giving me enough time to get my feet.

"Not a fucking chance," I shrieked, falling full-force downward, my knee stabbing into his stomach and making all his air whoosh out of him. My hands moved to his throat and closed around it. Just like him, I was good. But unlike him, I wanted him to pass out so I pressed and I pressed hard, pushing into the carotid artery. Eight to ten seconds, that was all it took for unconscious to take over. Once he was out, I had maybe two minutes to find a way to kill him.

The easiest way would be to continue to cut off his air supply. For that, I needed three minutes of no air getting into his body. Three minutes and he would be gone. But that being said, there was always the chance of him gaining consciousness and fighting back.

There were no sharp objects around. There was nothing to stab him with. But there was the pot and pan in the kitchen. It would take forever and drain me, but I could bash his head in. He would be unconscious from one good blow to the side of the head, just beneath the ear. He wouldn't regain consciousness.

Six. Seven. Ei...

The side of his hand slammed forward into my throat, making me choke hard and drop my hands.

Fuck.

There went my advantage.

I was thrown off of him, pinned under his weight. There was a split second before I felt his fist in my face. Familiar, Christ, the sensation was so fucking familiar it made me sick. I tasted blood in my mouth and, with what was probably not a smart amount of anger, spat it in his face.

His hands went up to wipe his face, giving me the chance to drag my legs up from behind him, cursing at the weight of the chain, and cross them over his throat, pushing him backward with the strength in my thighs. The chain pushed into his throat as he twisted to the side, wrangling away. He hit the floor and my leg kicked out, my foot colliding with the side of his face. His grunt of pain was like the voice of God to my ears. Especially because I knew I had gotten a few good shots in, but that he was going to overpower me. I was going to get my ass kicked again.

"Stupid bitch," he said, sitting back on his heels and wiping the blood off his lip. "I know what kind of lesson I need to teach you," he said and his hands moved downward.

When I saw what they were seeking, I felt a sweat break out over my whole body. His belt. He was going for his fucking belt. I had taken a lot of beatings during my time with him. I'd felt his bare hand on my ass. I'd felt his fist in every soft place in my body. I'd felt his feet stabbing into my stomach and ribs. But nothing, literally nothing ever hurt as bad as that belt on my skin.

"Just like that first time," he smirked, pushing the hook free from the hole and slowly pulling the leather from the loops. It was then that I noticed it *was* going to be just like that first time... because it was the same fucking belt.

CASH

For the first five strikes, I had the protection of my shirt. Damian, frustrated by the fact I wasn't shrieking in absolute agony, dropped the belt long enough to grab my shirt and tear it off, leaving the skin of my back bare save for the band of my bra.

Then, well, there was screaming.

I didn't want to. It hurt somewhere deep in my soul to do it, but the pain was unlike anything else life had to offer, somehow feeling both blunt and sharp and burning all at once. I fought, don't get me wrong. I twisted, turned, scrambled away. But I could only get so far so fast with the shackle at my ankle. And each time he caught up to me, the lashes got more vicious until the tears were streaming down my face as the skin at my back finally broke open and the lashes didn't stop.

My throat hurt, raw from crying out and I collapsed forward on the floor, unable to draw up any energy to fight anymore. I was done. Done done done. I just wanted it to end. I wanted to go back in time and drag that knife up my forearms. I wanted everything to...

My thoughts trailed off when I heard the belt drop down beside my body, followed by the sound of his fly being pulled down. Yep, just like the first time. The only difference being this time... I couldn't delude myself into thinking what was about to follow wasn't rape.

I closed my eyes tight against that idea, trying to will my arms to push me up, but they stayed limp at my sides as I saw the belt get picked up again a moment before it slipped around my neck as a noose and tightened. He held it one-handed, the other going to the back of my pants and slipping into the waistband, trying to drag them down.

I didn't hear the door slamming open.

I didn't even hear the boots on the steps.

But I did hear something.

I heard the most beautiful sound I had ever heard in my life.

CASH

I heard Cash's voice.

It was then that I realized I had fallen asleep.

Because only in my dreams did Cash come rushing in to save me.

So I closed my eyes and smiled, sinking into the dream.

TWENTY-TWO

Cash

There are moments in your life that, when they happen, you know they are going to be burned into your memory, that they will always come back to you in bright, flawless, technicolor perfection.

Throwing the storage shelf out of the way and finding a door behind, having to wait for Malcolm to use some kind of device to break open the code thing, then charging down those steps and seeing what I saw... mother fucking *burned* into my mind.

Forget that the basement had been changed into some freaky apartment that I had a sneaking suspicion must have had some kind of significance to Lo's old life. I barely even fucking took that shit in. Because right there in the center of the floor with a god damn slave chain around her ankle, was a face-down Lo, her entire back torn open with gashes, her blood seeping down to her sides and puddling on the floor beside her. A belt was wrapped around her throat and was being pulled mercilessly as Damian fucking Crane, pants down and hard dick out, tried to pull down Lo's pants.

That was a sight I never wanted to fucking see.

And now I would never be free from it.

"Lo," I heard myself call, but it was a strange, raw, crackling sound.

I didn't even think of the fucking gun nestled in the small of my back. I didn't take heed to the half dozen Hailstorm men and women coming down the stairs behind me. Because, quite fuckin' frankly, this fight was between me and the mother fucker who dared put his hands on what was *mine.*

"This is gonna' be fun," I growled as Damian tried to wrestle his cock back into his pants and got to his feet.

I got one second to notice that Lo had closed her eyes with an odd, sweet smile on her face before I charged at Damian. Malcolm and the rest of them would get her up and out of there. They would start to do something about the wounds on her back. They would do a much better job at that than I could. And I, well, I was going to do the better job at making Damian Crane pay for ever even thinking about putting his hands on her.

I took him down with a running crouch to his center, his yell suggesting Lo had already gotten a good hit or kick to his ribs. I felt a swell of pride at that- my girl was a fighter, as I pounded my fist into the bastard's face, enjoying the spurt of blood out of his nose.

Behind me, I could hear Malcolm giving out orders and the hair-raising sound of Lo's shriek as they, presumably, moved her.

Damian bucked and I was flying to my side, landing with a grunt.

Something clattered to the ground next to me and Malcolm's voice called. "We need to get her back to Hailstorm. She's losing a lot of blood."

But I wasn't paying much attention because I finally realized what had flown down next to be: the asshole's belt. I felt a sick smile pull at my lips as I grabbed for it and got my feet, turning back to see Damian closing in on me.

Oh, yeah. Talk about justice.

I was gonna see how much *he* liked getting a strap taken to him.

"Shoulda' kept your hands off what belongs to me," I said, swinging back, then snapping the belt forward, the blow landing in the center of his chest, giving me a grunt.

"She's *mine.*" And, well, that was just the wrong damn thing to say.

I cocked my arm back again, then swung forward, this time aiming a helluva lot higher. His whole body jerked back as the belt smacked across the side of his face. His hand went instinctively up to cover the raising welt and I took that opportunity to nail the back of his hand too- his guttural howl sending off a shock of pleasure through my system.

I wasn't that guy. I didn't have that dark of a soul. I didn't get off on pain. But, hell, I was half hard listening to this fuck getting what was coming to him. For Lo. For the years of damage he had caused her. For the shields she felt she had to wear around herself because of him. For the fear such a strong, formidable woman like Lo was forced to live through every day of her life.

His face half swollen, Damian lunged, taking us both down, making me land beneath his weight with a hiss on the hard floor. Right hand lamed by the belt strike, he raised his left and got a half-force punch to the side of my face before I knifed up, throwing him down and taking my feet.

I cocked back the belt and swung one last time. My aim was off by the barest of inches and the lash took him across the eye, making a cry that was only half-human escape him as a swirling feeling started in my stomach.

Enough. That was fucking enough.

I flew across the floor as he cradled his face and grabbed the chain that had been around Lo's ankle and dragging the heavy as all fuck thing across the floor, clamping it around Damian's ankle before he could even stop howling enough to try to stop me.

"Let's see how much you like being held against your will, you sick fuck," I said, taking off toward the stairs, my heart pounding hard in my chest. Anger drained, all I felt was the kind of worry that settled in your belly and felt like it hollowed you out inside.

"He dead?" the only leftover Hailstorm guy asked as I got to the top landing, left there, I imagined, in case Damian got away from me because this guy was a mammoth of a man... he looked like he'd give Wolf a run for his money.

"No. But I bet he wishes he was. Can you lock this thing back up?" I asked, gesturing toward the door as Damian's swears of vengeance drifted up the stairs.

"Yeah," he said, pulling something out of his pocket. "Changing the code though," he said, pressing away as he kicked the door closed. "So you're keeping him down there?" he asked, turning back to me, pinning me with his freakishly blue eyes.

"Figured Lo might want a shot at him once she's up and moving again," I shrugged, knowing she would. Once the pain and embarrassment faded, she would be spittin' mad. And she would want him to pay for ever making her feel weak again. There was no way I was going to deny her that. "She okay?" I asked, not bothering to hide the rawness in my voice.

"She's gonna be hurting for a while. Her back was completely cut open. Has some marks on her face and her ribs looked like they got worked over again. But she'll be alright. They know what they're doing."

With all the shit they got themselves into, all the damage that must have been done to their crew, I imagined that was true.

"I need to see her."

The guy nodded, jerking his head toward the front of the store. "Let's go."

With that, we moved outside. And I saw why I had missed the basement windows in the first place. He had put bricks the same color as the foundation in the holes. If you looked close, you could tell they didn't fit, but when you were in a panic looking for your girl, they barely stood out at all. Lo's guy took off in his Jeep and I took off on my bike, both of us pushing twenty over the speed limit until we finally pulled up to the gates which swung open.

"Where is she?" I demanded from the first person I saw, grabbing the front of his shirt when all he did was raise a brow at me and look over my shoulder at the guy I pulled in with. "Listen, mother fucker... I'm not in the mood for your gam..."

"Yo," the guy behind me said, clamping a hand on my shoulder. "I'll take you. Relax."

"Maybe you should get him calmed down first, Leo. He can't be charging into the sick room balls out mad..."

"Try to stop me, I dare you. I just fucking blinded the last man who stood between me and Lo. You really want to do this?" I asked, shoving his chest, stepping back with drawn-in brows when all he did was laugh.

"Malc was right," he said, nodding over my shoulder at Leo.

"Yep," Leo agreed then moved to look at me. "Come on, let's go."

With that, I followed him into the storage container maze that was the innards of Hailstorm. By the fourth container, I was certain that if you didn't know the layout, you genuinely could get completely lost. Half of the rooms were all but empty, jutting off into what looked like deadends. Past the barracks-style bedroom, we finally arrived at a door with a small glass window through which I could see a naked to the waist Lo lying on her stomach on a hospital bed while one of her men, dark-skinned, shaved head, wearing a white tee and jeans, sat over her with white gloves on his hands, pressing something into the broken-open welts on her back.

CASH

Leo pushed open the door and led me inside. Beside the man bent over Lo, the only person left in the room was Malcolm whose face was in severe lines. The air around him seemed to be buzzing with a mix of rage and concern. It was a feeling I knew well.

"She's not moving," I said, getting close to the side of the bed.

"Knocked her out," the guy pressing compresses to her wounds said, not looking up. "She'd skin me if I let us all hear her cry through this," he added, gesturing toward the suture kit he had laid up beside him.

"Fuck," I said, looking down at her perfect back ripped to shreds. "I was there," I said, shaking my head, feeling the realization settle heavy inside. "I had been there and she was one fucking floor beneath me. I could have saved her from this!" I yelled, grabbing the metal stool beside me and hauling it across the room.

"Don't go there," Malcolm said, shaking his head as he watched me.

"How the fuck can I not go there? I was *there.* I should have looked harder for a door. I should have noticed the fucking basement windows from outside..."

"It's not your fault some sick bastard tortured her. That's not on you. That's on him. She doesn't need your anger. She needs you to be here for her. She's not a victim. Don't treat her like one. At least... not if you want to be able to be in her life in the future, that is."

"I'm gonna be there," I said, a kind of certainty in my words I never usually felt, let alone expressed. I was going to be there, in her future, even if I had to claw my way into it.

It made no sense. True, I'd met her a year... closer to two years before. But I only got to really know her the past several days. But it didn't matter. I never claimed it was rational. All I knew was, she was mine. And she wasn't 'mine for the night' or 'mine for the time being' like women had been in the past... she was mine without an expiration date. Because I had never met a woman like her- a woman covered in steel but so soft inside. I'd never met a woman who liked to fight as much as she liked to fuck. And speaking of fucking... I needed more of that with her. Like... a lifetime of it.

So, yeah, it didn't make much sense. But what in my life did? I'd always made decisions flippantly, recklessly. I always threw myself into whatever felt right in the moment. That was how I lived. I wasn't someone to sit around and write fucking pro and con lists and hem and haw every situation, every choice to be made, every repercussion of each choice. I went with my gut.

And my gut was telling me that I was going to be in Lo's life.

So that was the way it was going to be.

I watched, hands curled into fists, as the guy with the gloves went about stitching Lo back together.

"Relax, Cash," Malcolm's voice found me, though one look at him and he didn't look much less stressed than I did, "Mike here knows what he's doing. He was an EMT in his life before."

Feeling marginally better, I sucked in a breath, slanting my head toward Malcolm with a wry smile. "For a bunch of survivalist nutjobs... you all have normal fucking names."

Malcolm snorted, shaking his head, trying to fight the twitching of his lips. "Hey we can't all be Reign, Cash, Wolf, and... Repo now, can we?"

"Think you maybe want to get your face fixed up?" Mike asked, surprising me because I was pretty sure he hadn't looked up at me since I came in.

"I'm fine."

"Sure, sure," he said, nodding. "No big deal. Just a bloody, open wound dripping down your face. No big deal. You probably won't get sepsis and die."

At that, I felt an unexpected laugh rise up. "Fine, I'll clean up my face. Got any whiskey laying around?"

At that, his gaze finally came up. "Please don't tell me you pour booze on your cuts normally."

"Okay... I won't tell you that," I grinned.

"It's amazing you're not covered in nasty scars."

"Hey... battlefield medicine, man."

"In what military are the soldiers carrying around alcohol?"

"I dunno," I smiled, rocking back on my heels. "The Russians. Can't imagine them going into battle without a shit ton of vodka in their bloodstream."

Mike smiled, shook his head, and went back to working on the blissfully unconscious Lo while Malcolm waved a hand toward the bathroom at the far end of the room.

I went in, put some peroxide on the cuts, put on a couple butterfly sutures, and swabbed on some antibiotic cream before washing the dirt and blood off my hands and looking up at my reflection in the mirror.

There was a tightness around my eyes that I made an effort to release before I made my way back out of the bathroom. Mike was standing, fiddling around with some kind of huge sheet of gauze, slathering something onto it, then taking the giant dressing and laying it across Lo's entire back.

"When she wakes up, we're going to need to get her up and wrap some gauze around her to keep this on," he explained. "But there's no use trying to get her up when she's unconscious. She'll be out for hours." With that, he snapped off his gloves and shrugged at us. "She'll be fine in a couple days. I'll take the stitches out in a week or two depending on how everything heals, but she will be up and moving in a day or two."

We nodded and Malcolm thanked him and he walked out. Alone, Malcolm sighed loudly, looking down at Lo. "I hate to leave her, but I have some stuff I need to see to..." he paused, looking at me, "and you'll be here for her, right?"

"Of course," I said, sitting down on the stool Mike had vacated and brushing my hand down the side of her bruised face. I couldn't wait until I could see it undamaged again, until I could touch her without having to worry about hurting her.

I heard Malcolm's feet retreat and the door open and close and we were alone. "Fucking sorry, baby," I said quietly, my hand running down her arm.

I watched her slow, steady breathing for a long time, until my eyes got too heavy to stay open anymore and I dozed off, slumped over the side of her hospital bed.

I woke up to my hair being tousled sometime later. My eyes snapped open, immediately alert. And there was Lo, laying on her stomach, her face turned to me, her lips turned up in a small smile.

"I thought it was a dream," she said in a groggy voice.

"You thought what was a dream, gorgeous?"

"You saving me. I had a dream that you saved me the night before and I thought... I thought I had passed out from the pain and was dreaming again."

"Wasn't a dream. Of course I came to save you. There was never any question about that, Lo."

"Stupid fucking carpet store," she said, getting her spirit back. "How did I miss that?"

"Who would think he would buy a place and sit on it for years, never once contacting you? Shit don't make any sense."

"He wasn't sitting on it. He was making a replica of our old apartment, down to every last kitchen towel and the position of my perfume bottles. He's out of his mind."

"He raised his hands to this perfect fucking face," I said, running my pointer finger down her cheek. "I think that proved how fucked in the head he was."

Lo offered me a small smile. "How bad is it?" she asked, waving a hand lazily around. "I can't feel anything still, but I know it can't be good."

"It's nothing. Mike got you all taken care of."

Lo's brow arched up and her eyes got small. "Don't talk to me like I'm a fucking child, Cash. I can handle it."

There was my girl. I felt my lips curving up. "Fine. It's jacked. You're held together with stitches at this point. That what you want to hear?"

"Yes, actually, if that's the truth."

"It's the truth."

"Okay," she nodded, taking a deep breath. "It's gonna hurt like a bitch when I wake up again, isn't it?"

"Yeah," I nodded. "But they'll just come back in here and shove a needle in your ass and it will all be better."

She snorted, wincing a bit as her smile spread. "They'll give me pills, you idiot."

"I like it my way better," I laughed.

"You just want to see my ass," she smiled.

"Hell fuckin' yeah. Nice and plump and..."

"Bite-able," she supplied, letting out a quiet version of her tinkling laugh.

"I still haven't gotten the chance to bite it yet. You know... we're alone in here..."

"Go to sleep, Cash," she said, shaking her head.

"Really, I could just pull your pants down real quick and..." I paused, seeing tears rise up in her eyes unexpectedly. "What?" I asked, my thumb brushing one away as it broke free of her lashes.

She shook her head a little. "You'd make a pretty good leading man, Cash," she said oddly, closing her eyes without further explanation.

With nothing left to do, I did what I was told, I went to sleep.

TWENTY-THREE

Lo

I came awake suddenly in the early light of the morning, the pain a searing, awful thing that felt like it spread from my back and took over my entire body. My breath hissed out loudly as I tried to shift slightly to ease the crick in my neck.

"Fuck," I groaned, flopping back down.

"Babe," Cash's voice reached me, sounding annoyingly awake. I tilted my head to see him walking toward me from the bathroom, his hair wet from the shower, dressed in clothes that didn't belong to him- charcoal gray work pants and a faded green Army shirt. There were fresh butterfly sutures down the side of his face where a bruise was visible under the cuts. He was the most beautiful sight I'd ever seen. "Don't," he said when I went to push up and fell again on a cry. "Fucking Christ, woman," he said, attempting annoyed but it came off as concerned nonetheless, "I get it, we all get it- you're a badass and don't need nothing from no one, but you gotta let people help you out sometimes."

"Where's Mike and Malcolm?"

"They're not helping you with this," he said, shaking his head, a small smirk playing at his lips.

"Why not? They're both trained. Malcolm had training in the military and Mike was..."

"An EMT."

"Exactly. So they would be more qualified to..."

"They aren't seeing your tits, babe. Sorry."

"What?" I half-accused, half-laughed.

"Those might be on your body and all... but they're mine now. And neither Mike or Malcolm are getting to see them."

"They probably already did. You noticed I'm shirtless, right?" I asked, fighting the smile because I didn't want him to know that his possessiveness was giving me the warm and tinglies.

"Sure. But that was then. This is now and I'm gonna be the one to help you stand and wrap those bad boys up."

"You're ridiculous," I said, but I was smiling.

"You love it," he countered with a wink.

I had a sneaking suspicion that might be a little too true.

"Right so now... we're gonna get you up on an arm and then swing your legs off the bed. Then you can just sit there while I wrap you up." His hand went under one of my arms and pulled as I pushed, biting hard into my busted lip to keep from crying out. "Seriously? With the stoic shit?" he asked, watching my face. "Not gonna think less of you if you curse and spit about it, babe."

So then, I did. And I earned a smile for it to boot.

Fifteen minutes later, Cash took a few steps back, watching me while he held his chin in his fingers.

"Was it completely necessary to make a fucking tunic out of the gauze?" I laughed, looking down to where I was wrapped from pelvis to five inches over my breasts. Hell, there were even straps.

"Yep," he said easily, moving back toward me and extending his hand. "Bathroom?" he asked with a shrug when I furrowed my brow at his hand.

"Right." There were things you didn't want to admit to a man you were sleeping with, especially only a few days into said naughty-bits-rubbing, and one of those things... was telling them you had to pee. But, given the fact that I was pretty sure I'd double over in pain if I tried to make the journey myself and the fact that I really did have to go, well, I took his hand.

The move across the floor was excruciating in both actual pain and slowness. I felt like every time my foot landed that the sensation shot up my back. By the time we reached the bathroom, still steamy from Cash's shower, I was sweaty and clutching painfully into Cash's arm for stability.

He walked me over toward the toilet and didn't let go.

Okay. I was willing to admit to him that I needed to go, but there was no way in hell he would get firsthand knowledge of that experience.

"I got it from here," I said, letting go of his arm, which made me need to slam my hand down on the cool surface of the sink counter.

"Babe... seriously..." he tried, looking uncharacteristically serious.

"No. We are *so* not at the point where I am going to let you watch me pee. In fact," I went on as he started grinning, "I don't think we will ever be at that point."

"Honey, I don't see how you'll be able to lower yourself down, let alone get back up if I'm not..."

"Then I will just... live here," I said, shaking my head.

"Lo..."

"Cash... out!" I said, my tone a little too sharp, but well, just standing there was painful enough for me to want to pass out and he was just dragging the whole process out.

Cash sighed, shaking his head at me like I was being stupid, then slowly moved out of the room and closed the door.

I knew his ass was waiting right outside the door and that was sweet and all... but he could hear. So I turned on the tap high as I moved to try to get myself to the toilet. I was pretty sure I heard his chuckle from outside the door, but frankly, I was hurting too much to care if he thought I was being ridiculous.

Ten absolutely horrifyingly painful minutes later, I had handled my business, gotten up, and was washing my hands and ignoring the tears streaming down my face when the door opened and there Cash was.

"Baby," he said, coming up beside me and watching my reflection. "Was your modesty really worth it?" he asked, reaching up and wiping my cheeks before handing me a towel to dry my hands.

"Yes."

"Women..." he said, shaking his head, but he was giving me a soft smile. "Know this is probably fucking salt in the wounds," he said, turning me slightly, "but I have to do it..."

"Do wha..."

The last of my word was hushed by his lips landing on mine, soft, so gentle it was barely a touch at all, but damn if I didn't feel it down to my toes. My hands moved up, grabbing his cocked arms as his hands held the sides of my head and his tongue moved between my lips to stroke mine, sending a jolt of desire so strong through my body that my legs felt wobbly. I moaned softly into his mouth and he pulled away.

My eyes opened slowly to see him smirking. "What?" I asked, close to being offended and he hadn't even *said* anything.

"You moaned..."

Oh, hell.

"Yeah, so?" I said, attempting indifference though a part of me was dying a little inside.

"So..." he said, his smile spreading wider, "for a minute there... you weren't hurting."

The swirling, uncomfortable feeling subsided, replaced with a rush of warmth. Christ, he really was just too... good at times.

"I guess."

"Know what?" he asked, his smile taking a turn toward the scandalous.

"What?" I asked, smiling back.

"I can think of a *lot* of ways to naturally kill the pain..."

My sex clenched hard and I felt a rush of wetness between my thighs. It was so easy with him. All he had to do was talk to me. Hell, even just look at me.

"Oh yeah?" I asked, my hand sliding up his bicep to toy with the long strands of hair falling toward his neck.

"Oh... *yeah,*" he said confidently as his hand moved down over my chest. Even under endless layers of gauze (seriously, he never wanted anyone to even see a hint of tit), my nipples hardened as his hand kept moving downward. He paused for the barest of seconds, watching my face, enjoying my reaction, before his hand moved between my thighs and cupped my sex. "Bet every gun at the compound that your pussy is already drenched."

"You'd win that bet," I said with a smile, moving my hips slightly against his palm, ignoring the stab of pain up my back.

His fingers crooked inward and pressed against my clit, making a surprised moan escape my lips. "Best fucking pussy I've ever..."

"Seriously?" Mike's voice called from the other room, making me straighten. Cash just smiled, pressing into my clit again, taking a sick kind of pleasure at the half-shocked, half-aroused look on my face. "She shouldn't be up walking without pain meds," Mike scolded, his voice getting closer.

"Should I tell him about our new little version of pain management?" Cash asked with a devilish smile as he stroked over my clit again, making a soft whimper escape my lips. "Nah," he said as Mike's feet stopped just outside the door, "let's keep this between the two of us, yeah?" he asked, moving his hand from between my thighs to under my arm. "Keep your panties on. She had to pee for chrissakes."

Oh my God.

If I was capable of blushing, I'd have been beet red right that minute. Cash swung the door open and Mike went from annoyed to concerned in a blink, offering me his other arm which made the process, admittedly, less painful on the way back to the bed where I was planted, handed two pain pills, then pushed back onto my belly which got a loud grumble from me.

"What?" Cash asked as Mike walked out.

"So you know my tits?" I asked, looking at him. It was literally all I could do in that position.

"You mean my top two favorite parts of your body?" he asked, biting slightly into his lower lip, making me wonder if it was on purpose or subconscious. Either way, it sent another rush of desire through my system, making me all the more grumpy because there was nothing that could be done about that in this position either.

"Top two?" I asked, unable to help myself.

"Tits, smile, cunt, eyes, ass," he answered on a shrug.

Well, then.

"So, being your top two favorite parts of my body," I repeated with a smile, "I'm sure it hasn't exactly escaped your notice that they are on the..."

"That they're way more than a fucking handful?" he asked, with a full smile.

"I was going to say on the large side, but yeah, essentially. So... laying on them like this... not fucking comfortable in the least."

"No?" he asked, standing suddenly and reaching for me. Too surprised (and drugged) to react, I simply sat back on my ankles like he was pushing me to do and watched as he slipped into the hospital bed where my head had been lying a moment before. He reached for the remote to the bed and messed with it until it curved upward, putting him in an almost upright position, before he reached out for me and pulled me against his chest, his hands wrapping around my ass and holding me to him. "How's this then?" he asked and his voice sounded husky. It also didn't escape my notice that he was hard beneath me.

"Mmhmm," I murmured, too satisfied to manage anything else.

"Know what else is good about this position?" he asked.

"What?" I asked, burying my face in his neck and breathing him in- the slightest hint of the soap we stocked at Hailstorm, but mostly, just him.

"This," he said, rocking his hips beneath me, letting his cock stroke up my cleft. Maybe I should have objected, should have told him to save it for a time when I could ensure a satisfying end for him as well, but, well... I was the one with her back torn open and he had unfairly gotten my engine running in the bathroom so... he owed me.

It didn't take long. I was feeling good from the meds and I was soaked from his hand playing with my clit. His cock maybe hit my clit five or six times before the orgasm ripped its way through my body, making me cry out against his neck as one of his hands moved to the back of my neck and pushed me closer to him.

"Never get fuckin' tired of hearing you come," he said quietly, his fingers stroking my hair and I should have pushed him away because it was dirty and greasy from not being washed, but it felt too good and before too long, I was fast asleep and couldn't care less about things like greasy hair.

Aside from short breaks for me or him to hit the bathroom, that was the position we stayed in for three days. Some of the time, I slept. Some of the time, we both slept. A lot of the time, we talked- about my past with Damian, about how I decided to build Hailstorm, about his past in the MC, funny stories about stupid shit he had pulled when he was younger.

He held my arms reassuringly when Mike came in and unwrapped me and tended to my wounds, then helped balance my weight off the side of the bed when I finally insisted it was time to wash my hair and Aggie, one of the girls who worked in skips, came in to do it with a bucket over the side of the bed. I took whore's baths when Cash left me alone in the bathroom and had started to feel reasonably more human by the third morning.

I was also absolutely, one-hundred percent certain on that third morning that I was completely, overwhelmingly, irrationally... in love with him.

"Hey, ah, Cash," Mike came in, looking almost sheepish, with an odd smile.

"What?" he asked, sitting up a little straighter.

"Someone is at the gate for you."

"Someone?" he repeated, brow lifted.

"Your brother," he specified. "And, ah, man... he's kinda pissed."

At that, Cash let out a strange laugh-groan hybrid. "He would be. I haven't checked in in almost five days and the last anyone saw of me, I was charging in all badass to save the day," he said with a grin. "Let me up, babe," he said, patting my ass, and I moved a leg from over him and moved to sit off the edge of the bed. "Well, this is gonna be fun," he said, stretching and leaning in to plant a quick kiss on my forehead before following Mike out.

And I was left there thinking the most insane two thoughts I had probably ever had cross my mind before: What would Reign, badass biker MC president, think of his kid brother dating the leader of Hailstorm? And also- would he be able to accept me into his weird little miss-matched family?

See? Insane.

Because no matter how sweet Cash had been to me, how caring, how silly when I needed it, how stalwart when I bitched at him, how strong to withstand all of my crazy moods... he wasn't that kind of guy.

I went and fell for the carefree manwhore that, in fiction, met and fell in love and came out the other side completely reformed.

But this wasn't a romance novel, this was real life.

And in real life, well, he wasn't leading man material.

And that was the saddest realization I had ever come to terms with.

TWENTY-FOUR

Cash

I was fucked and I knew it. Fucked in a multitude of different ways. First, I was fucked because something was happening with Lo, something I wasn't stupid enough to not recognize, but something I *was* stupid enough to think I would never let happen.

Second, I was fucked because what I just pulled with Lo, Damian, and Hailstorm at large, well, it put me in hot fucking water with The Henchmen. You never, as in ever, pulled dangerous shit behind their backs. Mostly because they wanted to be in on it. But also because it was disloyal to keep that kinda stuff from them.

So I didn't even need to see Reign's face to know he was pissed.

But when I walked up the front path to see him standing outside the gates, arms crossed over his chest, his light green eyes piercing into me, one of his dark brows raised like he couldn't believe what he was seeing, yeah, I knew I was fucked.

"You fucking serious?" he asked when I got to the gate.

"Shit move, not to call," I admitted on a shrug. There was nothing I could do about that. It was after the fact. But it was wrong.

"You didn't answer your cell so I went to your place."

"Fuck," I groaned, running a hand up the shaved side of my head.

"Yeah... fuck. I get there and it's torn the fuck up and there's blood on the wall and a gun tucked under the fucking couch and you're MIA."

"Wasn't my blood," I clarified, though the cut on my face was a spot his eyes kept finding. "It was Lo's. She was staying with me."

Reign sucked in a breath, looking to the side for a long minute. "She was the chick who was screaming up the gates about a favor owed, wasn't she?"

Well, at least that probie hadn't given me up fully. I owed him a marker for that shit. No one lied to Reign, no one. "Yeah. Did they tell you about her face?" Reign winced and I had my answer. "Whatever they said it was, it was worse. And she could barely move her ribs were so bruised. I took her to my place because, for reasons I didn't know at the time, she didn't want to involve Hailstorm in her mess. And we *did* owe her."

"Yeah," he agreed, nodding. "But that was my place to repay that debt."

"You have more to lose than I do. And I was there. And she was in bad shape. I made a decision. Try to tell me you didn't do the same exact fucking thing with Summer." I paused, taking in his tight jaw, knowing I was pushing it. "Tell me it wasn't just as against the code for you to do it."

"It was different."

"Yeah, given that I actually knew Lo, and Summer was just some random chick in the middle of the road in a hurricane."

"Careful."

"Know you love her and I love her for you, but at the time... she was no one to you. You went ahead and pulled some crazy shit, some action movie shit to get her out of her situation."

"I'm assuming there's a point to this."

"I didn't bring any possible trouble to the club. This was just me, Lo, her fuckhead of an ex and some of the Hailstorm guys." There was a cough to Reign's side and I saw the person in the security booth was a young woman named Katie who was giving me a brow raise. "And girls," I clarified.

"Her ex?" Reign asked and I felt a small stab of guilt. Lo would probably be pissed that I was sharing that shit.

"Yeah," I agreed, needing to tell him despite the hell she was going to give me about it. "She married young. Wasn't long before he started beating her. He was especially fond of a belt."

"Fuck," Reign said, looking down at his feet.

"One day, she had enough, stabbed him, then got shot of him. Or at least, that was what she thought. Apparently, he was just hanging out around here, setting up the basement of the old carpet store to look like their old apartment, waiting for her to make a mistake so he could get her. Caught her alone at her old safe house, beat her. I took her. He found my place and took her back."

"Kill 'em?"

I shook my head. "Chained him down in that basement like he did to her after going at him with his belt for a while. Figured once Lo is up and moving, she'd want a go at him."

Reign nodded, an evil little smirk toying with his lips. "Should send Wolf down there if you want some real vengeance."

I chuckled, shaking my head. "He almost went postal on me when he thought I was the one who fucked up Lo."

Reign smiled slightly before it fell. "You're fucking her," he guessed, rightly.

I looked down at my feet, not able to face him when I

admitted, "More than that."

"Eyes, bro," he commanded and I reluctantly looked up. "Oh, you're so fucked!" he broke off laughing. "Lo, man? Fuuuuuck."

"She's not who everyone thinks she is."

"She got your balls in a vice grip, she'd have to be something pretty fuckin' exceptional."

He had no idea. Stripped of the chance to run away from me, pain making it impossible to keep her shields reinforced, she had opened up to me. She told me about her shit father and his shit gender roles, the way he used to punish her when she fucked up- making her do endless hours of push-ups, sit-ups, force her to do suicides until she puked or fainted, made her clean up the vomit, then start all over again. She told me how she saw the boy next door asking her to marry her as a way out of the prison she was raised in. She cried when she told me about the first time he beat her, how she almost killed herself to be free of him, how she was terrified anyone knew those things because she thought everyone would look at her differently then, like she was a victim instead of the badass bitch (her words) she had worked so hard to be.

She let me in.

I got to see the whole person for the first time and I realized with the same kind of clarity that Reign did, that I was *so* fucked.

"Repo ain't too happy about you slamming him up against a wall the other day."

"He's a loyal fuck. Gotta appreciate that about him. I'll talk to him."

"He's keeping this between us, but he's gonna have some major trust issues, you picking a chick and Hailstorm over us. Especially with Wolf being off doing fuck-knows what too. Things aren't looking good at the top over there right now."

"Wolf's business is Wolf's business," I specified, not willing to break that trust either, "but we all know we can trust him to make the right decisions too."

Reign sighed, his shoulders slumping a bit, barely noticeable if someone didn't know him as well as I did. The weight of leadership, he was feeling it. "Whatever he's got himself into, is it bad?"

My gut was telling me *yes*. He was edgy and being way too protective of Janie. He wasn't showing up at the clubhouse. It was all pointing to something serious. "He's got his head on straight from what I can tell so far."

Reign snorted. "So far."

"Yeah," I agreed, both of us knowing there were times, albeit infrequent, but no less terrifying, that Wolf flew off the handle, went full on ape-shit crazy, nearly blacked out in his rage and did shit we didn't even want to think about.

"I get that you got shit going on here," he allowed and I felt a wave of relief. He wasn't going to directly order me back and force me to defy him which would lead to all kinds of problems. No, he saved me from that. Yet again, fuckin' looking out for me like always. "But I need to see your face, the *men,* fucking *Repo* need to see your face in church. And I need to know you're keeping an eye on the Wolf situation. Last thing we need is his bloody, law-enforcement-attention-grabbing trouble at our doorstep. Now you got your shit sorted, things are calm again. Don't want to be rocking the boat."

"Got it," I agreed.

"And answer your god damn phone," he added with a smile.

"Will do."

"She alright?" he asked after a long pause.

"It was fucking bad, man," I admitted, not caring that the emotion was leaking into my tone. If there was one person who understood how it felt to see the woman you cared about battered by another man, it was Reign. "Her entire back was ripped open and her face was busted again. But she's stitched up and healing fast. She'll be up raising hell in no time."

"Sometime like now?" he asked, nodding over my shoulder.

I turned, curious, to find Lo standing by the front door to the compound talking to Malcolm. She had on a loose-fitting white tee that must have belonged to one of the men and I had a sneaking suspicion it was Mike's and a pair of black yoga pants tucked slightly into her heavy-looking black combat boots.

"Fucking seriously?" I asked, looking up at the sky.

"Gonna have your hands full with that one," Reign remarked and it sounded like he was smiling.

I turned back to him to find he was. "Like you should talk. Still got fuckin' bullet holes in the side of the compound."

"Lucky I don't have bullet holes in me," Reign laughed, shaking his head. "Never met a woman so infatuated with guns."

"Good she's shacked up with a gun runner then," I smiled back.

Reign nodded, his face soft at the idea of Summer. "Go see to your woman. Get her fuckin' ass back in bed before she falls over," he said, getting back on his bike. "See you at church."

I gave him a small wave, waiting for him to pull away before I turned to stalk back over to Lo.

"Serious, woman?" I asked, shaking my head at her.

"I'm fine."

"Twenty minutes ago you were lying against my chest, too sore to move." And I fuckin' liked having her there too.

"Yes, well, twenty minutes ago I didn't have an elephant's dose of feel-good meds coursing through my bloodstream," she smiled. But her eyes weren't cloudy and her words weren't slow. She wasn't flying high on any pain killers.

"Baby..."

"I want to see him, Cash," she said, lifting her chin.

"He's got food and shit down there. He'll live a couple more days."

"You're taking me or I'll have one of my men take me," she warned, brow raised, daring me to push it.

"One more day," I tried to reason as Malcolm grinned down at me like an idiot knowing, like I knew as well, that I was going to lose.

"One hour," she countered, looking a bit like she was trying to stop a smile.

"Listen here," I said in a very dad-tone, trying not to laugh when her eyes widened, "Willow 'Lo' Swift, I am absolutely not taking your ass all busted up into town to pound on the guy who put you into a hospital bed. You need to heal up."

"Know what I don't need?" she started, lifting that damn brow again. "Aside from time to 'heal up', that is? I don't need a man thinking he can be telling me what and when I can do things. So tone that shit down, get in on this, or get the fuck out of my way."

I was annoyed, sure, that she was risking her healing by getting up so soon, but I respected her stubbornness, her urge for revenge. They'd have to strap me to a bed if I were in her position. "Oh, I'm in on this," I agreed, rocking back on my heels, slipping my hands into my pockets. "Just wanted to make it clear I wanted my woman to get her ass back in bed and heal and all that shit that I'm supposed to say."

"Your woman?" she asked, forehead wrinkling up, but there was no mistaking that melty-softness I saw in her eyes. She liked that. She wanted that... to be mine.

"Yep."

"What if I don't *want* to be your woman?"

"Well that's just too damn bad because you already are, Wills."

She stiffened suddenly, her whole body going ramrod straight and fuck if I knew for what. She took a breath and noticeably forced herself to relax. "You think so, huh?" she asked, but the teasing was out of her voice.

Beside her, Malcolm was pressing his lips together to keep from smiling as I closed in on Lo, getting my front all up against hers as I pressed my fists into the wall behind her, caging her in. My head tilted and dipped toward her ear so only she could hear. "Second I got a taste of that sweet pussy, baby, you were mine. And, what's more, you wanted to keep being mine."

Her breathing was a little shallow and I felt my cock twitching at the idea of getting to be inside her again once she was all healed. "Pretty sure of yourself, huh?"

I pressed a kiss against her neck and smiled there. "Fuckin' A."

Her chest shook with a little silent laugh.

I pulled back, still caging her in, and laid it down. "I get you gotta do this. Can't blame you. I got my shots in and I'm still itching for more and the fuck didn't do shit to me." Her hand raised to the side of my face and touched the outline of my cut, her eyes like a challenge. "Like I said... ain't shit." She smiled and rolled her eyes at me. "Like I said, I get it. I ain't gonna try to keep you here. But we go, you say your piece, you put a bullet between his eyes... whatever the fuck you need. But you don't do anything to rip open those stitches and then you get your ass back here and get back into that bed, yeah?"

"Depends," she said with an almost dainty shrug.

"On?"

"Are you gonna be in that bed with me?" she asked with a coy smile.

"If I ain't got somewhere better to be," I teased and tried not to smile when her face went hard. Her emotions were like a switch being flicked and it was fuckin' cute as all hell. Not that I would ever tell her that. She'd probably balk at that word, but it was the damn truth. "Babe, there ain't nowhere else I'd rather be," I leveled with her, my tone soft, my eyes on hers.

Her shoulders slumped a little and she gave me a ghost of a smile. "So are we done gabbing like a couple chicks so we can go kick some ass?" With that, she took off toward the cars parked to the side of the property.

"Any chance I can keep her from kicking shit?" I asked Malcolm, knowing what the answer was going to be.

His smile was almost paternal as he watched her walk away for a second before turning his gaze to me. "I'll let Mike know she's probably gonna need to be stitched up again," he said, slapping a hand on my shoulder then walking away.

"Fuck," I said, shaking my head at life in general as I ran to catch up to her, pushing her reluctantly toward the passenger side. "Babe, you can't even sit back. Not safe for you to drive."

With that, and only a small grumble at being 'treated like an invalid' (that was her new favorite phrase when she got into a mood about people telling her she shouldn't do something), she got in and let me drive.

"Just saying... if this is some macho 'my ass is in the car, I'm driving' bullshit... it's not gonna fly long term. I like to drive."

"Of course you do," I smiled at the windshield.

"What's that smile for?"

"Nothin', babe," I lied. "And don't worry. I'm comfortable enough in my masculinity that if my woman wants to drive, I will happily plant my ass passenger. But we're on my bike? I'm driving."

"That's reasonable," she said, nodding for emphasis.

"I'm nothing if not accommodating," I added with a wink, pretending to ignore the fact that we were outlining some parameters to a relationship. Yeah, I didn't need to be thinking about that shit right then. Or ever. It was all new and foreign to me and if I gave it any kind of goddamn thought at all, I'd probably be freaking out about it. My only saving grace seemed to be that Lo seemed as equally awkward and uncomfortable with the idea too. So we had that going for us. Though I was pretty sure having a mutual fear of commitment was probably not the greatest trait to share, but whatever.

I pulled into the parking lot with a weighted feeling in my stomach. True, I wanted to see the fucker hurt. Hell, I wanted to make him hurt again. And I damn sure wanted to see Lo get her payback. But something just didn't feel right. As we climbed out of the car and made our way in through the cracked front window where a pool of water had gathered from the torrential downpour we had had the night before, I tried to convince myself it was only fear for Lo's well being that was making me feel almost queasy.

"You know the code?" she asked as I punched it in, her brows drawn together.

"Leo changed it," I clarified with a shrug as I pulled the door open. "Need help down?"

Her head snapped to me with what I could only describe as horrified shock. "Not a fucking chance," she said, like I was an idiot to offer. It was then that I realized sickbed Lo was gone. Hell, she wasn't even normal day-to-day Lo anymore. No, she was Lo, the badass lady boss of Hailstorm and offering her help was insulting. She could handle her own shit, no matter how bad she was hurting, she was going to go in there like she didn't have a care in the world.

Fucking sexy as hell.

"After you," I said, waving a hand out dramatically and she smiled at me before making her way down the stairs, slow, but steady. She even managed to make it look like she was casually holding the railing instead of using it to help her keep her footing.

"Ah... Cash," she said when she reached the bottom step. I was several feet above her, the half wall of the ceiling to the floor above still blocking my view.

"Fuck... is he dead already?" I asked, but voice too light. "It's cool. Won't judge you for beating on a corpse."

CASH

"Oh my God. No no no..." she cried out as she moved around the room.

My heart skipped up into my throat as I flew down the last few stairs and took in the scene before me. That scene being... an open fucking ankle cuff and no Damian in sight.

"No fucking way. No fucking way," I said, looking around helplessly, my fists curling up. "The door was locked. New code, all that shit. No fucking way."

"There must have been another way out," she said, almost too calmly and when I turned to face her, she was sitting on the side of the bed, looking down at the floor, her shoulder slumped forward and I knew it was hurting like fuck to sit that way, but I guessed whatever she was feeling was hurting worse so she didn't even register it. "He was smart like that. I didn't have a lot of time to look around but there must have been another way out." I picked up the ankle cuff, seeing the scratches near the lock and throwing it down in anger. "He used the belt," she offered.

"What, babe?" I asked carefully, wondering if this was going to be her recounting some of the trauma again. I thought she purged that, crying into my neck as her body shook violently. But maybe that poison buried deep. Maybe she would always need to let it out, little by little.

She sighed loudly and lifted her head to me, waving a hand toward the floor. "To pick the lock. I wasn't able to find the way out, but I had done enough snooping around to know that there was literally nothing in here to use to pick that lock. So he had to use something he had on him."

"Fuck," I growled, wanting to hit, kick, smash something. I left him the belt. I was such a fucking moron. Why would I leave the belt?

"It's not your fault, Cash," she said, her voice suddenly softer, losing all of the badass lady leader and going right back to sweet, soft Lo. "There was so much going on. I was carried out of here. You were worried. The other guys didn't think to secure the area either and I trained them to do that shit. Everyone was all over the place. It's not your fault."

"He got away," I said helplessly.

"Yeah, but it's alright. We'll find him eventually. We have all the time in the world to track him down."

"You shouldn't be so calm about this," I said, sitting down next to her, my hand landing on her thigh and squeezing.

"I've spent a hell of a lot of time being angry with him, Cash. Honestly, I'm just sick of it now. I want to move on." She leaned into me, her head resting on my shoulder and I heard the words she left unspoken: she wanted to move on... with me.

"But this isn't done, right? We're not going to let this fuck walk, are we?" Honestly, even if she told me that that was exactly what she wanted, no fucking way was I going to let that happen. I'd keep her out of it, keep her blind, but I was going to hunt the bastard down and slaughter him like the animal he was.

"No. This isn't done. But I also just... I don't know. I don't feel the need to be the one to do it, to take him down. You know?"

"Honest, honey, no I don't know." I still wanted his blood.

"You know he's a war hero, right? He's been honored and all that. He has buddies still in the Marines. They wouldn't let his disappearance go without an investigation. Too much leads back to me and, through me, to you. We can't risk that."

"You want to bring someone else in on this."

"It's the smartest option."

"Wolf would be itching for the job," I offered.

"Wolf leads back to you who leads back to me. Same problem. It can't be people in our organizations. I know a lot of people who can do contract work like this if..."

"Shooter," I supplied with a shrug.

"What?" she asked, picking her head up to look at me.

"Shooter. Used to work for Breaker. He's a friend. He gets

word of this, he'll be all over it."

"You're sure you trust him? I haven't really done any work with him or Breaker. I know the jobs they pull, but personally..."

"I'll bring him in," I shrugged easily. "You talk to him, get a feel for him. You don't like him, we call in one of your guys. But, babe, he's the best fucking shot I've ever seen. If there's anyone who can clock him and take him out without Damian getting a scent of him, it's Shoot."

She nodded, no doubt having heard the stories of the insane, impossible shots Shooter had pulled off. "Call him in," she agreed, moving to stand up. She reached inside the nightstand and pulled out a necklace. At my curious look, she shrugged. "My mother's."

I gave her a small smile, knowing her mother wasn't even much of a memory to her, but losing mine young, I knew that kind of wound. It was a kind of hollow inside that never felt filled. "You ready to head back, babe?"

"Everything hurts," she admitted, leaning her forehead into my chest.

My hands moved up and down her arms, wishing I could wrap them around her. "Then let's go get you all drugged up."

"Know what I was thinking?" she asked, following me up the steps.

"What?"

"That maybe I could use that... alternative cure for pain you introduced me to."

I turned back, my cock twitching to life at the thought. "This time you let me eat you, though," I said and she let out a surprised yelping laugh. "Been too long since I tasted you. Got a taste for that cunt, baby."

"Okay shut up," she said, stopping for a second on the step below me and I realized she was pressing her thighs together.

"Like that idea huh?" I teased, taking her hand and pulling

her up the last step.

"Cash..." she said, looking downward, pushing against my chest.

"You're all wet thinking about my tongue sliding up your wet slit, teasing over your clit until it's throbbing then sucking on it 'till you come hard, screaming out my name."

"Shut up and get me back to Hailstorm."

I shut up, then I got her back to Hailstorm, made Mike check out her back, then I fucking delivered on my promise.

–

Later, Lo asleep on her stomach, flat on the bed, zonked from a handful of pills Mike had tossed at her an hour before, I moved into the bathroom and pulled out my cell.

The call rang and went to message, as I expected to, as it always did with professionals. His voice said simply, "Shoot," then the beep for the message chimed.

"It's Cash," I said simply then hung up.

I didn't call him often. Hell, I think the only time I ever actually did call him was one night when we were all drinking at Chaz's and one of the guys from the club went home with a chick who ended up having a dick and that shit was too fucking funny not to pass on.

I waited, five, ten minutes before my phone started vibrating in my hand. "Yo," I said as greeting.

"You're just full of pleasantries tonight, huh?" he asked back, his voice teasing, sarcastic, as it almost always was.

"Where the fuck you at, man?"

"What?" he asked and, if I wasn't mistaken and I fucking wasn't, there was a guarded sound in his tone that I had never heard there before.

"All hell breaks loose around here and I hear you are off on some road trip with Breaker and some chick."

"Winter, man," he said, sounding lighthearted again. "Fucking miserable, coming on fast. We wanted a change of pace."

Fuck. He was still out of town.

"Please tell me you aren't off in the Canary Islands somewhere."

"Fuckin' wish," Shoot laughed. "Mexico, man. Place is a hellhole right now, but fuck there are some ripe, lush ladies down here."

I laughed, surprised when it felt like it had been forever since skirt-chasing seemed like my top priority. "You set on staying there?"

"Why? What's up?"

"Got a job."

"What kind of job?"

"Your kind of job. Need someone who is air and can hit a target from as far as possible."

There was a short pause. "What'd you get yourself into that your brothers can't get you out of, man?"

"It's not my shit. It's Lo's shit. And since she belongs to me, it's by proxy... my shit and I want it handled by someone I trust."

"Lo? As in... Hailstorm?" he repeated and I heard surprise in his voice.

"That'd be her."

Another pause, followed by a low whistle. "Fuck, man. That's some grade-A pussy. Best tits I've ever seen..."

"And you haven't even seen 'em," I added with a smile.

"Lucky fuck," he added and I could practically see him smiling. "So you're like... *with* her?" he asked, his tone similar to how mine would have been a week or so back if he came up and told me he got himself shacked up with some chick. That wasn't what we did. We partied, drank, fucked. We took life as it came and we took it easy, no strings, no stress.

"First Shane, then Reign, then Breaker, now you... who the fuck am I gonna skirt-chase with when I get the fuck back there?" he laughed.

"I think Repo's got a few years left in him," I mused.

"Christ," he laughed.

"What?"

"Man, he's like eight years younger than me. Can't have young bloods as my competition."

I rubbed a hand up the side of my head. "Guess we're getting a little old for that shit, huh?"

"Speak for yourself, Cash. How is Repo gonna handle all of these hunnies by himself? I have to do my part... for womankind." He paused. "I'll talk to Break and see if I can get a plane into the city tomorrow then I'll rent a car and drive back. Meet day after tomorrow?"

"Sounds good. Hailstorm?"

"With bells on," he agreed and disconnected.

TWENTY-FIVE

Lo

"Sugar, honey, darlin'," were the first words Shooter mysterious-no-last-name said to me as he stood at the gates sliding open, "you sure you want to be with this guy? You can do so much better."

With that, I was charmed. Putty in his hands charmed and I didn't know a damn thing about him. I felt bad for all of single womankind. They didn't stand a chance.

And not just because he was good looking, but he was. He was tall and a lean kind of strong in his black jeans, worn on the tight side, just shy of hipster, a v-neck white tee, a beaten up black leather jacket, and black creepers. Yes... creepers. Though it was cold out and he was mostly covered up, I could see ink on his hands, creeping across his chest, and culminating in an eagle tattoo, wings spread wide, across his throat. His face was on the thinner side, his eyes a sharp, dark green, his hair teetering between blond and brown, cut close on the sides and slicked back down the center.

His ears were gauged. His eyebrow pierced.

Hot.

He was insanely, unfairly hot in his weird modern punk kind of way.

But it wasn't the hotness. It was the way he carried himself- calm, casual, sure of himself without seeming too cocky, and there was a sweetness underneath it all that made you want to let him put an arm around you and whisper sweet, sweet nothings in your ear, fully aware that was all you would ever be to him- a sweet nothing.

"I think maybe Cash is the one getting the short end of the stick in this situation," I admitted honestly. I was a mess and I came with so much baggage and he was just so... good. So sweet. So giving.

"Barely know you, but I know that isn't the truth," he said, moving toward me, shocking me when he reached out and grabbed my pinkie with his and pulled me along with it. I looked over at Cash who was wearing a huge, amused grin. Seeing my confusion, he shrugged. It didn't bother him in the least that his friend was sort-of holding hands with me. He wasn't the jealous kind. I liked that. I liked that a lot. Because that meant he trusted me, even with his charming as all hell, attractive as all get-out friend, he trusted me... and there was nothing more important than that. "So I hear you got yourself into some trouble," he said, flawlessly skirting around mentioning that he could *see* that I got myself into some trouble, saving my vanity. God, he was smooth.

"That would be an understatement."

It didn't escape my notice that he was walking me into my own compound like he owned the place, not me. That was how at-ease he was with himself and his surroundings. He even made walking down one of my many dead-end halls look like he meant to do it, dipping his head down to my ear and pretending to whisper (though he was talking in his normal voice so he was sure

Cash could hear), "I see what you did there, walking me down to a private place," he teased and I found my smile making my bruised cheeks hurt. "But I am a good, Christian boy," he said, dropping into a Southern accent that sounded natural, surprising me, "I will not be tempted by your wicked womanly wiles."

I felt my giggle well up, uncontrollable. I looked over to see Cash rolling his eyes, but his lips were twitching. "Alright alright," he said, finally breaking in for the first time since before his friend showed up. "We get it. You're slick. Now get your face away from my woman's neck."

"Hand to God," Shooter said, dramatically putting a hand to his heart, "I can't help myself. Look at her."

"I have. Extensively," Cash said, his smile in place but there was a bit of steel in his words. I found myself liking that. He trusted me; he'd let me hold hands with his friends. But he also felt possessive and had no problem making that point clear.

"Point taken," Shooter shrugged, nodding at Cash and winking at me. He dropped my pinkie then, no joke, he booped my nose, like people do to kids, but somehow, it managed to be both sweet and sexy. "Now lay it on me, sweetheart."

With that, I did, and I didn't wince or shrink away from the truth like I would have done a week before, desperately trying to save face, to not let anyone see my damage. I just... gave it to him like I gave it to Cash over the days spent in my hospital bed.

Done, Shooter hissed out a breath, looking down at his feet for a second so I couldn't see what was going on with his face, what he was thinking or feeling. Then his eyes slid up to mine again and I saw a sort of fierce determination there. "Nothing fucking worse than a man who raises his hand against a woman. Even worse when the bastard gets away with it. So you give me a name and a picture," he said to me, then turned to Cash, "and you get me the kind of gun I can work with." Cash nodded and Shooter pinned me again with his intense gaze, "And in twenty-four fucking hours, he won't be breathing easy anymore. Mainly because the fuck won't be breathing at all."

It was then that I saw the professional underneath the real man. I saw him for what he was. I saw how he earned his name. Shooter. That was what he was. That was what he did. It was easy to forget that when he was smiling and touching you and being sweet-sexy enough to make a nun blush. It was easy to forget what he was: a killer. A very good, very experienced killer.

It wasn't the skin he lived in. It wasn't something he wore on his sleeve, but it was a part of him.

"Unless you want him plugged but breathing. I can make that happen too. I don't like to do that, but in this case... I can make an exception."

"I want this over," I said with a simple shrug. I was over it. I wanted the loose ends tied off so I could finally move on.

"It won't trace back to me or Cash or you," he assured me, then added, "I don't collect bodies."

Meaning, he was going to shoot him and leave him. He didn't do the hands-on work. "That works for me."

"Okay," he said, the professional persona slipping away immediately as he clapped then rubbed his hands together, a devilish smile playing with his lips. "So where are the rest of these femme-fatales hiding?" he asked, slipping an arm through mine and leading me back out of the dead end.

"Don't do it, gorgeous," Cash warned, falling behind us. "'Less you're stocked up on tissues and ice cream and whatever the fuck you ladies need when a guy hits and quits."

Shooter craned his head over his shoulder, smirk still intact. "Oh, come on, Cash. You know me better than that. I always leave the ladies with a smile."

Somehow, I did not doubt that in the least.

Cash snorted, shaking his head as we stopped in the front yard again. "Can't wait to see how you're smirking when some chick gets you by the balls, man."

I felt my lips quirking up at that. Suddenly, I wanted to see that too.

Shooter let go of my arm as he stepped in the gateway, turning to face us, smile wide. "That's never gonna happen," he said, booped my nose again, and was on his way.

"What's so funny?" I asked, watching Cash chuckle at his friend driving away.

"Babe, I used to say the same thing," he said, smiling down at me.

"You're saying I have you by the balls?" I asked, grinning big.

"Baby..." he said, as if that was answer enough.

"Well," I demanded, brows going up expectantly. I wanted to hear him say it.

He exhaled his breath through his nose, shaking his head up at the sky. "Fuck me," he said to no one in particular before letting his eyes land on mine. "Balls, dick, heart, brain, baby, you got it all."

Heart.

He said heart.

He'd kinda snuck it in there. But it *was* in there.

He said I had him by the heart.

At that, I felt my own trip over itself frantically.

It wasn't *those words,* but it was.

I opened my mouth to respond, to tell him that I felt the same, that he was the only person I had ever felt safe around, the only man I could let myself care about, the most surprising, wonderful person I had ever met.

But the front door burst open and Malcolm was running out, phone pressed to his ear. At the silent question in my eyes, he called, "It's Janie." At that, my heart, already pounding, went into a near attack. Janie. Janie was calling Hailstorm. Maybe she was coming back. Maybe... "She needs to talk to Cash."

Oh.

I tried to hide the disappointment in my eyes. At this, I failed judging by the small shrug Cash gave me as he took the phone.

"Hey kid, what's up?" he asked, his sweet smile in place and I liked that. I liked that he got on with Janie, that he got on with Malcolm and Mike and everyone else in my life. But then his head snapped up and his eyes pinned me. "Calm down." Okay. It wasn't weird for Janie to be, well, *not* calm. She was mercurial. She went from calm and focused to off the handle in two-point-five seconds. Then she went from off the handle to laughing in two-point-fifteen. So it wasn't unusual for her to be worked up. What was unusual was the fact that Cash went from calm and happy to stern and worried.

"What's going on?"

He shook his head at me, a plea for silence.

"When? Fuck. Shit goddamn it," he said, the words savage. "Be there as soon as possible." He paused, looking at me. "I'm bringing Lo to sit with you." With that, he hung up. But he didn't talk to me. Instead, he turned his attention back to the phone and dialed fast. His eyes found mine as the phone rang. "Reign. Get Repo and get your fucking asses on your bikes. Wolf went AWOL. No... he's hunting. Yeah, the human kind. I know. Yeah. His place. Thirty minutes."

Not many people knew Wolf's background. I, on the other hand, did. So if he was AWOL and he was hunting the human kind of prey, it absolutely warranted the stony, resigned worry taking over Cash's normally carefree face.

"You need to sit with and calm down your girl," he told me, already making his way over to the cars.

"Okay." I could do that. "Do you need me to bring Hailstorm in to back up you and your guys?"

"Only the three of us on this. Anyone else would be

potential collateral damage."

I understood that too. So I silently got my ass into the passenger seat and let him have the silence he needed to get himself together. We parked at the bottom of Wolf's hill and I grabbed his hand before he could swing out and talk to Reign and Repo, already parked with their bikes, looking every bit as anxious as Cash did.

"Yeah?" he asked, the sound a little clipped, but I understood too well what he was feeling to be offended.

"You'll be careful." It wasn't a question or a plea. It was practically a demand.

"'Course," he said, reaching out to touch my face. We turned and got out of the car. "I need to walk her up and then I'll be down," he said to Reign and Repo who both looked at me with angry eyes, taking in my busted face.

"No. Get going. I'm fine."

"Lo..."

"It's not that far."

"You got stitches all up your..."

"I said I'm fine. Go get your boy. I need to go calm down my girl."

He nodded reluctantly, grabbing the back of my neck to pull me slightly to him and kissed the side of my head. "I'll call."

"You better," I shot back then pulled away. "You guys be careful too," I said to Reign and Repo as I turned and slowly made my way up the hill with gritted teeth. I told him I was fine and I was determined to make it look that way, no matter how much it hurt. I was right, it wasn't *that* far... for a normal person. For someone with stitches tracing their back, well, it felt like fifteen football fields.

I got to the door and heard the bikes and, presumably, the car pulling away. I paused, hand raised to knock, finding myself suddenly nervous. To see her, which made no sense. She was the best friend I had in the world. We shared so much. Though, there was probably just as much that we kept from each other and it was time to come clean, it was time to admit that I had been hiding my past from her, that I didn't trust her with it before but that it was time for that to change.

So I forced my hand to knock.

When I heard nothing from inside, no moving, no TV, no nothing, I felt the hairs on the back of my neck standing on end. I reached for the handle and found it unlocked, another thing that had me worried. Janie was practically OCD about locks. She checked every door inside Hailstorm before she went to sleep at night. I understood why. No one would blame her. Not once in all the years I had known her had she forgotten to check. And Hailstorm was a fortress, made of unyielding metal and surrounded by barbed wire gates and protected by guard dogs. So leaving the door open at some random little cottage in the woods? Yeah, so not Janie.

"Janie?" I called, pushing open the door and stepping in carefully. "You in here, babe?"

My eyes took a second to adjust to the light in the darkened room and when they did, I finally saw her, curled up in the bed under the covers, cuddled into a protective little ball, crying.

Crying.

Once. I had seen her crying once in all the years I knew her- the night I met her. After that, she tucked it away, she locked it up tight; or she dealt with the tears in private, but she never shared them. Not with me, not with anyone.

"Honey," I said, my voice a worried whisper as I moved to sit down on the side of the bed by her body. My hand moved out to touch her shoulder and she shrieked and flew back from me, scooting up in the bed to lean up against the headboard. "It's me. Hey, it's me," I crooned, holding my hands up, palms out.

Janie took a deep breath, closing her eyes, tilting her head to the ceiling. The air shook in her chest as she let it out, her eyes opening slowly as she focused on me. The tears were gone and I had a moment to admire the kind of self-control it took for her to go from the depths of hell of emotions to almost robotically blank in the course of a few seconds.

"You alright, honey?" I asked, knowing her response would be surface, would be empty and knee-jerk.

"Your face," she said instead, choosing not to lie.

"Back is worse," I shrugged, feeling the pulsing pain start up again. "Your arm," I said, gesturing toward the white gauze. Her eyes flew down to the limb in question, her eyes closing again for a moment. "Burn, right?" I asked and her head snapped up, surprised. At that, I let myself smile. "Know you like a little sister," I explained. "Did you really think I'd miss the Jstorm signature? No one does explosions like you, babe."

Her hand rose, shaking a little as she ripped it through her hair roughly. "You knew," she accused quietly and I nodded. "How long?"

"Since about the minute after I picked myself up off the ground."

Janie exhaled loudly. "You weren't supposed to be there. You were supposed to be at Reign's. I told Summer..."

"No effing way," I laughed, unable to help myself. "Oh, that makes so much more sense now."

"What does?"

"That ridiculous dinner party. None of us understood why the hell we were there except that Summer threw a holy fit at any of us who said we weren't going to be able to make it."

"I wanted to keep you all safe."

"While you created chaos."

"I didn't want any of the friendleys thinking it was any of the other friendleys doing the dirt," she said, using the silly term she always did for The Henchmen or the Mallicks. Summer's father,

Richard Lyon, was not included in that list, but I imagined she felt the need to protect Summer's feelings by protecting her father.

I paused for a second, trying to find the right words, trying to not push the wrong buttons. "That night, babe, that night is burned in my memory," I started, knowing she knew I didn't mean the night of the bombs. I meant the night I met her, the night she became the biggest part of my heart.

"When I close my eyes, some nights, I still see it clear as I did then. You were too young to be that broken. Sixteen with scars a grown woman would never be able to walk around wearing. And not just all these ones," I said, running my hand down the tattoos on her arms, tattoos she got to cover up what was underneath. "I mean the ones you wear on the inside. I didn't know you. You couldn't even speak to me your face was so swollen, but I knew you. I understood. Our souls spoke in the same language- the language only women can fully understand, babe. And the second I picked you up off that street, I knew I would give anything to see you able to carry your own weight again one day, to see you smile or laugh, to see you start to heal."

"I tried, Lo," she said, her voice a small, desperate whisper.

My hand went to hers, grabbing it hard and not letting go. "No. You didn't *try*. You succeeded. It took a long time, years, but you healed from the outside in. But because I spoke your language, babe, I knew that there were some scars, the ones marked deep down on your soul, that might never heal. I understood that. I never expected you to live one day like all of that never happened to you. It would be hypocritical of me to expect that of you when I didn't expect it of myself."

"Lo..." Janie broke in, her tone clear: I didn't need to talk about it if I didn't want to.

But I wanted to. I was done hiding. Maybe if I stopped hiding, she could too. "I was wrong to hide it. I was wrong to think that what happened *to* me would define the way others would see me. It wasn't my fault that I married someone who wasn't who I thought he was. It wasn't my fault he beat me, that he pushed himself on me. It wasn't even my fault that I stayed. I was young. Older than you were, babe, but way too young to deal with that. I didn't see a way out. But when I finally did, I took it."

Her hand squeezed mine. "Lo, I know about Damian..."

My body jolted before I forced it to relax. "Cash told..."

Her head shook immediately. "I snooped, Lo. I know I shouldn't have, but I could never sleep. There were only so many books I could read, so many articles I could browse. I looked into all of you at the beginning. I knew you were married. I knew you left him. I didn't know he beat you." Her lip trembled slightly before she forced it to relax. "But you're right- it didn't change the way I thought about you. It doesn't define you. You're you. You're the baddest bitch I've ever met and you taught me so much about how to be strong, how to overcome, even though I didn't know there was something like that for you to overcome, I think I felt it. I felt it in my gut."

"Wolf is hunting Lex, isn't he?" I asked, knowing my answer, but wanting the confirmation.

"Yes," she said, nodding the slightest bit.

I paused for a second, taking a breath. "I know it's not right of me, but I really hope he finds him before Reign, Cash, and Repo catch up."

Janie exhaled a sharp breath. "Me too."

I nodded, moving to lie down next to her, on my stomach but propped up on my arms. "Then let's just sit here and be not-right together, yeah?"

"Yeah," she agreed, snuggling back down on the bed.

A while later, listening to nothing but each other's breathing and the wind outside, I turned my face to watch her profile. "One night," I started and her head cocked slightly to look at me, "Cash came in while I was sleeping and picked up one of my books..."

"Oh, no..." Janie groaned, knowing of my penchant for romance novels, something she teased me mercilessly about because she buried her nose in classics.

"Then he started reading one of the sex scenes. Out loud."

Then Janie did something I hadn't seen her do in way too long, she threw her head back and laughed. "Were you mortified?"

"Words can't even describe."

"Did he tease you about it?"

I felt my smile grow soft and, judging by the way her eyes did the same thing, she noticed. "No. He tried to force me to relax, not be embarrassed. Then, well, stuff happened."

Her smile turned a little devilish, "Stuff, huh?" she asked with an eyebrow wiggle. "Is he as good as the word on the street?"

"God, babe... so much *better.*"

She laughed a little, trying to sober her face and failing. "It's good his STD check came back clean last month then."

It was my turn to burst out laughing and it felt good. It felt especially good to be sharing it with her. "We should probably stop monitoring him so closely from now on."

"Hey, if he's got nothing to hide then he shouldn't..."

"I think I love him, Janie," I broke in, letting the words trip out before I could force them back. When she didn't immediately respond, I gushed on, "I know it's fast. It's... too fast. It doesn't make sense and..."

That was when Janie's head shook and her eyes went as wise as her words. "Lo, when has love *ever* made any kind of sense?"

I felt my head nod and the silence lapsed again. "I think he loves me too," I admitted, my voice a little hopeful.

"He fucking better," was her immediate response, making me smile. "He doesn't see what a prize he's got with you, he's an idiot. I mean... he *is* and idiot..."

"Hey," I broke in, trying for offended, but I was smiling too much.

"I'm kidding. He's good people, Lo. You know I'd tell you otherwise if I didn't think he was."

And, boy would she ever. Keeping her opinions to herself was never a problem she suffered from.

"Janie... I know he's got a wicked reputation of being a vicious son of a bitch," I started, keeping my eyes on her, looking for a reaction, "but I think Wolf is a good man too."

I wasn't imagining it when her face went a little soft again.

And I felt myself hoping that, one day, she would tell me their story. Because I was sure it was a doozy.

Eventually, me tired from pain, her tired from whatever battle she was struggling with inside, we both slept.

I woke up to no call from Cash.

We had a whole day.

I went to sleep with no call from Cash.

I woke up again and my phone was ringing. I flew upward, ass to heels, and dug it out of my back pocket. "Cash?" I called desperately into the receiver.

"Ouch," was the response and it wasn't Cash. "Sugar, honey, darlin'," he drawled and despite being worried as shit about Cash, I felt my lips curving up. "You forgot about me already?"

"As if that is possible," I answered truthfully.

"Are you flirting with me, pumpkin?" he asked and I laughed. Then he did too.

"What's up, Shooter?" I asked and Janie's head snapped up, watching me with really intent eyes.

"News. Channel five. Right now."

"Janie, news, channel five," I relayed and she reached for a remote and brought it up.

"... Damian Crane, a decorated war hero, was shot dead in the doorway of his car early this morning..."

I didn't hear the rest. I didn't need to. It was done. It was over. I was finally, finally free.

"Shot him in the dick first," Shooter said casually, making me choke on my own saliva for a second.

"What?"

"Between the eyes, peaches? Too fast, too clean, too good for the fuck. Shot him in the dick, gave him about fifteen seconds to come to terms with never being able to use that particular organ ever again, then took him out."

"You confuse me," I admitted, shaking my head at myself.

"I got a little rage I can tap into now and again," he shared, openly, easily, a trait I truly admired, "but that's rare. Mostly, it's just the devilishly handsome ladies man you have come to know and love."

I smiled. "I think it's impossible not to love you a little bit, Shoot."

"That's what all the ladies tell me," he answered back and I could hear the smile in his voice.

"I bet they do," I agreed. "By the balls one day, Shooter. Can't wait to see that."

"Never gonna happen."

"Famous last words," I said back immediately. "Thanks, Shooter. You got me free of him finally. I can't say how..."

"Thank Cash," he cut in, unwilling to accept my gratitude. "He called me in. I'm just a scope and a finger. He made the call. So go find him, jump him, give it to him nice and sweet. And... try not to think of me while you do it," he teased.

"Oh, I don't know... that might be difficult."

"I know, sweet pea, but you're going to have to try," he laughed and disconnected.

I took a second, letting the reality settle into me, felt it wipe away the smoky air inside like a gust of fresh wind, before I turned to Janie who was watching me and making no attempt to act like she wasn't.

"One day," she said, her words heavy, "when I'm ready... we need to have a talk. The girly kind... with feelings and shit. There's a lot you need to know. Not just about what happened to me way back then... but about what I have done since then, behind everyone's backs. For the greater good, I think, but still. Not good stuff. Not clean."

"Babe... nothing in our lives is clean. It's dirty and bloody and we have to fight so hard for everything we get, but it's that fight that makes it worth it in the end."

I heard it then. Not my phone, not the call I was promised, but boots outside. I was up and on my feet just as fast as Janie, reaching for a gun I didn't have. But just as I thought that, one was flying across the bed at me and Janie was already turned toward the door, arms raised. I wasted no time getting my safety off and following her lead, legs spread, arms steady.

The door burst open and I realized Janie didn't lock it again, taking that thought and its accompanying question and burying it to be asked at a later date. My finger slipped to the trigger as three men walked inside.

"You were supposed to fucking *call!*" I snapped before I even got the gun lowered, not bothering to look at Reign or Repo, and focusing solely on Cash.

"Things got hot. We didn't have time."

"Oh, no? The whole ride back from wherever-the-fuck you were... you couldn't call?"

"No," he said, shaking his head, looking almost amused as he made his way across the room toward me.

"Why the hell not?"

"Because I was trying to focus on the road and not die on my way back to you."

Well then.

I guessed that was a rational reason.

"I'm still mad at you," I grumbled, but I wasn't.

"I guess I'll have to live with that," he smiled, pressing his front into my front, his hands sliding down my arms then wrapping around my ass before his mouth came down on mine. It wasn't a quick peck either. It was long and wet and deep and his tongue stroked mine until I was clinging to him, blissfully oblivious to the three other people in the room.

"Mind if we get this over with so I can go home and kiss my woman like that and Repo can... go and kiss his cars or whatever the fuck he does?" Reign asked, making me jump away from Cash, embarrassed it had gotten so hot and heavy in public.

Cash seemed to not be of the same mind as his head ducked down and started running his tongue down the side of my neck in a way that my legs nearly buckled.

"Get what over with?" I asked, ignoring the breathlessness in my tone.

"We found Wolf," Reign said, looking at Janie, guessing or knowing the situation, giving her the news she needed. "He's... working through some shit," he said, vaguely.

"Are any of us going to have to worry about an FBI raid?" I asked.

"Janie, wanna go see him?" Reign asked, his tone soft as he held an arm out to lead her outside, Repo following behind.

"That's not an answer!" I called at their retreating forms and Cash chuckled. "Come on, babe, we need to get you back. Mike is gonna be pissed he hasn't changed those dressings."

"Stop trying to distract me," I demanded as he led me outside and down the hill. Everyone else was nowhere in sight. "Where did they all go? Is Janie going to be alright with him? Is he off the handle? We need..."

"You need to be quiet, shut down the boss-lady shit, and let your man get you taken care of, yeah?"

I tried to remember I was mad at him. I really did. But really, all there was was relief. So I let him lead me to the car that was a sight more beat up than it was when I had last seen it, then drive me back to Hailstorm.

Later, in the bed, my chest to his, my legs on either side of his hips, our lips pressing memories into each other, our bodies melting toward each other, for the first time in what felt like forever, he slowly slipped inside me. I took him to the hilt on a quiet moan, my head tilting back for a second, silently hoping it would always feel like it did right then- perfect, right, beautiful. His hands moved up to my face, cradling it gently.

"Ride me, baby," he urged and my hips surged immediately, drawing a husky groan from his lips. His hands went to my hips, his face buried in my neck. "Fuck yeah. I missed this."

God, I did too. "Me too," I whimpered, my body driving up fast, too fast, so fast that my breathing felt strangled in my chest already.

"When your back is better," he said, using his fingers to dig into my hips and pick up my pace, "I am taking up real estate in this pussy," he said with a smile as I drove my hips down and my orgasm broke through my system, my mouth opening on a surprised cry as I convulsed around him, milking him, bringing him with me, groaning into my neck as he came.

"I have no objections to that plan," I admitted, my arms holding him tight to me.

"She agrees with me," he said and I could feel him smile into my throat. "Halle-fucking-lujah."

"Hey Cash," I said a minute later and his head lifted at my suddenly serious tone.

"Yeah, babe?"

"Thank you," I said, thinking of Shooter's words. I gave it to him nice and sweet, it was time for me to open up.

"For what, Wills?" he asked and I only stiffened slightly at that nickname.

"I'm finally free. You got me free."

He thought on that for a second. "And you gave me you. The real you. We're even, yeah?"

I felt my lips curve.

"Yeah," I agreed.

Easy. Uncomplicated.

Two things I never knew before.

Two things only Cash could give me.

Free. Finally.

EPILOGUE

Cash- two weeks

Days, Hailstorm got her. They got their badass boss lady. They got her strong, her hard, her smart. Then night came, her ass landed in my bed, and I got it *all*. Her strong, her hard, her smart, but also her sweet, her sassy, her cute, her awkward, her sexy. I got every piece.

Her ass was in my bed because my ass wasn't too keen on sleeping in a barracks with a couple dozen other men and women because I wanted my woman free with me. And by 'free', I meant naked. And by 'naked' I meant bare-assed and pressed all over me.

I made good on my promise and I took up real estate in her pussy. Her stitches out, her back only tender when she overdid it in training, I got her on her back again finally. I felt her legs wrapped around me while I pounded hard and deep, no bruised ribs to worry about, nothing to keep us from completely consuming each other so that was what we did. We fucked, barely out of the doorway every time she came over. We ate. I ate her, I fucked her again in the shower. We talked, we shared war stories. I fucked her again in bed.

I woke up most mornings to her climbing on me. The mornings I didn't, I woke her up with my face between her legs.

We didn't talk about her scumbag ex being dead. She knew, I knew. It was over. She was free. That shit didn't need to be dissected. She was moving on and that meant we were moving on... together.

Lo- three months

We were sitting on the front porch, drinking coffee, bundled up against the February cold, looking like a normal couple- not a gun running biker and a leader of a camp full of heavily-trained fighters, killers, and fixers. I was just thinking how close to clean it felt, how close to average. It didn't seem possible, to be who we were, criminals, not bad guys, but not legitimately good citizens either, but still be able to have average, have normal.

CASH

Yeah, I was just thinking that thought when a snowball came flying across the front yard and splattered right between Cash and my feet.

The girls across the street let out a string of giggles from where they were hiding behind my car. Cash's face snapped up, playful smile already fully engaged (and let me tell ya', that smile was a sight to see) as he did a full on spy roll across the front yard like his mission to get hidden behind his bike was the most important one of his life.

I then watched as a snowball fight to end all snowball fights commenced, Cash taking the hits on purpose to keep things fair as he pummeled the squealing girls with the soft, fresh snow until they mother came to the doorway, smiling at the scene and calling the girls in for hot chocolate. A good call seeing as their faces were stained bright pink from the cold.

Cash came back to me out of breath, dropping down on the chair beside me and warming his hands with his coffee cup.

It was time.

For that talk.

One I had been avoiding because I knew it was awkward and it was dangerous.

"You're good with kids," I said, looking off into the yard, not able to meet his eye yet.

"Babe, what's with the tone?" he asked, knowing me too well.

I forced my face toward him. "I can't have them."

His head jerked a little, but I didn't see disappointment, just surprise. "Can't?"

I knew what he was asking. Because he knew me. He knew all of me. And that included my menstrual cycle. He knew I still got it. So he was asking if I was barren. "Biologically, I probably could. But, Cash... I'm thirty-nine. I know you're younger and I know..."

Not missing a beat, not letting me finish, he cut in, "Didn't you notice, baby? Reign and Summer fuck like bunnies. I'll have half a dozen nieces and nephews to screw around with in a couple years. The best part?" he asked, leaning close, giving me his gaze where I saw nothing but honesty, "when they get tired and whiny... we send them back to their parents. Then *we,*" he said, grabbing the back of my neck and pulling me close, "can fuck like bunnies."

He kissed me then, soft, sweet, then harder, needier. Coffee got abandoned, so did our heavy winter clothes all up the stairs as we tried to make it to the bed.

We didn't. We fucked right on the floor in the hallway, loud, wild, giving and taking everything from each other.

And all I could think afterward, lying there, catching my breath was: mine. He was so good, so caring, so sweet, so sexy, so... unexpected and he was all mine.

Cash- one year

I liked her there, in the church, by the altar, holding flowers.

I liked it a whole helluva lot. And I realized I'd have liked it a whole lot more if she wasn't in the rose-colored dress she was wearing. I'd have liked it more if she was in white.

But there was time for that.

This was Summer's turn to wear white.

The song switched and my brother's woman stood in the doorway, her father on her arm, smiling fucking huge at Reign who was shaking his head at her, no doubt thinking what the fuck he had done in his life to deserve her. I knew that feeling well.

Richard kissed Summer's cheek, he shook Reign's hand, and the couple turned back to us.

"I'm just going to go ahead and say what everyone else here is thinking," I said quietly and everyone's eyes turned to me, lips already twitching, knowing what was coming. "This has got to be the weirdest fucking wedding that has ever happened," I smiled, looking out at the scene behind us as everyone tried to stifle their laughs.

Because, it was.

On one side, we had Henchmen, wearing black, wearing their cuts, looking like a bunch of crazy mother fuckers. With them, we had the Mallicks, every last one of those dark haired, light-eyed bastards, Shooter, Breaker and his woman, Alex. On the other side, there was Richard Lyon and a couple of his bodyguards, all in suits worth thousands. Mixed in with them, there were all the people from Hailstorm, and a few of Summer's high-brow friends from her life before it took a veer off into uncharted territories.

It was the craziest fucking hodgepodge of people ever to congregate in the same room at the same time.

But crazy things brought crazy people together. Crazy, unstoppable things like the love that brought Reign and Summer together and, by doing so, me and Lo, and Wolf and Janie.

CASH

Lo

"You're supposed to be giving a speech," I gasped as his hand slid up my dress and yanked my panties down. We were in the coat room. Not original, but the only other choice was the janitor's closet and I didn't feel like fighting off a broom to get it on with my man. Because that was what we were doing, despite my objections, we were *so* going to do it in the coat room at Reign and Summer's wedding.

"Please, Reign dragged Summer away as fast as he could to get in his wife's panties. We have time," he reasoned, reaching for his zipper and freeing himself.

He pushed into me fast and hard, burying to the hilt and I let out a quiet moan.

That was when there was the sound of a throat clearing and I felt Cash stiffen as my eyes went wide. "Don't worry," the same voice called, a very familiar voice. A very *lovable* voice. "You get your wedding jollies off. I'll stand guard. I'm not listening. Or imagining. Nope. Not at all," Shooter's voice called.

Against me, Cash's chest was shaking he was laughing so hard and I felt my own smile spreading wide.

"If you need some help in there, Lo, all of my digits and appendages are yours to exploit for your pleasure."

"Think we're good in here," I called, my choked laugh ending on a gasp as Cash surged inside me.

"You sure 'cause I got to say I..."

"Fuck off Shoot," Cash called, his voice still laughing.

"Alright alright. Fine. Have good orgasms!" he called just as loudly as he pleased, making humor and mortification well up into a strange cocktail inside.

Cash thrust forward again and both feelings rushed away with the feel of him.

"I love you," I whimpered, pulling him tight.

"I love you too, Wills," he said and I didn't flinch at all.

Freedom was different than what I had thought. I had thought it would be waking up every morning thinking that I had won, that I had beat him. But that wasn't it at all. In fact, he very rarely ever crossed my mind.

Freedom was this- it was wild sex in a coat room interrupted by a friend who was all too happy to call us on our wantonness. It was holding back tears as I watched Reign slip his ring on Summer's finger. It was watching Wolf stand guard of Janie as if he planned to be in the way of any danger that might ever come her way. It was waking up in the morning next to Cash.

You see, there were five moments in my life that made me into the woman I turned out to be: My father telling me women didn't belong in the military, giving me the passion to prove him wrong in my own way. Watching love get ripped away from two people and believing to my marrow that I would never experience that kind of passion. Feeling the fist of a man who was supposed to protect me smash into my face. Finding Janie on the street one night. And, finally, realizing I was wrong about moment number two- when I fell so completely, consumingly, irrationally in love with Cash.

No, freedom wasn't what I thought it would be.

It turned out, it was way, way better than I could have ever imagined.

CASH

XX

DON'T FORGET

If you enjoyed this book, go ahead and hop onto Goodreads or Amazon and tell me your favorite parts. You can also spread the word by recommending the book to friends or sending digital copies that can be received via kindle or kindle app on any device.

ALSO BY JESSICA GADZIALA

The Henchmen MC
Reign
Cash
Wolf
Repo
Duke
Renny

The Savages
Monster
Killer
Savior

--

DEBT
For A Good Time, Call...
Shane
The Sex Surrogate

CASH

Dr. Chase Hudson

Dissent

Into The Green

What The Heart Needs

What The Heart Wants

What The Heart Finds

What The Heart Knows

The Stars Landing Deviant

Dark Mysteries

367 Days

Stuffed: A Thanksgiving Romance

Dark Secrets

Unwrapped

ABOUT THE AUTHOR

Jessica Gadziala is a full-time writer, parrot enthusiast, and coffee drinker from New Jersey. She enjoys short rides to the book store, sad songs, and cold weather.

She is very active on Goodreads, Facebook, as well as her personal groups on those sites. Join in. She's friendly.

STALK HER!

Connect with Jessica:

Facebook: https://www.facebook.com/JessicaGadziala/
Facebook Group: https://www.facebook.com/groups/314540025563403/

Goodreads: https://www.goodreads.com/author/show/13800950.Jessica_Gadziala
Goodreads Group: https://www.goodreads.com/group/show/177944-jessica-gadziala-books-and-bullsh

Twitter: @JessicaGadziala

JessicaGadziala.com

CASH

<3/ Jessica

<<<<>>>>